ANYWHERE BUT HERE

NATIONAL BESTSELLING AUTHOR
MYUNIQUE C. GREEN

Copyright © 2025 by Myunique C. Green

All rights reserved. This book or any portion thereof may not be reproduced or used in any manner whatsoever without the express written permission of the publisher except for the use of brief quotations in a book review. To protect the privacy of parties involved some names have been changed.

Anywhere But Here is a work of fiction. Names, characters, places, and incidents either are the product of the author's imagination or are used fictitiously. Any resemblance to actual persons, living or dead, events or locales is purely coincidental.

ISBN: 978-1-300-61796-9

Produced by iWriteBooks Publishing.
iWriteBooksPub.com
MyuniqueGreen.com

Praise For
ANYWHERE BUT HERE

"The brilliance of Anywhere But Here lies in its details—every shadow, every whispered exchange, every locked door that dares you to open it. Myunique C. Green doesn't just build a setting; she engineers an experience, one that feels both hypnotic and claustrophobic. This is horror that seeps under your skin, that makes you question what's real and what's merely been rewritten. A chilling, beautifully crafted descent into generational secrets and scientific nightmares." —Dark Ink Literary Magazine

"A suffocating, hypnotic descent into a town that refuses to let go. Myunique has crafted a masterpiece of creeping horror." —The Horror Review Journal

"Few novels capture the uncanny with the precision of Anywhere But Here. Green's Darbonne is not just a town, but a living organism, one that ensnares its residents in a web of history, science, and something far more sinister. With prose as sharp as a scalpel and an atmosphere thick enough to suffocate, this is psychological horror at its finest. Anywhere But Here is the kind of book that whispers to you in the dark." — Southern Horror Quarterly

OTHER BOOKS

Available in Digital & Paperback

Young Adult Fantasy
Everything That Glitters (Bloodlines Book 1)
Dead to Rights (Bloodlines Book 2)
Awakened (The Reignmere Chronicles Book 1)
Reaping 101

Sci-Fi & Dystopian
Cipher (Hybrid Horizons Book 1)
Talia (Hybrid Horizons Book 2)
Grand Rising
Zombies Anonymous

Literature & Fiction
Psinder
Hysteria
Professional Development
Linked By Ink (Available as Audiobook)
Hearts, Hype & Other Hoaxes

Women's Non-Fiction
The C is for Complex
To Mend a Broken Heart (Available as Audiobook)
Sweet Savage
Girl, It Hasn't Happened Yet!
Love Letters to Heaven

Thriller & Suspense
Chopped & Skrewed (Available as Audiobook)
Last Seen (Available as Audiobook)
Compulsive
Anywhere But Here

For a complete list of titles visit: iWriteBooksPub.com

Anywhere But Here

DEDICATED TO MY MUSE AND GREATEST ADVENTURE.

CHAPTER ONE:

Connection

Dr. Nia Wallace sat before the soft glow of her computer screen, the pale light casting long shadows across the neatly arranged papers on her desk. The lab was quiet at this hour, save for the rhythmic hum of the ventilation system and the occasional electronic beep from one of the machines monitoring the latest batch of genetic sequences. She had been at it for hours, methodically analyzing the results of her most recent study, her fingers moving over the keyboard with practiced precision. The numbers, the patterns, the raw information—it all absorbed her completely, lulling her into the focused trance that had become second nature over years of research.

Outside the lab's windows, the city stretched beyond the tinted glass, its lights flickering in the distance like stars grounded to the earth. It was late, later than she had intended to stay, but she was on the verge of something—or at least, she felt as though she was. The dataset before her was unlike any she had encountered before, the sequences forming a pattern that was both familiar and elusive, a puzzle missing its final pieces. She adjusted her glasses, scrolling back through her notes, the meticulous documentation of her research marked with notations in the margins, personal reminders of theories she had yet to explore.

At thirty-eight, Nia had built a career on precision and discipline, on the belief that DNA held stories more profound than history books and more immutable than memory. She had spent years perfecting the art of tracing ancestral lineages, mapping the silent echoes of genetic inheritance. Her colleagues admired her focus, though some found her intensity isolating. But Nia had long made peace with the solitude of her work. Scientific inquiry had never required the warmth of companionship, only the rigor of thought and the certainty of evidence.

She leaned back in her chair, exhaling slowly as she rubbed her temples. The day had been long, filled with lectures, grant proposals, and the unspoken pressure of expectation. Her name carried weight in the field of genetic research, and with that came an endless cycle of inquiries, invitations, and obligations. She welcomed it, in her own way—after all, this was what she had worked for. Yet, as she sat in the stillness of her lab, surrounded by the data that had defined her life, there was an odd weight pressing at the edges of her mind, a quiet whisper of exhaustion she refused to acknowledge.

A notification blinked in the corner of her screen, breaking the steady rhythm of her thoughts. She glanced at it absently, expecting another routine update from one of her research partners. But the sender's name was unfamiliar, and the subject line was even stranger: **A Connection You Never Expected.**

Nia hesitated. Emails with vague, dramatic titles were almost always some form of academic spam or a marketing ploy disguised as a groundbreaking revelation. But something about this one gave her pause. A part of her—buried beneath years of scientific pragmatism—was oddly compelled to open it.

Nia's fingers hovered over the mouse before she clicked open the email.

The subject line was unassuming; a standard alert from the ancestry database she had contributed to years ago, more out of professional curiosity than personal interest. She received dozens of these a month, distant cousins, barely traceable connections. Usually, she ignored them.

But this one was different.

The screen refreshed, and there it was—her own name in bold, right beside another. Danielle Mercer. A sibling match.

Her breath caught, though she wasn't sure why. This wasn't possible. It had to be a mistake.

She clicked into the detailed report, eyes scanning the shared DNA percentage. A staggering 48.7%. Not a distant relative. Not some third cousin twice removed. This was immediate. Direct. The kind of match that didn't leave room for interpretation.

She pulled up her raw data, comparing the markers side by side. The numbers aligned almost too perfectly, the inheritance pattern unmistakable. Her mother's side, her father's side—both represented.

She checked the sample ID, confirming it had been processed through a legitimate lab. No errors. No anomalies in sequencing.

She ran the comparison again. The same result.

And again.

Still the same.

Nia sat back, the faint whir of the centrifuge dulling into static in her ears. The air inside the lab shifted, thin and sharp, pressing against her skin in a way that made her shiver. Her fingers, still gripping the desk, felt distant, like she had lost sensation without realizing it. This wasn't shock. It was something deeper, something *wrong*—a tectonic shift in the foundation of her life, slipping just beneath her grasp.

A sister.

She had a sister.

No. That wasn't right.

She didn't have any siblings. She had never had siblings.

Her mother had been clear on that, as clear as she had been about everything else. Nia was an only child, raised with the quiet understanding that their small family was just that—small. Complete.

And yet, the proof was right in front of her.

The email included a message. A simple, casual introduction.

Hey, Nia. I know this might come as a surprise, but it looks like we're related. I'd love to talk whenever you're ready. No pressure. Just curiosity. Hope to hear from you. – Danielle.

Nia reread it, the words blurring slightly as her focus wavered. She flexed her fingers, exhaling slowly as she forced herself to sit up straighter.

There had to be an explanation. A mistake in the database. A misattributed sample. *Something*.

She wasn't in the habit of questioning science. She trusted her field, trusted the data. But right now, staring at the screen, she wasn't sure she trusted any of it at all.

The sharp trill of her phone cut through the silence, vibrating against the polished surface of her desk. Nia blinked, momentarily disoriented, before glancing at the caller ID. Malcolm.

She exhaled through her nose, debating whether to let it go to voicemail. The thought of talking right now, of engaging in anything that required more mental effort than staring blankly at the screen, felt exhausting.

But she knew Malcolm. If she ignored him, he'd just keep calling.

With a resigned sigh, she swiped to answer, tucking the phone between her ear and shoulder as she rubbed her temples.

"Hey," she said, her voice coming out rougher than she intended.

"Tell me you're not still at the lab."

Nia closed her eyes. She could picture him perfectly—standing in their kitchen, barefoot, leaning against the counter with that exasperated tilt to his head. Probably nursing a glass of bourbon, because he always had one when she worked late.

"It's not that late," she deflected, knowing full well that was a lie.

Malcolm scoffed. "It's after midnight, Nia."

She frowned and checked the clock in the corner of her monitor. 12:17 AM.

Shit.

"Lost track of time," she admitted, stretching her neck to work out the tension settling there.

"Shocking," he drawled. "Should I assume I'll be sleeping alone again tonight?"

There was a teasing edge to his voice, but underneath it, she could hear something else. A hint of irritation. Maybe even concern.

Nia sighed, pinching the bridge of her nose. "No, I'm coming home."

There was a pause. "You sure?"

"I'm sure," she said, already reaching for her bag.

Another pause. Softer, this time. "You okay?"

Her fingers hovered over the strap. She hesitated. Not long, but long enough.

"Yeah," she lied. "Just tired."

Malcolm didn't push, but she knew he caught it—the slight hesitation, the too-casual deflection. He was too perceptive for his own good, which was both a blessing and an occasional annoyance.

"Alright," he finally said. "Drive safe."

"I will."

"Want me to wait up?"

She considered it. "No, go to bed. I'll see you soon."

Another beat of silence, then a quiet, "Okay."

She hung up before she could say anything else, staring at the darkened screen for a moment before setting the phone down.

Her eyes drifted back to the email, the name Danielle Mercer still glaring at her in bold.

She could deal with it tomorrow.

Right now, she just wanted to go home.

Nia shut down her computer, watching as the screen dimmed into nothingness before she grabbed her bag and shrugged on her coat. The lab, once a place of comfort and routine, suddenly felt sterile in a way that made her eager to leave. The rhythmic hum of machines had lost its usual soothing quality, replaced by a hollow sound that echoed in the quiet.

She flicked off the desk lamp, casting the room into the pale glow of emergency lighting before heading toward the exit. Her heels clicked against the polished tile, the sound sharp and isolated. The building had emptied hours ago, the usual bustle of researchers and lab techs reduced to ghostly traces—half-full coffee cups abandoned on desks, whiteboards filled with half-solved equations, the scent of chemicals lingering in the air.

As she stepped into the hallway, she passed by the glass wall of another lab, the reflection catching her for a moment. She looked at herself—her dark brown skin washed out in the fluorescent light, exhaustion softening the edges of her features. Her hair was still pinned back, though a few loose strands had escaped, curling at her temples. There was something unreadable in her own expression, something heavy, like the weight of the past hour had finally settled in.

She shook it off and kept moving.

The automatic doors hissed open as she stepped into the cool night air. The parking lot was nearly empty, just a handful of cars scattered beneath the flickering glow of overhead lights. The world outside felt vast after so many hours enclosed in the lab, the quiet pressing in differently—less controlled, more unpredictable.

Her breath curled in the air as she dug through her bag for her keys. She found them tangled in her headphones, pulled them free with a frustrated sigh, and unlocked her car with a beep that echoed in the stillness.

Sliding into the driver's seat, she shut the door with a solid thunk and let out a slow breath. The silence of the car felt almost too thick, so she reached for the radio, flipping to a late-night jazz station. The soft, mournful notes of a saxophone filled the space, smoothing out the edges of her frayed thoughts.

She started the engine, the low rumble vibrating through her hands as she gripped the wheel.

The drive home was familiar—muscle memory guiding her through empty streets lined with darkened storefronts and dimly lit intersections. The city had settled into its quiet hours, the chaos of the day replaced by an eerie stillness. Occasional headlights passed in the opposite lane, faceless drivers moving through the night like ghosts.

Nia's mind drifted as she drove, her fingers drumming idly against the steering wheel. The email lingered at the edges of her thoughts, a persistent buzz she couldn't quite tune out. Danielle Mercer. The name felt foreign yet unnervingly close, like a piece of a puzzle she didn't remember losing.

She tightened her grip on the wheel, forcing herself to focus on the road. Not now. She would think about it tomorrow.

The streetlights cast shifting shadows over her dashboard as she turned onto her street, the familiar row of brownstones coming into view. She pulled into the driveway, shutting off the engine but lingering in the car for a moment.

Inside, Malcolm was probably asleep by now. Or maybe not.

She sighed, rubbing a hand over her face before finally stepping out. The cold night air bit at her skin as she locked the car and made her way to the front door.

Home.

For now, that was all she needed to think about.

The lock clicked softly as Nia pushed the front door open, stepping into the dimly lit foyer. The house was still, the only movement a flicker of shadow as something small and warm darted toward her.

"Hey, Dinga," she murmured as the cat wove between her legs, purring loud enough to fill the silence. The sleek black feline stretched, arching her back before pressing her head against Nia's shin in an insistent greeting.

Nia bent down, running a hand over Dinga's soft fur. "You missed me?"

Dinga meowed in response, then turned and trotted ahead, leading her deeper into the house as if guiding her back to the life she'd left waiting.

She set her bag down near the door and toed off her shoes, flexing her sore feet against the hardwood floor. The house smelled faintly of Malcolm's cologne, warm and familiar, mixed with something richer—probably whatever he had made for dinner. A dinner she'd missed.

Moving quietly, she padded down the hall toward the bedroom. The door was slightly ajar, just enough for her to see Malcolm sprawled across the bed, half-covered by the comforter. His arm rested over his chest, his breathing slow and steady.

For a moment, she just stood there, taking him in. His hair was slightly messy, the sharp lines of his jaw softened in sleep. He looked peaceful, unaware of the strange spiral she'd found herself in tonight.

She thought about sliding into bed beside him, burying herself in his warmth and pretending the world outside their home didn't exist. But her stomach had other plans, a hollow ache reminding her that she'd skipped dinner.

Sighing, she turned away and headed toward the kitchen.

Dinga followed, her tail curling at the tip as she trotted alongside Nia, clearly hoping for a late-night snack of her own. The kitchen was dark except for the glow of the microwave clock—12:56 AM—and the faint glimmer of city lights filtering through the window.

Nia opened the fridge, staring blankly at its contents before spotting the glass container of lasagna.

Malcolm's cooking. That explained the lingering scent of tomatoes and herbs in the air.

She pulled it out, peeled back the lid, and set it in the microwave. The low hum of the appliance filled the silence, and she leaned against the counter, rubbing her temples.

Dinga leapt onto a stool, watching her with unblinking green eyes.

"I know, I know," Nia muttered. "Too late to be eating."

Dinga flicked her tail as if to say she didn't care, so long as Nia shared.

The microwave beeped.

She took her plate and settled at the small breakfast nook, the heat from the lasagna warming her fingers as she picked up her fork. The first bite was good—rich, comforting. It grounded her in the present, in the simplicity of eating a home-cooked meal at an unreasonable hour.

But her mind wasn't in it.

Her gaze drifted to the phone she had placed beside her plate. The email sat there, waiting.

She swallowed the last bite and reached for her phone, her thumb hovering over the reply button. She could wait. She could let it sit, pretend she hadn't seen it. Or she could respond now, while the thought was fresh. Before she had the chance to overthink it.

Her fingers moved before she could second-guess herself.

Danielle,

This is definitely a surprise. I'm not sure what to say yet, but I'd be open to talking. Maybe we can set up a time. – Nia

She stared at the message for a long moment, then hit send.

The email disappeared into the ether, and with it, any illusion that she could pretend this wasn't happening.

Dinga stretched, then jumped down, brushing against Nia's leg before disappearing into the darkness of the hallway.

Nia sighed, pushing her plate away. The lasagna was still warm, but she'd lost her appetite.

Nia sighed and pushed back from the table, the chair scraping softly against the floor. The house was quiet, save for the distant hum of the fridge and the soft rustle of Dinga settling into her favorite corner.

She picked up her plate and carried it to the sink, rinsing it under warm water before placing it in the dishwasher. The motions were automatic, something to keep her hands busy while her mind raced in endless loops. She wiped down the counter, folded the dish towel over the oven handle, and took a final glance around the kitchen before turning off the light.

The hallway stretched ahead, dark and inviting, the glow of the bedroom barely visible through the cracked door. Nia moved toward it, her body finally registering the weight of exhaustion pressing down on her shoulders.

Inside, Malcolm hadn't shifted much since she last peeked in. He was sprawled on his back, one arm still resting over his chest, his breathing deep and steady. The sheets were rumpled around his waist, the room carrying the familiar warmth of shared sleep.

She slipped out of her clothes and pulled on one of his t-shirts from the dresser, the fabric soft and worn against her skin. As soon as she slid beneath the covers, Malcolm stirred, shifting toward her with the kind of instinctive ease that came from years of knowing exactly where she would be.

His arm curled around her waist, strong and sure, pulling her in until her back was flush against his chest.

"Missed you," he murmured against her shoulder, his voice thick with sleep.

She smiled, though he couldn't see it. "I'm here now."

Malcolm exhaled, his breath warm against her skin as he pressed a lazy, lingering kiss to the curve of her neck. His lips traced a slow path up to her jaw before he settled against her again, tucking her closer into his embrace.

Safe. That was how she felt in his arms. A solid, steady presence grounding her in the now.

But her mind was still a hive of activity, buzzing with the weight of the email she had just sent, the questions left unanswered, the reality she hadn't yet processed.

Her phone vibrated on the nightstand.

Nia stiffened slightly, but she didn't lift her head to check it. She could guess who it was.

Danielle.

Malcolm's arm tightened around her as if sensing the shift in her body. "Sleep, Nia," he murmured, already drifting again.

She closed her eyes, willing her thoughts to settle.

Tomorrow. She would deal with it tomorrow.

For now, she let herself sink into Malcolm's warmth, the steady rhythm of his breathing lulling her toward rest, even as the unanswered questions lingered, waiting for her in the dark.

CHAPTER TWO:
IMPRESSIONS

The morning greeted Nia with the soft glow of daylight seeping through the curtains, casting lazy golden streaks across the sheets. Malcolm was already up—the empty space beside her still warm, the faint scent of his cologne lingering in the air. She stretched, her muscles stiff from too little sleep, then pushed the covers back and swung her legs over the edge of the bed.

Dinga was waiting by the door, tail flicking, clearly expecting breakfast.

"Morning, demanding one," Nia murmured, scratching the cat behind her ears before padding toward the bathroom.

The mirror above the sink reflected tired eyes and hair that needed more attention than she had been giving it. Her locs, thick and well-maintained for the most part, were due for a retwist. New growth had softened the parts at her scalp, making them look slightly unkempt—not quite wild, but not as polished as she preferred.

She ran a hand through them, pulling a few forward to inspect. She needed to set aside time for it, but like most things outside of work, it had been pushed to the back burner. There was always something more pressing, something more urgent.

With a sigh, she pulled them back into a loose bun and turned on the shower.

The hot water was a blessing against her skin, steam curling around her as she let the warmth seep into her muscles. She took her time, letting the steady pressure of the water wake her up fully. The scent of her eucalyptus body wash filled the space, fresh and clean, a small indulgence in a morning that already felt heavy with lingering thoughts.

After drying off, she went through the routine she could do in her sleep—moisturizer, a light serum, a cooling under-eye cream she always swore she didn't need but used anyway. The routine grounded her. There was something meditative about the familiar steps, a way to prepare herself for the day ahead.

She slipped into a fitted black long-sleeve and a pair of soft gray joggers before making her way to the kitchen, the scent of butter and warm sugar already filling the house.

Malcolm stood at the stove, barefoot, his broad shoulders relaxed as he flipped pancakes with practiced ease. A pot of coffee brewed beside him, the rich aroma mixing with the scent of eggs sizzling in a separate pan.

"Blueberry pancakes?" Nia asked, coming up behind him and wrapping her arms around his waist.

He smirked, flipping the pancake onto a growing stack. "Figured I'd make something special since I was abandoned last night."

She huffed a laugh against his back. "I wasn't that late."

"You were late enough," he countered, turning slightly to kiss the top of her head before nudging her toward the table. "Sit. Eat. Pretend you care about a balanced breakfast."

Nia did as she was told, grabbing a mug and pouring herself some coffee while Malcolm plated the food. The table was already set, forks resting beside folded napkins—a small detail that made her smile.

He slid a plate in front of her before sitting across from her, taking a sip of his coffee before digging into his eggs.

They ate in comfortable silence for a few moments, the occasional clink of silverware filling the space. The pancakes were fluffy, bursting with fresh blueberries, the eggs perfectly seasoned—because of course Malcolm wouldn't settle for anything less than perfection in the kitchen.

Nia was mid-bite when Malcolm let out a dramatic sigh and muttered, "You see the price of eggs lately?"

She snorted, shaking her head. "I knew it was coming."

"I'm just saying, at this point, we might as well get a damn chicken."

She sipped her coffee, arching a brow. "You? Raising chickens? The same man who won't even water the plants unless I guilt-trip you into it?"

"Chickens are different," he said, pointing his fork at her. "Chickens provide. The fiddle-leaf fig in the living room? That thing just sits there, judging me."

She laughed, reaching for another piece of pancake. "So, what, we just let a hen roam around the house? Dinga would have a fit."

Malcolm shook his head. "Nah, she'd be fine. She's already queen of the house. I bet she'd make the chicken her little minion."

Nia chuckled, shaking her head as she focused on her food. This was what she loved most about Malcolm. For all his success—the high-end real estate deals, the multi-million dollar properties he handled on a regular basis—he had never let it change him. He still talked about ridiculous things like getting a pet chicken, still made her laugh first thing in the morning before her brain had fully booted up.

He was a big deal in his world, but he never acted like it.

She reached across the table and gave his hand a squeeze. He glanced up, brow lifting slightly, but didn't ask why. He just squeezed back.

And for a moment, despite the chaos brewing in her head, everything felt simple.

They lingered at the table after breakfast, both nursing the last of their coffee as the morning sunlight filtered through the kitchen window. Malcolm leaned back in his chair, stretching his arms behind his head, his gaze settling on Nia with that easy, knowing expression of his.

"You're stalling," he said, smirking.

She rolled her eyes. "I'm not stalling."

"You are. You keep checking the time like you actually plan on rushing off to work. But I can tell you don't."

Nia exhaled, twisting her mug between her hands. He wasn't wrong. She had already decided she was going in late today. Her mind was too restless, too cluttered.

"A run would probably help," she admitted.

Malcolm's brow lifted slightly. "You want to run? With me?"

"Don't sound so shocked," she said, tilting her head at him. "We used to run together all the time."

"Yeah, like six months ago," he teased. "You're the one who bailed on our morning runs in favor of 'just a little more sleep.'"

Nia huffed, setting her mug down. "That was before work got crazy."

"Right. Because your job suddenly became *less* crazy overnight," he quipped, but there was no real bite to it.

She smirked, standing up. "Are you coming or not?"

Malcolm grinned and pushed away from the table. "I never say no to a chance to outrun you, babe."

The crisp morning air met them as they stepped outside, the familiar weight of movement settling into Nia's limbs as they started their run. The streets were quieter at this hour, with only a few other early risers stretching or jogging along the sidewalk.

The rhythmic pounding of their feet against the pavement fell into sync, the sound steady and grounding. For the first mile, they didn't talk, just moved together in a way that felt both nostalgic and necessary.

Eventually, Malcolm glanced over, sweat already starting to glisten on his brow. "So," he said, his voice slightly breathless, "are you gonna tell me what's actually on your mind, or are we just pretending this is a totally normal morning?"

Nia hesitated, her breath coming in controlled bursts. She had meant to bring it up, but now that the moment was here, the words felt heavier than she expected.

She slowed her pace slightly, and Malcolm matched her, his expression shifting to something more serious.

"I got an email last night," she finally said. "From a woman named Danielle Mercer."

He waited, giving her space to continue.

"Apparently, she's my sister."

Malcolm nearly tripped. "Wait, what?"

"Yeah." Nia let out a dry laugh. "That was pretty much my reaction, too."

They slowed to a walk, the momentum of their run replaced by the weight of the conversation. Malcolm wiped a hand down his face, still looking at her like she'd just told him the sky was green.

"But that—" He shook his head. "That doesn't make sense. You don't have siblings. Your mom—"

"I *know*," Nia said, running a hand through her locs. "I don't understand it either. But the DNA doesn't lie. It was a match. A direct match."

Malcolm was quiet for a moment, processing. "And you believe it's real? No chance of a mix-up?"

"I triple-checked," she said, exhaling. "It's real."

Malcolm let out a low whistle, shaking his head. "Damn. That's...wow."

Nia glanced at him, chewing the inside of her cheek. "I haven't checked my email yet. I don't know if she responded."

Malcolm gave her a pointed look. "And *that* is what you've been stalling on."

She sighed. He wasn't wrong.

Pulling out her phone, she unlocked it with a few taps and opened her inbox. And there it was—Danielle Mercer, Re: Surprising, but open.

Her stomach tightened.

"She responded," she murmured.

Malcolm shifted closer, peeking over her shoulder. "Well, don't keep me in suspense. Open it."

Nia inhaled deeply and clicked the email.

Hey Nia,

Thanks for writing back. I figured you'd be skeptical. I was, too. I don't know how much you know about your family history, but I'd really love to talk. I promise I'm not some scammer or some distant cousin hoping to claim relation. I just want to know the truth. If you're up for it, maybe we can hop on a call sometime? No pressure. Just putting it out there. Hope to hear from you. – Danielle

Nia stared at the message for a long moment. It was straightforward, no dramatics. Just…a person reaching out. A person who, somehow, was connected to her in a way she didn't understand.

Malcolm grinned. "See? She seems normal. This is good news."

She arched a brow at him. "Good news?"

"Yeah. Haven't you always wanted a sister, babe?" He bumped her shoulder lightly. "This is great, right?"

Nia wasn't so sure.

She slipped her phone back into her pocket, her thoughts swirling.

Malcolm saw it as something exciting. A gift. But all she could feel was uncertainty. Because if this was true—if she *did* have a sister—then it meant there was something in her past, in her *mother's* past, that had been hidden from her.

And she wasn't sure she was ready to find out why.

The rest of the run was quieter. Not in a tense way, but in a *processing* way. Nia could feel Malcolm stealing glances at her every so often, probably trying to gauge whether she was freaking out about the whole sister situation. She wasn't—not exactly. But she also wasn't as quick to jump to *this is great news* the way he had.

By the time they made it back home, their shirts were damp with sweat, their breathing evened out but still a little heavy. Malcolm unlocked the door first, stepping inside and immediately heading toward the kitchen for water. Nia followed, grabbing a cold bottle from the fridge and pressing it to her forehead before taking a long sip.

"Alright, I gotta shower and head out," Malcolm said, running a hand over his head as he leaned against the counter. "Meetings all morning, then a walkthrough this afternoon."

Nia nodded, still distracted, still working through the tangle of thoughts in her head.

He stepped closer, tilting his head. "You good?"

"Yeah," she said, forcing a small smile. "Just…still wrapping my head around everything."

Malcolm studied her for a beat, then pressed a kiss to her forehead. "Well, try not to overthink it."

She gave him a look. "Do you *know* me?"

He smirked, running his hands down her arms before resting them at her waist. "Yeah, I do. Which is why I also know you're gonna tell yourself you'll be home by ten tonight, and then I'll see you at, what, one? Two?"

Nia scoffed. "I will *not* be that late."

"You *will*," he countered, grinning. "But go ahead, lie to me."

She rolled her eyes, looping her arms around his neck. "*I will be home by ten.*"

Malcolm chuckled, clearly not convinced, but he kissed her anyway, slow and deep, before finally pulling back. "I'll see you when I see you."

"Love you," she murmured.

"Love you too," he said, grabbing his bag and heading toward the door.

The moment he was gone, the house felt quieter. She stood there for a moment, finishing the rest of her water, then set the empty bottle in the sink and pulled out her phone.

She settled onto the couch, tapping out a response to Danielle before she could talk herself out of it.

Hey Danielle,

I appreciate you reaching out again. This is still… a lot to process, but I think a call would be good. My number is (771) 359-5103. Let me know when you're free. – Nia

She hit send before she could hesitate.

Dinga stretched from her spot curled up on the armrest, blinking lazily at Nia before hopping down and trotting toward the kitchen.

"Yeah, yeah, I know," Nia muttered, following after her. "You require constant sustenance, otherwise, you'll waste away into nothingness."

Dinga meowed dramatically as Nia poured fresh food into her bowl, watching with rapt attention as if the act required supervision.

She had just finished when her phone rang.

Nia froze, glancing at the screen.

Unknown Number.

That was fast.

She wiped her hands on a dish towel before answering, pressing the phone to her ear.

"Hello?"

"Hey, is this Nia?"

Nia blinked.

The voice on the other end was bright, a little breathy, and undeniably... white.

Not "Black person code-switching to sound white." Not even "suburban Black girl with a private school upbringing" white.

No. This was full-on *Valley Girl* white.

"Oh my God, I'm so happy you picked up! I wasn't sure if you'd answer since, you know, this whole thing is probably super weird for you, but I just wanted to say hi and—"

Nia's brain short-circuited for a moment.

She had been expecting... she didn't know what exactly. But *this*? This had not been on the list.

"Uh," Nia managed, thrown completely off her game.

"Oh, sorry! I'm totally rambling, aren't I? I do that when I'm nervous. Anyway, it's so nice to finally hear your voice! This whole thing is *so* crazy, right?"

Nia rubbed her temple. She needed a second to recalibrate, to adjust to the whiplash of *expectation vs. reality*.

"Yeah," she finally said, slow, cautious. "It's... definitely something."

Nia paced slowly around the living room, phone pressed to her ear as she tried to make sense of what she was hearing.

"Darbonne?" she repeated, brow furrowing. "I've never heard of it."

"Yeah, not many people have," Danielle said, her voice carrying that same breezy, overly friendly tone. "It's this tiny town in Louisiana, kinda in the middle of nowhere. We have, like, one main street, and everyone knows everyone. It's actually super charming, though. You should visit sometime!"

Nia let out a quiet, bewildered laugh. "Right. I'll add that to my list."

This was already strange enough without adding a mysterious, unheard-of town into the mix.

"I was born and raised here," Danielle continued. "Whole family's from here. Well—our family, I guess. That still sounds so weird to say, like, *our family*. Oh my God, isn't this crazy?"

"That's one word for it," Nia murmured, sinking onto the couch.

A silence stretched for a moment, not quite awkward but definitely heavy with unspoken questions.

Danielle cleared her throat. "So, um, I know this might be weird to just throw out there, but—do you want to be friends on Facebook? I could send you some pictures of the family. You know, so you can see for yourself?"

Nia hesitated. Social media wasn't exactly her favorite place, but…

On the one hand, it was the easiest way to put some faces to all of this. To see if there was any resemblance. To start putting the pieces together without diving straight into a deep, emotional rabbit hole.

On the other hand, did she *want* to see?

She swallowed, fingers drumming lightly against her thigh. "Yeah. Yeah, that's not a bad idea."

"Cool! I'll send you a request. No pressure to look right away or anything."

Nia nodded to herself, even though Danielle couldn't see her.

There was another pause, shorter this time.

"So," Danielle said, a little softer now, "do you know which side of your family I'm from?"

Nia exhaled, pressing a hand to her forehead. "It's gotta be my dad's."

"Not your mom's?"

"No," Nia said, certain of that much. "My mom is a Black woman, through and through. And you..." She hesitated, not sure how to say it without sounding blunt.

Danielle, however, laughed. "And I sound like a sorority girl who just got back from brunch?"

Nia huffed a small laugh. "Something like that."

"Yeah, I get that a lot," Danielle admitted. "But if this is from your dad's side... does that mean you're biracial?"

The question hit Nia square in the chest.

She had never thought about it before. Never *had* to think about it. She had always been Nia Wallace, Black woman, raised by a Black mother. There was no ambiguity in her identity.

But if Danielle was her sister—her *half*-sister—then what did that make her?

She rubbed at her temple. "I have no idea what's happening right now," she admitted.

"That makes two of us," Danielle said.

The conversation wrapped up pleasantly enough, with Danielle promising to send the friend request and some pictures when she had a chance. They didn't set a time for their next conversation, but there was an understanding that there *would* be one.

Nia hung up and let the phone rest on her lap, staring blankly ahead.

Maybe she was overcomplicating things. Maybe this was one of those situations where it was best to let the DNA do the explaining. She could drive herself crazy trying to guess, or she could just wait and see where the facts led.

Still, one thing was clear—if her father had other children, then she didn't just have a sister.

She had an entire family she never knew about.

She sat with that thought for a moment, then grabbed her phone again, this time scrolling to her mother's contact.

Nia didn't want to confront her about anything—not over the phone, not like this. But she *did* want to ask about her father.

She pressed the call button and put it on speaker as she stood, moving around the house while it rang.

"Hello?"

Her mother's voice was softer now than it used to be, but still familiar, still warm.

"Hey, Ma," Nia said, making her way to the kitchen.

"Hey, baby," her mother said, and Nia could already hear the slight confusion in her tone, like she was trying to place the timing of this call. "You calling me from work?"

"Not yet. I'm heading in late today," Nia said, keeping her voice light. "Wanted to check in, see how you're feeling."

Her mother sighed. "Same as always, baby. Just taking it one day at a time."

Nia nodded, rinsing out her coffee mug and setting it on the drying rack. "Have you been eating?"

"Of course I have."

Nia arched a brow. "Are you lying to me right now?"

Her mother tsked. "Don't you start. I eat just fine."

Nia let it go—for now. "I was actually calling to ask you something," she said, keeping her tone casual. "About my dad."

A pause.

Her mother's voice came back slower this time. "Your dad?"

"Yeah." Nia leaned against the counter, watching as Dinga stretched out across the floor. "I realized I don't really know much about him. You never really talked about him."

Another pause. Longer this time.

"He was... a good man," her mother finally said. "A very good man."

Nia waited, but nothing more came.

"Okay," she said carefully. "Do you remember his name?"

Her mother exhaled a soft laugh. "'Course I do, baby."

Nia smiled slightly. "So… what was it?"

Silence.

Nia's stomach clenched as she realized her mother was thinking—*really* thinking. Trying to pull at a memory that should've been right there, but wasn't.

Finally, her mother spoke. "I don't—" She hesitated. "I don't remember."

The words sent a ripple through Nia's chest.

She closed her eyes briefly, pressing her fingers against the counter. "That's okay, Ma," she said gently. "It's not a big deal."

Her mother made a small, frustrated sound. "I swear, I knew it just a minute ago."

"You're fine," Nia reassured her. "I was just curious. No pressure."

Her mother sighed again, softer this time. "I'm sorry, baby."

Nia swallowed around the lump in her throat.

She hated this. Hated watching her mother struggle to grasp pieces of her own life, watching memories slip through her fingers like sand. Early-onset dementia had crept in slowly at first, but now, these gaps were becoming more frequent.

"Don't apologize," Nia said, forcing her voice to stay light. "We can talk about it another time."

"Okay," her mother murmured, but there was still something distant in her tone.

They talked for a few more minutes—small things, light things—before Nia finally let her go.

When the call ended, she stayed standing in the kitchen for a long time, staring at nothing.

She wasn't sure what answer she had been hoping for. But somehow, *nothing* felt worse than the truth.

CHAPTER THREE:

BIRTHMARK

The steady hum of the sequencing machine filled the lab, an ever-present rhythm that underscored the quiet focus of the space. Nia sat at her workstation, her eyes scanning over the familiar genome maps, her fingers methodically flipping through pages of raw data. The logical part of her brain told her there had to be an explanation—something buried in the numbers, in the chains of proteins and markers that made up the foundation of who she was.

If there was a mystery, she would solve it.

She had spent years deciphering genetic puzzles for other people, tracing lineages, identifying mutations, mapping out complex ancestry for clients who longed for a connection to something bigger. Now, for the first time, she was her own case study.

Lena had handled most of the morning workload, giving Nia the freedom to dive back into the DNA results without distraction.

"By the way, I pushed your three o'clock to next week," Lena said, appearing in the doorway, a tablet tucked under her arm. "You looked deep in it, and I figured unless it was an emergency, you weren't coming up for air."

Nia glanced up, offering a small smile. "You know me too well."

Lena smirked. "I know science you is a black hole of obsession. So, am I leaving you to it?"

"Yeah," Nia said, rubbing her forehead. "Thanks for holding things down."

Lena nodded and disappeared down the hallway, leaving Nia alone with her thoughts.

She turned back to her screen, shifting in her chair.

She pulled up the raw DNA file again, staring at the markers that had thrown her world off course. The sibling match was there—undeniable, unwavering. She had already run the data against every possible explanation. No contamination, no sample mix-up, no errors in sequencing.

The truth sat right in front of her, but it didn't fit.

A notification popped up on her screen.

Danielle Mercer sent you a friend request.

Nia exhaled sharply. She clicked the notification and opened Danielle's profile. And there she was.

Danielle Mercer, 29 years old. Public profile set to limited, but enough was visible for Nia to get a good look at the woman claiming to be her sister.

She studied the picture closely, the way she would if she were analyzing genetic similarities in clients.

Danielle was blonde—*naturally* blonde, not the kind that came from a salon. Her hair was fine, the soft kind that caught in the wind too easily, the kind that never had to fight against gravity to stay in place. Long and wavy, the loose strands framing her face were the color of warm honey, bright even in the casual lighting of the photo.

Her skin was fair. Not just fair—but fair, *fair*. Sunburn-easily fair. Ivory smooth, almost translucent in certain places, where veins were visible beneath the surface.

She had delicate features—a softly rounded chin, a gentle slope to her nose, high cheekbones that caught the light just enough. Her eyes were light, a sharp, icy blue that stood out even in the low-resolution of the profile picture.

Nothing about her face screamed *Wallace*.

Nothing about her face looked like Nia at all.

And yet…

Nia's gaze drifted lower, over the exposed collarbone in the photo, down to the right side of her shoulder, where just barely visible against the pale skin was a small, distinct birthmark.

A heart.

Small, naturally imperfect in its shape, but undeniably a heart.

Nia's own hand moved instinctively to her own mark, resting just at the curve of her right shoulder. She had always thought of it as something unique—something no one else had. And yet, there it was.

On Danielle.

Her chest tightened, her breath coming slower as her brain struggled to make sense of the impossibility. This wasn't just genetics. This wasn't just *some* match.

She and Danielle weren't just linked by numbers in a database. They had been stamped with the same mark, carried the same silent proof on their skin.

Nia sat back in her chair, staring at the screen. For the first time since this started, she didn't know what to do.

Nia exhaled, clicking the Accept Friend Request button before she could talk herself out of it. Danielle's full profile opened up instantly.

She scrolled through cautiously at first, then more fluidly, easing into the rhythm of digital sleuthing. Danielle *seemed* normal. Not some shadowy, vague figure with only a handful of curated posts—no, she was very much a *real* person.

Her timeline was filled with snippets of life, small and sentimental. She shared quotes about love and longing, the kind that felt like they belonged in the margins of a well-worn journal.

"Some people arrive and make such a beautiful impact on your life, you can barely remember what life was like without them."

"The hardest part about family is missing someone who's still alive."

Nia frowned at that one, but kept scrolling.

There were photos of Danielle with friends—smiling, laughing, clinking glasses over candle-lit dinners, squinting into the sun on some beach, always surrounded by warmth. Coffee shop check-ins, tagged locations from travels—Paris, New York, Austin. A post from two years ago about visiting New Orleans for the first time, even though she was a Louisiana native.

"NOLA stole my heart this weekend. How did I grow up so close and never come here?"

No crazy stalker vibes.

But then again, wouldn't a *crazy stalker* know how to scrub their profile? Wouldn't they know exactly how to appear normal?

Nia exhaled sharply, rubbing her temples. Now *she* sounded like the crazy one.

This was a real account. A real person.

The photos went back at least five years, and nothing seemed fabricated or overly curated. She clicked through an album labeled Family & Home and found pictures of Danielle and an older woman—her mother, presumably.

They stood side by side in front of a house with a wraparound porch, Danielle grinning while her mother rested a gentle hand on her shoulder. Another showed them at Christmas, twinkling lights in the background. The woman had graying blonde hair, sharp blue eyes like Danielle's, but softer features.

White.

Very, very *white*.

Nia's stomach twisted.

This wasn't her mother. Which meant this had to be from her *father's* side. The same father she knew nothing about.

Would that make her—?

She shook her head. No, she wasn't going down that path *right now*. The thought of reconfiguring her identity in real-time was too much to layer on top of everything else.

Her phone rang, breaking through her spiraling thoughts.

She grabbed it off the desk and glanced at the screen.

Malcolm.

She swiped to answer, exhaling. "Hey."

"Hey, beautiful," he said, his voice smooth and easy. "Figured I'd catch you before you buried yourself in research all day. How about a lunch rendezvous?"

Nia smiled despite herself. "A rendezvous, huh?"

"Yeah, you, me, somewhere that doesn't smell like disinfectant and lab-grade ethanol."

She glanced at the clock. It was already past one. She had been sitting here longer than she realized.

"Okay," she said, rolling her shoulders to loosen them. "I could use a break."

"Good, because I already made a reservation at that spot you like. La Belle Bistro, two o'clock."

She shook her head, amused. "You just assumed I'd say yes?"

Malcolm chuckled. "I assumed you'd need food at some point today, and I was betting on my chances of making that happen."

Nia let out a soft laugh. "Fair enough. Plus, I have new information to share with you."

"See? Perfect timing," he said, pleased. "I'll see you soon."

She hung up, staring at her screen for a moment before locking it.

Danielle Mercer wasn't a figment of the internet. She wasn't a scam. She was real. And the more real she became, the less sense any of this made.

The Wallace Genomics & Ancestry Lab—her domain, her battleground, her sanctuary.

Nia had spent years building her reputation within these walls, not just as another researcher, not just as an expert in genetic lineage tracing, but as a leader. She had fought for every inch of space she occupied, pushing through the barriers that had been quietly, sometimes *not* so quietly, set against her.

And she had won.

A polished gold plaque outside her office bore her name:

Dr. Nia Wallace, Ph.D.

Director of Genetic Research & Ancestry Mapping

The title carried weight, but she never let it define her. She had seen too many people let prestige inflate their egos, too many academics become untouchable in their own minds. That wasn't her.

She was proud, but not prideful.

The lab was divided into two main sections—the Research Wing and the Analysis & Data Division.

The Research Wing was the heart of the operation, filled with cutting-edge sequencing machines, climate-controlled sample storage units, and teams of technicians running tests that would shape the future of genetic science. The sterile scent of ethanol and chemicals clung to the air, mixed with the low whir of centrifuges and the quiet beeping of computers processing genetic code.

Then there was the Analysis & Data Division—the cubicle section, as some called it. Less sterile, more lived-in, this area buzzed with analysts and bioinformatics specialists parsing through massive data sets. Screens glowed with genome maps, migration patterns, and ancestry charts. Some cubicles were covered in family photos, research posters, and the occasional stress-relief toy (Lena had a ridiculous collection of rubber ducks on her desk).

And above it all, Nia oversaw everything.

She had revolutionized this field with her research, mapping ancestry with unprecedented accuracy, uncovering links between genetics and historical migrations that no one else had. She had been awarded for it—prestigious recognitions that cemented her legacy in ways she hadn't fully processed yet.

But she wasn't in it for the awards. She was in it because she knew what it felt like to *not know*. To crave answers about your own blood, your own history.

For people like her—Black women in a field still heavily dominated by white men—knowledge was power. She had fought to break the door down, not just for herself, but for the ones coming up behind her.

For people like Lena.

Speaking of—

"Going out for lunch," Nia called as she passed by her assistant's desk.

Lena, seated at her monitor, barely looked up. "You taking a real break, or is this one of those *'I'm going to sit in a restaurant but still work the whole time'* situations?"

Nia smirked. "Define real break."

Lena arched a brow. "Are you taking your laptop?"

Nia hesitated.

"Uh-huh," Lena said, unimpressed. "At least bring me back something good if you're gonna pretend to be normal."

"Fine," Nia said, rolling her eyes. "What do you want?"

"Surprise me," Lena said, then, with a sly grin, "but *if* that surprise happens to be fries from La Belle Bistro, I wouldn't be mad."

Nia chuckled. "Noted."

Lena turned back to her work, but there was a quiet admiration in her gaze, one she tried not to make obvious. Nia saw it, though. She knew what it meant.

There weren't many Black women in this space. And seeing someone like herself—someone who had *made it*—meant something.

Nia had fought hard to be here, but she wasn't fighting just for herself. She was making sure the door she kicked open never closed again.

Nia stepped out of the lab and into the crisp afternoon air, rolling her shoulders as if physically shedding the weight of the morning. The transition from sterile, fluorescent-lit workspaces to the real world always felt abrupt, like stepping from one dimension into another.

The city bustled around her—cars weaving through midday traffic, pedestrians moving with purpose, the occasional honk or muffled conversation drifting through the air. She pulled her coat tighter around herself as she crossed the parking lot, the slight chill biting against her skin despite the sun hanging high overhead.

Sliding into her car, she let out a slow breath, resting her hands on the steering wheel for a moment before starting the engine.

La Belle Bistro wasn't far, maybe a fifteen-minute drive, nestled in a part of the city that felt more old-world European than metropolitan. It was one of those places Malcolm had introduced her to when they first started dating—back when she still had a habit of skipping meals in favor of work and he had made it his mission to drag her out of the lab at least *occasionally*.

The drive was uneventful, save for the hum of the city passing by her windows. She flipped on the radio, letting jazz fill the car as she maneuvered through traffic, her mind still turning over the last hour.

The birthmark.

The sheer impossibility of all of this.

She drummed her fingers against the wheel as she pulled up to the restaurant, sliding into a parking spot near the entrance. The street was lined with boutique shops and cafés, their awnings casting long shadows across the sidewalk.

As she stepped out of the car, she caught a glimpse of Malcolm through the restaurant's front window—seated at their usual table near the back, already half-focused on his phone. Always early, always composed.

She allowed herself a small smile before making her way inside.

The warmth of the restaurant enveloped her instantly, the scent of butter and fresh herbs mingling with the low hum of conversation. Soft music played in the background, the kind of instrumental melodies designed to make people linger over their meals.

She spotted Malcolm before he saw her, the sharp lines of his suit jacket contrasting against the relaxed atmosphere of the bistro. He was scrolling through something on his phone, his brow furrowed in mild concentration.

As she approached, he glanced up, his face shifting into that familiar easy grin.

"Right on time," he said, setting his phone aside.

Nia slid into the seat across from him, exhaling. "You doubted me?"

He smirked. "Not at all. But let's be real, the promise of food *definitely* helped."

She rolled her eyes, but couldn't argue.

As she settled in, unwinding her scarf, Malcolm leaned forward slightly, studying her.

"You look like you've been thinking too hard," he said.

Nia let out a quiet laugh. "Always."

He tilted his head. "This about our mystery sister?"

She nodded, reaching for the menu even though she already knew what she wanted. "I have more information. And you're not gonna believe this."

Malcolm sat back, gesturing. "Lay it on me."

She took a breath, steadying herself.

And then, she told him everything.

Nia set her menu down and leaned back in her chair, fixing Malcolm with a steady look. "Okay, so first—Danielle finally sent the friend request."

Malcolm nodded, intrigued. "And?"

"And she's *real*."

He lifted a brow. "Real real, or just social-media-real?"

Nia smirked. "Both. The profile isn't new—posts and photos go back at least five years. I scrolled through everything, and it all checks out. Family pictures, travel photos, random memes about coffee addiction—nothing weird, nothing staged."

Malcolm sat forward, his hands clasped together on the table. "Alright. That's good, right?"

Nia hesitated, glancing down at the polished wood surface before meeting his eyes again. "It should be. But then I saw something."

Malcolm tilted his head slightly. "Something bad?"

"Not bad." She exhaled. "Just… impossible."

A waiter appeared before she could continue, smoothly interrupting their conversation.

"Good afternoon! Can I get you started with anything?"

Nia glanced up. "I'll have a cocktail—um, the French 75."

Malcolm smirked. "Day drinking now?"

She gave him a look. "It's one cocktail, Malcolm."

He chuckled. "Alright, alright. I'll have a bourbon neat."

"And for food?" the waiter asked, scribbling down their drinks.

"I'll do the crab cakes," Nia said. "Not too heavy, not too light."

"Good choice," the waiter said before turning to Malcolm.

"I'll take the steak frites," he said, handing back the menu.

"Perfect. I'll get those started for you."

As soon as the waiter left, Malcolm leaned in, giving Nia a pointed look. "Okay, what's the impossible part?"

She pulled in a breath. "Danielle has *my* birthmark."

Malcolm frowned. "Come again?"

Nia turned her shoulder slightly, gesturing to the curve where her shirt dipped just enough to reveal the small, heart-shaped birthmark on her skin. "This. *She has the exact same mark. In the exact same place.*"

Malcolm blinked. "No way."

"I saw it in one of her photos." Nia shook her head, still unable to wrap her mind around it. "I've had this my whole life. I always thought it made me *unique*. I've never seen another person with the same thing. And now, suddenly, here's this woman—who's supposedly my sister—with *the same damn mark?*"

Malcolm let out a slow whistle. "Okay. That's wild."

Nia sighed. "It doesn't feel like a coincidence."

"No, because it's *not*," Malcolm said, shaking his head. "That's some genetic-level connection right there."

She ran a hand over her locs. "I just don't get it. My mom is Black. Full Black. There's no way Danielle is from her side. Which means this is about my dad."

Malcolm studied her. "You ever think about getting answers from him? Or... I don't know, tracking him down?"

Nia let out a dry laugh. "Yeah, well, I tried calling the only person who *would* know something, and guess what?"

He lifted a brow. "Nothing?"

"Nothing," she confirmed. "My mom couldn't even remember his name."

Malcolm's expression softened. "Dementia?"

She nodded. "It's getting worse."

"I'm sorry, babe." He reached across the table, squeezing her hand briefly before leaning back.

She let out a long breath. "I just— I don't even know what I want to get out of this. Do I just accept it? Move on? Dig deeper? I don't know where the line is between 'this is interesting' and 'I'm about to drive myself crazy.'"

Malcolm shrugged. "You always say 'let the DNA do the explaining.' Maybe you should take your own advice."

Before she could respond, their food arrived.

The waiter placed her plate in front of her, the aroma of perfectly seared crab cakes mingling with the light tang of citrus. Malcolm's steak frites followed, but she was already focused on her plate, picking up her fork and slicing into the golden-brown crust.

The first bite was *perfection*. The crisp exterior gave way to a soft, delicate center, the flavors bursting with just the right balance of seasoning and freshness.

She closed her eyes for a second, savoring it.

Malcolm laughed. "Damn. Should I leave you two alone?"

Nia smirked, opening her eyes. "You don't understand. *This* is exactly what I needed."

"Apparently," he said, cutting into his steak. "I was about to ask if you wanted to switch meals, but I feel like I'd lose a hand in the process."

"Correct," she said, taking another bite.

They both laughed, the tension breaking for just a moment.

For now, at least, food and laughter were enough to keep the questions at bay.

Malcolm cut into his steak, chewing thoughtfully before setting his fork down and shifting his gaze back to her. "Alright," he said, "let's switch gears a little."

Nia arched a brow. "Oh? Are we done talking about my newfound *possibly-maybe* sister?"

"For now." He smirked, taking a sip of his bourbon. "I trust you to figure it out. You always do."

She exhaled, shaking her head. "I wish I had your confidence."

"I have confidence in *you*."

His words were simple, but they settled deep in her chest. She looked at him for a moment, appreciating the steadiness in his eyes, the quiet belief he always had in her.

"What's on your mind?" she asked, recognizing the shift in his tone.

Malcolm rested his elbows on the table, considering his words. "Got a call this morning. An opportunity came up."

She tilted her head. "Good opportunity or 'ugh, I have to smile through this' opportunity?"

He smirked. "Good. Maybe great. A new commercial development in Atlanta—big names involved, big commission on the table. But I'd need to be there in person. Probably for a couple of weeks."

Nia took that in, nodding slowly. "When?"

"End of the month," he said. "It's not *final* yet, but it's looking pretty locked in."

She twirled the stem of her cocktail glass between her fingers, letting the information settle.

Malcolm wasn't the type to jump at just any opportunity. He was careful, strategic. If he was considering this, it meant it was worth it.

"You should go," she said, meeting his eyes. "If it's a good move for you, do it."

"You sure?" He studied her. "I don't want to just leave you here dealing with all this alone."

She let out a soft laugh. "Malcolm, I get lost in work when you *are* here. If anything, this just means you won't have to listen to me rant about genomes for a little while."

He smirked. "So you're saying you won't even notice I'm gone?"

Her face softened. "You know that's not true."

Malcolm's expression shifted slightly, something quieter, more thoughtful settling there.

"You're the one solid thing in my life, Mal," she admitted. "The only thing that's ever made sense in this world."

His gaze didn't waver.

"You *get* me," she continued, her voice steady. "Not just the surface stuff. Not just what I let people see. You really *get* me."

A small, almost imperceptible smile tugged at the corner of his lips. "That's because you let me."

She sighed, reaching for his hand across the table, lacing their fingers together. "So, if this is something you want—*really* want—I'm not going to be the one to hold you back."

He squeezed her hand gently. "I appreciate that, babe. But you know I'd turn it down if you needed me here."

She gave him a look. "And *you* know I'd never let you."

He exhaled a quiet chuckle. "Fair enough."

They sat like that for a moment, the warmth of his palm against hers, the hum of the restaurant fading into the background.

They had been together for nearly three years now—long enough to know each other's rhythms, each other's tells.

Long enough to trust that no amount of distance, even for a few weeks, would change anything between them.

Finally, Malcolm leaned back, giving her an easy grin. "Alright then. I'll go, make some money, close some deals, and you'll—"

"Bury myself in work until I forget to eat and Lena has to force-feed me," she finished dryly.

Malcolm pointed at her. "*Exactly.*"

She rolled her eyes. "I hate that you know me so well."

"No, you don't," he said smoothly, taking another sip of bourbon. And damn it, he was right.

CHAPTER FOUR:
Tomorrow

Nia sat on her couch, legs tucked beneath her, a throw blanket draped loosely around her shoulders. It was *relatively* early for her—only a little after nine—but she had been home for over an hour already, which was practically unheard of.

She had tried to work, tried to focus on anything that would keep her mind occupied, but it had been a losing battle all day. The numbers blurred, the reports seemed redundant, and even the DNA sequencing—a task she usually lost herself in—felt distant, unimportant.

Danielle lingered in the back of her mind.

Her messages. Her voice. The impossible connection between them.

With a sigh, Nia grabbed her phone and opened their chat.

Nia: *Hey, you free to talk?*

It didn't take long before the typing bubbles appeared.

Danielle: *Yes! I was wondering if you'd reach out. I know this whole thing is crazy for you.*

Nia: *That's an understatement.*

Danielle: *Lol fair.*

A short pause. Then another message.

Danielle: *I know I already said this, but you should really come to Darbonne.*

Nia smirked slightly, shaking her head. She had expected Danielle to push the visit idea again. It was clear she wasn't just making an offhand suggestion—she *really* wanted Nia to see the town for herself.

Nia: *You're persistent.*

Danielle: *Only when it matters :)*

Nia bit her lip, considering.

Nia: *Just like I scrolled through your profile, I'm assuming you've been doing the same with mine?*

Danielle: *Oh, absolutely. Lol. I had to know what kind of sister I was dealing with.*

That made Nia smile. Of course Danielle had been looking, just as curious, just as intrigued.

But as much as Danielle's profile had given Nia a glimpse into her life, something stood out—there was *nothing* about work. No job updates, no posts about hating Mondays or coworkers, no mentions of a career.

Nia hesitated, then typed:

Nia: *I noticed something, though—you never mention work. What do you do?*

A few seconds passed.

Danielle: *Oh, I'm my grandparents' caretaker. Full-time.*

That wasn't the answer Nia had expected.

Nia: *Really?*

Danielle: *Yep. I actually went to college and left home for a while, but when my grandparents' health started failing, I came back. They needed someone, and my parents are older too, so they weren't exactly reliable for it.*

Nia absorbed that.

Nia: *That's a lot of responsibility.*

Danielle: *It is. But I love Darbonne. It's home. Always has been, always will be.*

Nia frowned slightly at that. The way she said it, so matter-of-fact, so *final*.

Most people she knew—especially people from small towns—left and *stayed* gone. Or if they did return, it was with a heavy heart, a reluctant acceptance of circumstances.

But Danielle… she didn't just *live* in Darbonne. She seemed *rooted* there. Like there was no other option.

No desire to leave again. No curiosity about what else was out there.

Nia: *You never wanted to leave again? Not even after being away for college?*

Danielle: *Nope. Darbonne is everything to me. It's where I belong.*

Nia stared at the screen, her fingers hovering over the keyboard. Something about the phrasing unsettled her.

Not *"I love it here."*

Not *"It's my home."*

But— *It's where I belong.*

Nia let out a slow breath and leaned back against the couch. This was becoming more than just genetics. She just wasn't sure what *exactly* it was yet.

Nia exhaled, tapping her fingers against the phone screen as she considered Danielle's latest message.

It's where I belong.

There was something about the certainty in those words, the way Danielle spoke of Darbonne as if it were more than just a town. Like it was *a person*. A presence. A force she couldn't—or wouldn't—ever separate herself from.

Nia: *Alright, let's say I do come visit. What exactly are you hoping I'll see?*

The typing bubbles appeared almost immediately.

Danielle: *Everything.*

Nia scoffed.

Nia: *Vague. Super helpful.*

Danielle: *Lol, okay okay, I just mean… I think you'd get a better understanding if you were here. This isn't the kind of place you can explain through a text. You have to experience it.*

Nia sat back, rubbing her temple. A visit wasn't the craziest idea. She *did* have some time off saved up, and she hadn't taken a real break in… well, longer than she cared to admit.

Lena could handle the lab in her absence. She had practically been running the place all morning anyway. And if anything came up, Nia would only be a flight away.

Plus, Malcolm was leaving soon.

The thought made her stomach tighten slightly, but she shook it off. He wasn't *leaving* leaving. It was just a couple of weeks. And while she hated the idea of coming home to an empty bed, she had to admit—it would be a little easier if she wasn't home at all.

She could take the trip, see for herself what this was all about, then return to normal life.

Simple.

Nia: *Alright. I'll come for a visit.*

Danielle: *Really?!*

Nia: *Yeah. I could use the time off anyway.*

Danielle: *This is amazing! When do you think you'll get here?*

Nia: *I'll check flights and get back to you.*

With that, Nia opened a new tab on her laptop and started searching.

The nearest airport to Darbonne was in Lafayette, Louisiana. Not a huge hub, but workable. She could get a direct flight from Houston, rent a car, and drive the rest of the way.

She leaned forward, scanning for accommodations. If she was going to do this, she'd at least book herself a nice Airbnb. Something comfortable, close enough to town but private enough to retreat to when she inevitably needed space.

Her fingers moved across the keyboard, entering search filters. But nothing came up.

She frowned, refreshing the page. Still nothing. No hotels. No bed-and-breakfasts. No *anything*.

That was... odd. Even the smallest towns had *somewhere* to stay.

She tried another site.

Same result.

With a deepening frown, she switched to a general search: Where to stay in Darbonne, Louisiana.

Nothing.

She drummed her fingers against the table, chewing the inside of her cheek before switching back to the chat.

Nia: *Hey, weird question, but... does Darbonne not have hotels? Or Airbnbs? I can't find anything.*

The response came quickly.

Danielle: *Yeah, we don't really have those. Most people just stay with family.*

Nia hesitated.

Nia: *Okay, well, what do visitors do?*

Danielle: *We don't get a lot of visitors, tbh.*

That was *really* odd. Even small towns got visitors. If nothing else, *passing-through* travelers.

Before she could dwell on it, another message popped up.

Danielle: *You can just stay with me and my family! That way, you get the real experience.*

Nia blinked.

She hadn't exactly been fishing for an invitation.

She sat back, gripping her phone a little tighter.

Staying with Danielle and her family? That felt… intimate. A little *too* intimate.

She didn't even know these people. Hell, she didn't even know if she really *believed* these people were her family.

She chewed the inside of her cheek, trying to weigh her options.

Nia: *I don't know…*

Danielle: *Come on! It'll be fun. And I promise, we're normal. Well, mostly lol.*

Nia let out a slow breath, staring at the blinking cursor in the text box.

Was she really about to do this?

Nia hesitated, staring at the message. It wasn't that she thought Danielle was dangerous. At least, not in any obvious, *Dateline mystery* way. But there was something about the invitation that gave her pause.

She was a scientist. A logical thinker. And logic told her that staying in a stranger's home—even if that stranger shared half her DNA—wasn't necessarily the best idea.

She needed to talk this through. Maybe Malcolm would have a level-headed perspective. Or Lena, who always had a gut instinct for things like this.

Her fingers moved across the keyboard.

Nia: *Let me think about it. I'll get back to you.*

Danielle: *Of course! No pressure at all. Just let me know when you decide.*

Nia exhaled and locked her phone, setting it face-down on the coffee table.

She'd already committed to the trip, which was big enough. The details could wait until she had more clarity—or at least, until she wasn't sitting alone in her living room making decisions she wasn't sure about.

Yawning, she stretched her arms over her head, feeling the weight of the day finally settle into her muscles.

Tomorrow, she'd talk to Malcolm. And maybe, just maybe, he'd tell her exactly what she needed to hear.

Nia sighed, sinking deeper into the couch. Her mind was still running laps around the idea of Darbonne, of Danielle, of this whole situation she had somehow agreed to step into.

The sound of soft movement made her glance toward the kitchen.

Dinga.

The cat was creeping—sneaking—in that calculated way only cats could manage, moving low to the ground with the kind of deliberation that meant she was absolutely up to no good.

Nia narrowed her eyes. "Dinga…"

The cat froze mid-step, golden-green eyes flicking toward Nia with a look of absolute, feigned innocence.

Nia sat up slightly. "What are you doing?"

Dinga did not answer. Instead, she darted forward in a sudden, calculated burst—straight toward the kitchen counter.

"Dinga, no—"

Too late.

The little menace had launched herself onto the counter, landing with a quiet *thud* near the leftover chicken Nia had meant to put away.

"Excuse me?" Nia gawked, scrambling up from the couch.

Dinga, to her credit, at least had the *decency* to look guilty. But not guilty enough to abandon her mission. Her little pink nose twitched, eyes darting from Nia to the unattended food.

"Don't you *dare*."

Dinga, defiant, *dared.*

She reached one sneaky little paw forward—

Nia lunged.

Dinga bolted.

In a blur of fur and poor decisions, she leapt down from the counter and *skittered* across the floor, barely dodging Nia's reach before disappearing into the hallway.

"Unbelievable," Nia muttered, grabbing the plate and finally covering it. "You *eat* twice a day, you *have* treats, and you still act like a damn street cat."

Dinga peeked around the corner, tail flicking. No remorse.

Nia pointed at her. "I should revoke your snack privileges for that."

Dinga chirped in response, as if to say, *You won't.*

Nia exhaled, shaking her head. "Yeah, yeah. Go be sneaky somewhere else."

Dinga took that as permission to resume whatever silent rebellion she was planning next, trotting away with her tail high, victorious.

Nia rolled her eyes but couldn't help smiling a little.

At least Dinga was a *predictable* kind of chaos. Unlike, say, the very real possibility that she had a sister waiting for her in a town that apparently didn't believe in hotels.

CHAPTER FIVE:

SILENCE

Nia had buried herself in work for the past couple of days, letting the steady rhythm of the lab drown out the thoughts swirling in her mind. She hadn't talked to Danielle since their last exchange, hadn't texted or followed up about the trip. It wasn't intentional—at least, that's what she told herself—but the silence had stretched longer than she expected.

She had meant to check flights again. Had meant to call Malcolm and get his take. Had meant to at least *decide* if she was staying in some stranger's house in a town with no hotels.

But instead, she had done what she did best—she had worked.

Lena walked in mid-morning, tablet in hand, stopping just short of Nia's desk.

"Okay," she said, without preamble. "Before I add it to your calendar, you're definitely not going to be here next week, right?"

Nia frowned, looking up. "Wait, what?"

Lena sighed, flipping her tablet around to show her screen. "You told me a *few days ago* that you were going to take time off. Something about a family thing?"

And just like that, the realization hit Nia like a slap to the forehead.

Right. The trip. Danielle.

She had *completely* forgotten to follow up.

Lena, sharp-eyed as ever, caught the shift in Nia's expression and raised an eyebrow. "You *did* still plan on going, right?"

Nia exhaled, leaning back in her chair. "I don't know. I—" She hesitated, drumming her fingers against the desk before finally admitting, "I never actually booked the flight."

Lena gave her a flat look. "Of course you didn't."

Nia groaned, rubbing her temples. "It's just—ugh, I don't know, Lena. This whole thing is *weird.*"

Lena pulled up a chair and sat down, crossing her legs. "Alright. Spill. What's got you hesitating?"

And just like that, it all came pouring out.

Nia told her everything—about the DNA match, about Danielle, about the eerie, *too-identical* birthmark. She told her about Darbonne, the fact that there were no hotels, no rentals, no *trace* of a place for outsiders to stay. And then, finally, about Danielle's insistence that she stay with her and her family.

By the time she finished, Lena's eyebrows had practically disappeared into her hairline.

"Damn," she said, shaking her head. "This is some *real* soap-opera-level stuff."

"Tell me about it," Nia muttered.

Lena tapped her fingers against the armrest. "Okay, so… gut reaction. Do you *want* to go?"

Nia hesitated. "I don't know."

"Liar."

Nia sighed. "Okay, fine. *Yes.* I do. I want to see what this is all about, get some answers. But I also don't want to get there and feel like I've walked into something I *can't* walk out of, you know?"

Lena nodded slowly. "Yeah. I get that."

Nia glanced at her. "So what do you think? Would *you* go?"

Lena huffed a quiet laugh. "Girl, I don't know. On one hand, this is a *once-in-a-lifetime* kind of thing. You find out you have a whole-ass sister? That's huge. On the other hand… something about the whole *'we don't have hotels, just stay with us'* thing is giving me *get-out-while-you-can* energy."

"Exactly." Nia gestured toward her. "It's like, it sounds innocent enough, but also, why is there *nowhere* to stay? Why does no one visit this place?"

Lena tilted her head. "You *could* just visit and stay somewhere in a nearby town. Drive in for the day, see what it's about, and leave if you don't like it."

"That was the original plan." Nia sighed. "But there's nothing close enough to make that convenient. And Danielle really wants me to *immerse* myself in it. Says I won't *get it* unless I'm there for real."

Lena narrowed her eyes slightly. "That... sounds cult-y."

Nia snorted. "Right?"

"Like, *not obviously a cult*, but a *cult-adjacent* kind of vibe."

Nia let out a deep breath, rubbing the bridge of her nose. "I don't know what to do."

Lena studied her for a moment, then leaned forward. "You said Malcolm's leaving town, right?"

Nia nodded. "Yeah, in a few days."

"Okay. So, what's really holding you back? 'Cause from what I'm hearing, it's not the trip itself—it's the *staying with them* part."

Nia hesitated. "...Yeah."

"Then *don't* stay with them. If you really want to go, go. But be smart about it."

Nia crossed her arms. "You think I should do it?"

Lena shrugged. "I think if you don't, you'll regret it. You don't strike me as the type to let unanswered questions sit for long."

Nia let out a quiet chuckle. "No, I guess not."

Lena leaned back in her chair, tapping her fingers against her knee. "So, what's the move?"

Nia exhaled, grabbing her phone and staring at Danielle's last message.

Come stay with us.

She drummed her fingers against the screen, thinking.

Then, finally, she started typing.

Nia tapped out a response, her fingers hesitating for only a moment before she hit send.

Nia: *Alright, I'm booking my flight. Still figuring out where I'll stay, but I'll be there soon.*

A response came almost instantly.

Danielle: *Yay!! This is going to be amazing. And you know my offer still stands. You should stay with us.*

Nia let out a quiet sigh, chewing on the inside of her cheek.

She was still torn on that part. It felt like a boundary she wasn't sure she wanted to cross just yet.

Nia: *I appreciate that, really. Just let me figure out a few things first.*

Danielle: *Of course! Just let me know when you get in, and I'll come pick you up from the airport.*

Nia frowned slightly at that.

Nia: *I was thinking of renting a car.*

Danielle: *You could… but Darbonne is kind of tricky if you don't know the roads. No GPS past a certain point, and cell service is spotty. It'd just be easier if I drive you in.*

That made Nia pause.

No GPS? No service?

That didn't sound impossible, especially in rural Louisiana, but something about the way Danielle phrased it gave her pause.

She filed that bit of information away for later and responded carefully.

Nia: *I'll think about it.*

She put her phone down, exhaling as she turned back to Lena. "Well, I guess I'm doing this."

Lena grinned. "Oh, *you were always doing this*. You just needed someone to push you a little."

Nia huffed a laugh. "Maybe."

Lena gave her a knowing look. "So, you gonna tell Malcolm?"

"Yeah," Nia muttered. "Tonight, probably. I already know what he'll say."

Lena smirked. "Let me guess. 'Be careful, babe. Call me every five minutes. Don't get murdered.'"

"Basically."

Lena shook her head, still smiling. "Well, I guess I'll hold things down here while you go off and play detective."

"Thanks." Nia stood, stretching out the tension in her shoulders. "I owe you fries when I get back."

Lena gasped dramatically. "*From La Belle?*"

Nia smirked. "Obviously."

Lena placed a hand over her heart. "Now *that* is love."

Shaking her head, Nia grabbed her coat and checked the time. She still had a full workday ahead of her, but her mind was already halfway gone, spinning through the logistics of what she had just committed to.

She was really doing this.

She was going to Darbonne.

As soon as Nia stepped into her office and closed the door, she pulled out her phone and scrolled to Malcolm's name.

She tapped the call button and pressed the phone to her ear, pacing near her desk as the line rang.

"Hey, babe," Malcolm answered smoothly, his voice warm, familiar. "You calling to tell me you're actually coming home early for once?"

Nia smirked. "Not exactly."

There was a pause. "…That doesn't sound good."

She sighed, leaning against her desk. "It's not bad. Just… unexpected."

Malcolm hummed. "Go on."

Nia took a breath. "I decided I'm going to Darbonne."

A beat of silence.

Then— "For real?"

"For real."

Malcolm exhaled sharply, and she could practically *see* him rubbing the bridge of his nose. "Alright. Walk me through this. What changed?"

She hesitated, gathering her thoughts. "I don't know, exactly. I guess I just realized I *need* to see it for myself. I've spent days trying to make sense of it all from a distance, and it's not working. If I want answers, I need to go where the answers are."

"That makes sense," Malcolm admitted. "But you're sure about this? Because, not gonna lie, babe, this whole thing still feels *off* to me."

"It *is* off," she agreed. "And that's *why* I have to go."

Malcolm let out a low chuckle, but there was no real humor in it. "That stubborn scientist brain of yours. Can't just let a mystery sit, huh?"

"Absolutely not."

"Yeah, I figured."

She smiled slightly, then sighed. "I looked for places to stay, but there's literally nothing. No hotels, no rentals, no *anything*. Danielle says most people just stay with family, and she offered again for me to stay with her."

Malcolm *definitely* didn't like that. "And what did you say?"

"That I'd think about it."

Malcolm groaned. "Babe. *Really?*"

"I *know*," she said quickly. "I know how it sounds. But what choice do I have? I can't drive in and out every day if there's nowhere nearby."

"Or, hear me out," Malcolm said, "you just *don't go.*"

She huffed. "You *know* that's not happening."

"Yeah, I do," he muttered. "I had to try, though."

She softened. "I'll be careful. I promise."

Malcolm exhaled through his nose. "You better be. And you'll check in? Call me when you land?"

"Yes."

"And if anything *at all* feels off, you leave. No hesitation."

"I *will*."

He was quiet for a moment, then sighed. "I hate this."

"I know," she murmured. "But I need to do it."

"I know," he admitted. "Just… be smart, babe."

She smiled softly. "When am I not?"

Malcolm let out a tired laugh. "Do you *really* want me to answer that?"

She chuckled, shaking her head. "I'll book the flight tonight and send you the details."

"Good." His voice was quieter now, but still steady. "I trust you, Nia. I just don't trust… *this*."

She swallowed. "I get that."

A pause.

Then, softer— "I'm gonna miss you."

Her chest ached slightly, but she kept her voice light. "You *just* said I'd be too busy to notice you were gone."

"Doesn't mean I won't notice *you're* gone," he murmured.

She closed her eyes briefly, warmth settling in her ribs. "I'll be back before you know it."

"Better be."

They sat in silence for a moment, the distance between them stretching, but not in a way that felt insurmountable.

Then Malcolm sighed. "Alright, go book your flight. And, Nia?"

"Yeah?"

"If this turns into some *small-town horror movie scenario*, I am *personally* coming to drag your ass out of there."

Nia laughed. "Deal."

And with that, she hung up, staring at her phone for a long moment.

This was happening.

She was really doing this.

Now, all that was left was booking the flight… and figuring out whether she was actually going to stay with Danielle and her family.

After hanging up with Malcolm, Nia leaned back in her office chair, staring at the ceiling as she let the weight of her decision settle over her.

Darbonne.

A place she had never heard of until a few days ago, a town with no hotels, no Airbnbs, and apparently, *no visitors*.

She pulled her laptop closer and opened a new tab, fingers hovering over the keyboard before she typed:

Darbonne, Louisiana.

A few results popped up, but nothing particularly useful. There was no official tourism website, no city government page, no real online footprint at all.

The town had a Wikipedia entry, but it was *bare bones*—a brief history mentioning its founding in the mid-1800s, its population hovering around 1,200 people, and its economy once being built around timber and farming. There was no mention of any major businesses, no local attractions, nothing that explained how the town functioned in the modern era.

She clicked on Images, expecting at least a few recognizable shots—maybe a town square, a church, or a welcome sign.

Instead, the images were mostly outdated, grainy photos of dirt roads, weathered storefronts, and dense marshland. One of the few clear photos she found was of an old general store with a faded wooden sign reading Mercer's Market.

Her stomach tightened.

Mercer.

Danielle's last name.

Her family owned a business there.

She clicked on the image, but it didn't lead to anything useful. No website. No business hours. Just… an image with no context.

Frowning, she tried Mercer's Market Darbonne LA, but nothing came up besides that same old image and a few vague references on community message boards.

Nia chewed the inside of her cheek. That was *odd*. Even small, family-run businesses usually had *some* kind of online presence. A Facebook page, a Yelp review—something.

But Darbonne? It was like the town existed outside of time.

She switched gears and opened Google Maps, zooming in on Louisiana until she found the small dot labeled *Darbonne*. She tapped the satellite view, expecting to get a clearer picture.

The town was nestled deep within dense forest and swamp, with only a handful of roads cutting through the landscape. There was one main stretch that might've been the town center, but aside from that, it was almost all trees and water.

Nia narrowed her eyes, dragging the map around. No chain restaurants. No gas stations. No major roads leading in.

Just a few isolated houses and a couple of structures that could've been anything—a school, a church, maybe a post office.

Her chest tightened.

Where the *hell* was she going?

A knock at the door made her jump.

She snapped her laptop shut as Lena peeked in, raising a brow. "You good? You looked like you were about to get sucked into the Matrix just now."

Nia huffed, rubbing her temples. "Yeah. Just… trying to figure out what kind of place I'm walking into."

Lena stepped inside, flopping into the chair across from her desk. "And?"

Nia shook her head. "This town is *weird*, Lena. It's tiny. Like, *barely exists on a map* tiny. No hotels, no businesses with an online presence, no real anything.

And I just found out Danielle's family owns some kind of market there, but I can't find a single record of it being open or active."

Lena frowned. "Okay, *that* is sketchy."

"Right?" Nia exhaled, crossing her arms. "And on top of that, I couldn't even find a single visitor review. No blogs, no travel notes—nothing. It's like no one ever *goes* there."

Lena pursed her lips. "So let me get this straight. You're flying into a town that doesn't advertise itself, doesn't get visitors, and barely has a digital footprint— *to stay with a family you just met through a DNA app?*"

Nia winced. "When you say it like that, it sounds… *bad*."

"It *is* bad." Lena sat up, gesturing wildly. "Babe, you are literally walking into some *Stephen King-level small-town horror setup*."

Nia groaned, rubbing her forehead. "Look, I get it. But I can't shake this feeling that I *have* to go. That if I don't, I'll never get the full story."

Lena sighed dramatically. "Alright. But if you end up in some *cult situation*, I will personally drive down there to bust you out."

Nia laughed despite herself. "Appreciate it."

Lena pointed at her. "Just—*be smart*. And *please* don't turn your phone off the second you get there."

"Promise."

Lena eyed her, then sighed, pushing up from the chair. "Fine. Go do your detective thing. But if you end up needing a rescue mission, I'm bringing snacks."

Nia smirked. "Duly noted."

As Lena left, Nia glanced at her laptop again, her fingers drumming against the desk.

Darbonne wasn't just *small*.

It was isolated. Intentionally so. And the more she dug, the more she realized—this town didn't want to be found.

CHAPTER SIX:

Tinted

The moment Nia stepped off the plane, she was hit with a wall of thick, humid air—sticky and dense, clinging to her skin in a way that made her immediately regret wearing jeans. The airport smelled of fried food, stale coffee, and jet fuel, a strangely comforting mix that reminded her of travel but also made her stomach turn slightly after the long flight.

Pulling her carry-on behind her, she rolled her shoulders, trying to shake off the stiffness that had settled deep in her muscles. She had spent most of the flight mentally preparing herself for what was coming, committing fully to the experience. She wasn't going to half-step her way through this.

If she was going to Darbonne, she was going to do it right.

She pulled out her phone and typed quickly.

Nia: *Just landed. Gate B6.*

Almost immediately, the typing bubbles appeared.

Danielle: *Yay! I'm outside in passenger pickup. Black SUV.*

Danielle: *Also, welcome to Louisiana :)*

Nia smirked slightly, shaking her head as she made her way through the terminal.

The airport wasn't huge, but it wasn't exactly small either. The ceilings were high and industrial, with massive windows that let in a flood of natural light. Travelers bustled around her, dragging their own luggage, talking into phones, waiting impatiently at baggage claim. The sounds of shuffling feet, rolling suitcases, and muffled airport announcements created a low, constant hum in the background.

She made a quick stop in the restroom to freshen up, splashing cold water on her face before staring at her reflection in the mirror.

She looked good, even if she didn't quite feel it. Her locs were pulled back into a high bun, a few escaping around her temples, the result of travel fatigue. She adjusted her simple black tank top, wiping at a stray mascara smudge beneath her eye, before exhaling deeply.

Alright. No turning back now.

Grabbing her bag, she stepped back into the terminal and followed the signs toward Passenger Pickup.

The heat hit her again the moment she stepped outside, heavier than before, the kind that pressed against her like a second skin. The air smelled earthy and damp, a reminder that she wasn't in the city anymore—she was in the South, and the South had a way of making itself known immediately.

Her gaze swept the line of waiting cars until she spotted it.

Black SUV. Tinted windows. Parked near the curb.

Her stomach tightened slightly. She hesitated—just for a second—before walking toward it. As she got closer, the back passenger window rolled down, and there she was.

Danielle Mercer.

Blonde hair pulled into a loose ponytail, strands escaping in the humidity. Blue eyes that were even brighter in person, scanning Nia with an eager, open curiosity. She was smaller than Nia had expected, maybe an inch or two shorter, with a lean frame, delicate wrists.

And, just like in the pictures, she looked… white.

Which still didn't make any damn sense.

Danielle grinned, her entire face lighting up. "You made it!"

Nia swallowed down the unease rising in her chest and forced a small smile.

Yep. No turning back now.

Danielle practically bounced out of the SUV, her movements fluid and effortless as she hurried around to meet Nia at the back.

"Here, let me help," she said, reaching for Nia's carry-on before she could protest.

"I got it," Nia started, but Danielle had already grabbed it, hoisting it easily into the back of the SUV.

"You're my guest," she said, flashing a bright, toothy smile. "Let me do something nice for you."

Nia exhaled, nodding once. "Alright, thanks."

She slid into the passenger seat as Danielle hopped behind the wheel, the door shutting with a solid, insulated thud that muffled the noise of the airport outside.

"Hope you're ready for a bit of a drive," Danielle said as she adjusted the air conditioning, blasting cool air into the SUV. "Darbonne's about an hour and a half from here."

Nia smirked. "I figured. Nothing about this trip has been *convenient* so far."

Danielle laughed, shifting into drive. "Yeah, we're kind of... off the map."

That was an understatement.

As they pulled away from the airport, Nia took in the landscape around them. The city fell away quickly, replaced by expanses of open road, stretches of flat land and towering oaks draped in Spanish moss. The scenery was lush, green, the kind of untouched nature that felt like it had existed forever, unchanged by time.

"You hungry?" Danielle asked, glancing at her. "I can stop somewhere if you need to eat."

Nia shook her head. "I'm good. Had something on the plane."

"Cool. I just didn't want to kidnap you on an empty stomach," Danielle joked, shooting her a playful smile.

Nia gave her a look. "Let's not joke about kidnapping *just yet*."

Danielle laughed. "Fair."

They rode in companionable silence for a few minutes, the sound of the tires humming against the pavement filling the space between them.

Nia leaned her elbow on the door, watching as the road stretched ahead—long, winding, leading deeper into nothingness.

"So," she said, breaking the silence. "What's Darbonne actually like?"

Danielle hummed thoughtfully. "That's a tough one. It's… different."

"Different how?"

"You'll see," Danielle said, casting her a sideways glance. "It's got a history. People there don't leave often. When they do, they usually come back. It's the kind of place that just… gets in your bones."

Nia frowned slightly at that. "That sounds *ominous*."

Danielle grinned. "I didn't mean it like that. I just mean—it's home. Always has been, always will be."

Nia stared at her for a second, something unsettlingly familiar about those words.

She had said them before. In their texts.

Darbonne is where I belong.

The SUV continued down the road, the highway narrowing as they left behind the last remnants of modern civilization.

The trees grew thicker, the sky above shifting to a muted gray-blue, dense marshland appearing along the roadside.

They were heading somewhere quiet, somewhere deep.

And for the first time, Nia wondered—what exactly had she signed up for?

Nia watched the scenery shift, the road narrowing as civilization faded behind them. The further they drove, the more isolated it felt—less like they were heading toward a town and more like they were being pulled into some forgotten part of the world.

The towering cypress trees lining the road were draped in curtains of Spanish moss, their tangled limbs reaching over them like twisted fingers. The land was increasingly wet, patches of swamp water visible between dense clusters of trees. The air smelled heavier here, thick with the scent of damp earth and the faint, distant musk of something wild.

Danielle didn't seem fazed. If anything, she looked at ease.

"You don't get creeped out living way out here?" Nia asked, glancing at her.

Danielle chuckled, shaking her head. "No way. I love it."

Nia raised a brow. "You *love* being surrounded by nothing but trees and water?"

"It's not *nothing*," Danielle said, giving her a knowing smile. "It's *home*."

That word again.

Home.

Like Darbonne wasn't just a place, but something else entirely.

"So you never wanted to leave?" Nia pressed.

Danielle hesitated for a second, then shrugged. "I mean, I left for a little while. College. But the whole time, I missed it. The way the air smells after a storm, the way the trees sway at night… the quiet."

"The quiet?" Nia echoed, glancing out the window.

There was nothing but the rustling of leaves, the distant croak of frogs, the occasional chirp of cicadas.

"Yeah," Danielle said, smiling to herself. "Darbonne's not like the rest of the world. We don't have the same noise. It's… peaceful."

Nia wasn't sure she'd call it peaceful. Something about it felt too still.

The kind of stillness that wasn't calm, but watchful.

She shifted in her seat. "So what do people do for fun in Darbonne? No hotels, no visitors… is there at least a bar or something?"

Danielle laughed. "Oh, yeah. There's a bar. We've got a town square, too. A little church, a general store—my family's store, actually."

Nia nodded, remembering the faded sign from her online search. "Mercer's Market."

"Yep." Danielle glanced at her. "You looked it up?"

"Tried to. There's barely anything online about it."

Danielle shrugged, like that wasn't unusual. "Not much reason to have a website when everyone in town already knows us."

Nia frowned. "But what about people passing through?"

Danielle's fingers tightened around the steering wheel. Just slightly.

"We don't really get people passing through."

A small shiver crawled down Nia's spine.

She stared out the window again. The road had stopped feeling like a highway leading somewhere and more like a path closing in behind them.

"So… no tourists?" she asked, careful.

Danielle smirked. "Nope."

"Ever?"

Danielle's smile lingered, but something about it felt… off. "Not often."

The SUV rumbled along the worn pavement, the silence stretching too long before Danielle suddenly perked up, changing the subject.

"You know," she said, grinning, "I was thinking about what you said—how you scrolled through my profile? Well, I did the same to you."

Nia raised a brow, amused despite herself. "I figured."

Danielle laughed. "I mean, *of course* I did. I had to see what my long-lost sister was like."

"And?"

"And…" Danielle gave her a teasing look. "You're a workaholic."

Nia smirked. "Not *news*."

"No, but seriously, your life is impressive. The lab, the awards… you're kind of a big deal, Dr. Wallace."

Nia chuckled, shaking her head. "I don't know about all that."

"I *do*," Danielle said firmly. "You fought your way to where you are. I respect that."

Nia studied her, unsure what to say.

Danielle smiled. "And now you're here. A scientist in a town that probably hasn't changed much since the 1800s."

Nia exhaled, glancing at the dense trees that lined either side of the road. "Yeah… don't remind me."

Danielle laughed again, but this time, Nia noticed something in her eyes—something curious. Like she was studying Nia just as much as Nia was studying her.

Another twenty minutes passed before Danielle finally slowed the car, turning onto a narrow dirt road, trees closing in tighter around them.

Nia straightened in her seat.

This wasn't just a town.

This was something else entirely.

Nia let the silence settle for a few moments, watching as the landscape grew denser, the trees swallowing the last remnants of open sky. The road beneath them wasn't just narrowing—it was changing, the smooth pavement giving way to something rougher, older. The occasional wooden post marked the sides of the road, but there were no signs, no mile markers, no indication that this place was meant to be found by anyone who didn't already know where they were going.

She shifted, adjusting the seatbelt against her chest before finally asking, "So... what do you know about my dad?"

Danielle's hands flexed on the steering wheel, just slightly, before she let out a small breath. "Our dad," she corrected lightly, giving Nia a sidelong glance.

That sent a ripple through Nia's chest.

Our dad.

That wasn't the first time she had considered it, but hearing it said out loud made it feel more real than she was ready for.

Danielle smiled, but there was something carefully measured about it. "We'll talk about all that later."

Nia frowned. "Why not now?"

Danielle kept her eyes on the road, her expression calm but unreadable. "Because right now, I want you to see Darbonne. Take it all in before we dive into family history."

That felt like a deflection. A smooth, intentional redirection. But before Nia could press, the road curved, and suddenly—the town appeared.

It wasn't gradual. One second, there was nothing but trees, and the next, Darbonne revealed itself like a place tucked away in a fold of the universe. The first thing Nia noticed was the architecture.

The buildings weren't run-down, but they looked frozen in time—old-fashioned wooden facades, deep porches with rocking chairs, faded signs painted directly onto brick storefronts. Nothing about it was modern. No strip malls, no chain restaurants, no glaring neon lights.

People were outside.

More than she expected for a town so isolated. Some stood in small clusters, talking on sidewalks, while others sat on porch swings, watching the road. A group of kids on bicycles coasted past, their laughter bright and familiar, but something about it felt… too uniform.

Danielle waved at a few passersby, and every single person waved back.

Not just acknowledged her—but waved with warmth, with familiarity, as if she had been gone for a while and had just returned home.

Nia scanned the storefronts as they passed:

- Mercer's Market – The sign was the same one from the photo she had found online, faded but still standing. A few people were gathered near the entrance, chatting like it was more than just a grocery store—like it was a meeting place.

- Darbonne General – A hardware store, its windows packed with old farming equipment, oil lamps, and wooden barrels.

- Langley's Diner – A small café with a painted front, its chalkboard sign advertising "Beignets & Chicory Coffee – Today's Special."

- The Parish Hall – A large, two-story building with a bell hanging in a wooden tower.

If Nia had to guess, it was part government office, part church, part town gathering place.

Everything had that well-worn, lived-in look, but it wasn't abandoned. There was no dusty neglect, no sense of decay.

It was preserved.

Like someone had chosen to keep it exactly the way it had always been.

Danielle pulled the SUV down a narrower side street, where houses lined both sides—modest but sturdy, with deep porches and hanging flower baskets. The trees grew so thick overhead that the light here was softer, muted, like the sun itself had to push harder to reach the ground.

Nia exhaled slowly, her fingers curling against her knee.

This place felt untouched.

Like time hadn't been allowed to pass here the way it did everywhere else.

Danielle glanced at her with a knowing smile. "Not what you expected, huh?"

Nia shook her head, because it wasn't.

She had prepared herself for small-town Southern, for something like the rural Louisiana towns she had driven through before—gas stations with fading signs, a Walmart on the outskirts, maybe a fast-food place with a drive-thru.

But Darbonne was different. It wasn't just small. It was self-contained.

Like it wasn't part of the outside world at all.

The town stretched before them in a quiet sprawl, its roads winding through thick patches of cypress trees and swampy undergrowth. The deeper they drove, the clearer it became that Darbonne was a place untouched by time, a community preserved in a way that felt almost intentional. There were no fast-food chains, no grocery store parking lots filled with shopping carts, no signs of the outside world creeping in. Everything about it felt self-contained, as if the town had been built to sustain itself, with no need for anything beyond its borders.

The houses all carried a similar aesthetic—modest but sturdy, with wide porches and shuttered windows, the kind of homes meant to endure both heat and storm. The dirt roads that branched off the main path led to farmland and pastures, where neatly spaced rows of crops grew in rich, dark soil. Occasionally, a figure would appear—an older woman in a long dress sweeping her front porch, a group of men gathered near a pickup truck, their conversation easy and familiar. People here moved at a different rhythm, unhurried, as if time carried no weight.

Nia couldn't shake the feeling that everyone was watching her. Not in an overt, suspicious way, but with a quiet curiosity, the kind that comes with recognizing someone who doesn't belong. Their gazes lingered just a second too long before they turned away, their expressions neutral, unreadable. She had visited plenty of small towns before, knew the feeling of standing out in a place where everyone knew everyone. But this was different. There was an awareness in their eyes, a knowing. As if her arrival had been anticipated.

She shifted in her seat, glancing at Danielle, who seemed completely at ease. "How many people live here?" she asked, watching as they passed a diner with a hand-painted sign that read Langley's Café & Bakery. A few people sat outside drinking coffee, their conversations pausing briefly as the SUV rolled past.

"About twelve hundred," Danielle said, giving her a small smile. "It used to be more, but people don't leave as much as they used to."

Nia frowned slightly. "Don't leave?"

Danielle nodded. "Not permanently, anyway. Some go off for school or a little adventure, but most come back. It's just... home, you know?"

That word again. Home. She had heard it before, but never with the weight Danielle gave it. Darbonne wasn't just home in a nostalgic, small-town-America way. It was something deeper. A claim, an identity.

They passed what looked like the town square, a wide-open space surrounded by old brick buildings, their windows framed by wooden shutters. A large oak tree stood at the center, its sprawling branches casting shadows over a weathered wooden bench beneath it. There was a general store, a barber shop, and a small parish hall, its white steeple rising modestly against the backdrop of the trees. The people here weren't in a rush—some sat on benches, others walked slowly along the sidewalks, their conversations hushed but steady.

She had expected something more rural, more modern in certain places, but Darbonne wasn't just a small town. It was its own world, suspended in time.

"So what about you?" Nia asked, pulling her gaze away from the town and back to Danielle. "You said you left for college, but you came back?"

Danielle nodded, her expression warm but thoughtful. "Yeah. I went to school in Baton Rouge for a bit, thought about staying, but it didn't feel right. My grandparents needed me, and honestly, I missed this place. It's not for everyone, but for me, it's where I belong."

Something about the way she said it made Nia pause. There was no hesitation, no regret, just certainty. She had never felt that kind of certainty about a place before. Even now, with all her success, her apartment, her life, she didn't think of anywhere as truly belonging to her.

Danielle turned down a quieter street lined with oak trees draped in Spanish moss, their branches swaying slightly in the warm, thick air. "We're almost there," she said, nodding toward the end of the road.

Nia let her gaze drift to the houses they passed, all similar in structure, yet unique in the way time had settled into them. Some had peeling paint, others had perfectly manicured gardens, but they all carried a sense of permanence. These weren't places people moved in and out of. These were homes that had been passed down, lived in by generations of the same families.

A wooden sign appeared ahead, hand-carved and aged by the elements, its letters barely visible beneath years of wear.

Welcome to Darbonne. Founded 1852. Home to Generations.

The words struck her in a way she couldn't explain. Not *A Great Place to Live*. Not *A Historic Town*. Just Home to Generations. As if leaving wasn't part of the equation.

Danielle turned into a long driveway, the tires crunching softly over gravel. The house ahead of them was two stories, its wraparound porch adorned with hanging plants and a wooden swing swaying slightly in the breeze. A small vegetable garden stretched along the side, neat rows of tomatoes and peppers thriving under the afternoon sun. It was beautiful in a quiet, settled way.

Danielle put the car in park and turned to Nia, her smile bright, expectant. "Welcome home."

Nia swallowed, gripping the door handle.

She wasn't sure if it was exhaustion from the trip or the weight of stepping into something unknown, but the word *home* settled uneasily in her chest—this wasn't her home.

CHAPTER SEVEN:

Truly

Nia stepped out of the SUV, the late afternoon heat wrapping around her like a damp blanket. The air smelled thick with earth, wood, and something faintly floral, a scent she couldn't quite place. The house before her was larger than she expected, its structure old but well-maintained, with white wooden siding and a wraparound porch that sagged slightly at the edges, evidence of time and weather pressing against its bones. The porch swing creaked lightly in the breeze, and wind chimes—small, delicate ones—tinkled softly from a nearby beam.

Danielle moved ahead of her, stepping up onto the porch with ease, her keys jingling as she unlocked the heavy wooden door. It groaned on its hinges as it swung open, revealing the dim interior beyond.

"Come on in," Danielle said, pushing the door wider.

Nia hesitated for just a second, a small ripple of something uneasy passing through her chest, but she stepped forward, crossing the threshold into the house.

Anywhere But Here

The air inside was cooler than she expected, carrying the scent of aged wood, faint lavender, and something warm—like bread baking, but not quite. The floors beneath her were hardwood, well-worn, smooth beneath her sneakers. She glanced up at the high ceilings, where an old brass ceiling fan turned lazily, stirring the stillness in the air.

The interior had an old-world charm, but it wasn't outdated. It felt curated, like a place that had remained frozen in time on purpose. Framed black-and-white photos lined the hallway, the kind of pictures taken with film cameras—portraits of people dressed in styles that spanned decades, maybe even a century.

A long wooden staircase stretched up to the second floor, its bannister polished to a soft gleam. To the right, an open archway led into what looked like the living room—plush, antique furniture in deep earth tones, lace curtains drawn against the fading sunlight.

Danielle set her bag down near the stairs, shrugging out of her light jacket. "It's not much, but I love it," she said, smiling as she glanced back at Nia.

Nia stepped further inside, her fingers brushing the smooth wood of the hallway table. "It's beautiful," she admitted. "Feels... lived in."

Danielle grinned. "That's because it is. This house has been in my family for generations. My grandparents live here too, but they mostly stay upstairs these days. I'll introduce you later."

The word generations struck a familiar note in Nia's mind, tying back to the sign she had seen on the way in.

"Where should I put my stuff?" she asked, shifting her bag on her shoulder.

"Follow me," Danielle said, leading her through the hallway.

As they moved, Nia took in more details—a large grandfather clock ticking softly in the corner, shelves lined with old books, glass jars filled with dried herbs and other things she couldn't quite identify. There were no TVs, no electronics visible, just the quiet hum of the ceiling fan and the occasional creak of the house settling around them.

Danielle pushed open a door near the back of the house, revealing a guest bedroom. It was simple but welcoming—a four-poster bed covered in a handmade quilt, a small writing desk beneath a wide window, and a dresser topped with a ceramic lamp, its floral shade casting a soft glow.

"You'll be staying here," Danielle said, stepping aside so Nia could enter.

Nia set her bag down near the bed, running her hand over the quilt. The fabric was soft, slightly worn, the kind of thing that had been passed down rather than bought new. She glanced around, taking in the lack of personal decorations. No pictures, no clutter—just the essentials.

"It's nice," she said.

Danielle smiled. "Glad you think so. Make yourself at home."

That word again.

Home.

Nia exhaled, sitting down on the edge of the bed, the mattress firm but comfortable beneath her.

She had committed to this fully. No backing out now.

Danielle lingered in the doorway for a moment before saying, "Dinner should be ready soon. You hungry?"

Nia nodded, realizing she actually was. "Yeah, I could eat."

"Good," Danielle said, flashing a grin. "Come on, let's head to the kitchen. You can meet my mom."

Nia stood, brushing her palms against her thighs before following Danielle out of the room.

As they walked, the house creaked softly beneath their footsteps, as if shifting to accommodate her presence.

She wasn't sure if it was her imagination, but she couldn't shake the feeling that the house itself was watching her.

Danielle led Nia down the hall, the wooden floorboards giving a soft, rhythmic creak beneath their steps. The hallway was lined with tall, narrow windows, their panes slightly warped with age, filtering in the last golden light of the evening. A subtle floral scent lingered in the air, something old-fashioned—lavender, maybe, or dried rosemary—something that had seeped into the walls over time.

"This will be your room," Danielle said, stopping at the last door on the left. She pushed it open, stepping aside to let Nia in first.

The guest bedroom was simple but thoughtfully arranged. The four-poster bed sat in the center of the room, draped in a quilt made of deep earth tones, its fabric slightly worn at the edges but still soft-looking. A small wooden desk sat beneath a window, the white lace curtains billowing slightly from the evening breeze. Against the opposite wall stood a sturdy dresser, its top bare except for a ceramic oil lamp, casting a warm, flickering glow.

Nia stepped inside, letting her fingers trail across the quilt, feeling the raised seams of careful stitching. Everything about the room felt intentional, preserved, like nothing had been moved or changed in years.

"You can unpack if you want," Danielle said, leaning against the doorframe. "Or just relax a bit before dinner. It should be ready soon."

Nia glanced around. "Who stayed here before me?"

Danielle tilted her head slightly. "No one, really. It's always just been the guest room."

Nia turned toward the window, looking out. The view stretched into the trees, where the sky beyond had turned a dusky purple, the last traces of daylight fading behind the thick canopy. There were no city lights, no streetlamps—just the dark silhouette of cypress trees swaying slightly, their Spanish moss drifting in the wind like slow-moving specters.

No traffic. No distant hum of civilization.

Just quiet.

Nia set her bag down by the dresser, exhaling. "It's nice."

Danielle smiled. "Good. I want you to feel comfortable."

That phrasing felt deliberate.

Danielle lingered a moment longer before pushing off the doorframe. "I'll let you settle in. I'll come get you when dinner's ready."

She left the door open behind her, her footsteps fading down the hall.

Nia sat on the edge of the bed, testing the firmness of the mattress beneath her. She glanced around the room again, taking in the small details—the slightly uneven floorboards, the old brass keyhole on the door, the faint indentations on the wooden desk where someone had once pressed too hard while writing.

Everything in this house had history.

Nia sat on the bed for a long moment, her fingers idly smoothing over the textured fabric of the quilt. The quiet here was dense, but not in a suffocating way. It was layered, almost alive, the kind of silence that felt deliberate, settled, at peace with itself.

For once, she didn't mind it.

Her apartment back home was never truly silent—there was always the hum of the fridge, the distant rush of cars outside her window, the occasional thump of a neighbor moving around upstairs. But here, there was nothing but stillness, broken only by the occasional rustling of leaves outside and the soft tick of an unseen clock.

She exhaled, letting herself sink into it.

The last few days had been a whirlwind of overthinking, analyzing, trying to make sense of something that refused to fit neatly into any category she understood. Now that she was here, actually inside this world, it felt different than she had expected. Not *better*, necessarily, but calmer. More rooted.

She walked over to the window, pushing aside the lace curtain to get a clearer look. The land stretched out beyond the house, a mix of open fields and dense tree lines. Fireflies flickered near the grass, small golden pulses against the creeping dusk. It was the kind of thing she had only seen in childhood summers, visiting distant relatives in the South.

Out here, time felt slower.

She could see why Danielle liked it.

Turning away from the window, Nia moved toward her bag, unzipping it and pulling out a fresh shirt and some toiletries. A shower sounded nice—something to wash away the flight, the drive, the weight of the day settling into her shoulders. She wasn't exhausted, exactly, but she felt the need to shake off the last remnants of travel before facing whatever came next.

She stepped into the hallway, glancing in both directions. The house was eerily still, the soft glow of oil lamps casting long shadows along the wooden walls. For a second, she thought she heard something—a distant murmur of voices, but when she paused to listen, it was gone.

Shaking off the strange feeling, she made her way toward the bathroom, appreciating the simplicity of it all. No buzzing electronics, no glaring artificial lights—just quiet, and the faint, comforting scent of lavender and warm wood.

She could get used to this.

Maybe.

The bathroom was just as old-fashioned as the rest of the house—clawfoot tub, porcelain sink with brass fixtures, wooden shelving lined with neatly folded towels. The mirror above the sink had a slightly worn, cloudy edge, not quite warped but showing its age. Everything was well-kept but timeless, as though no one had ever felt the need to modernize it.

Nia turned on the faucet, letting the cool water run over her fingers before adjusting the temperature. The house might have been old, but the plumbing was surprisingly efficient. She undressed quickly, stepping into the shower, sighing as the warm spray loosened the tension in her shoulders.

The water smelled clean, crisp, like it had been pulled straight from a deep well. It felt good, rinsing away the weight of travel, the stiffness of sitting on a plane, the overthinking that had been running loops in her head since she arrived.

For a few minutes, she let herself just exist, listening to the steady rhythm of water hitting the porcelain tub.

When she finally stepped out, wrapping herself in a thick cotton towel, the air felt cooler against her skin. She wiped the fog from the mirror, catching her own tired but curious reflection.

She looked… different. Maybe it was just the soft lighting, or maybe it was the realization that she was here now, really here, doing something she wouldn't have even considered a week ago.

She ran her fingers along her scalp, feeling the new growth at the roots of her locs, slightly fuzzier than she liked. She was overdue for a retwist, something she had meant to get done before she left but had pushed to the side like so many other personal things. Work had always come first.

But now, here in a place where time felt slower, she had no excuses.

Maybe she'd finally take a breath.

She dressed quickly, pulling on a fresh shirt and leggings before stepping back into the hallway. The house still felt settled in its own silence, though now she could hear the faint clinking of dishes, the low murmur of voices coming from the kitchen. She followed the sounds, her bare feet cool against the hardwood floors, as she made her way toward the kitchen.

The closer she got, the more she felt it—the warmth, the scent, the quiet hum of a house that had seen generations of people pass through its walls. She felt like she was stepping into something bigger than herself.

The kitchen was warm and lived-in, the kind of space that had been used for generations. The walls were lined with wooden cabinets that had darkened over time, their surfaces worn smooth from years of use. The scent of slow-cooked meat and fresh cornbread thickened the air, mingling with something more herbal—bay leaves, maybe, or rosemary. A large pot simmered on the stove, steam curling toward the ceiling, while a cast-iron skillet rested on the counter, still glistening with oil.

Danielle stood near the sink, rolling up her sleeves as she dried her hands on a kitchen towel. She glanced up as Nia stepped inside and smiled. "There you are. I was about to come get you."

Seated at the wooden dining table were two older figures, their expressions neutral but observant. The woman, who had to be Danielle's mother, was in her late sixties, with sharp blue eyes and gray-streaked blonde hair pulled back into a low bun. She had a lean face, fine lines creasing her mouth and forehead, her hands folded neatly in front of her. The man beside her—Danielle's father, presumably—was broader, stockier, with a weathered face and tanned skin that suggested a lifetime of outdoor labor. He looked up from his plate, chewing slowly, taking his time before acknowledging Nia.

Danielle gestured toward them as she wiped her hands. "Mom, Dad—this is Nia."

Her mother was the first to respond. She stood, wiping her hands on a napkin before extending one toward Nia, her grip firm but not unfriendly. "Nice to meet you. I'm Claire Mercer."

Nia shook her hand, noting the roughness of her palm. Not just aging hands, but hands that had worked. "Nice to meet you too."

Her father didn't stand but gave her a slow nod. "Richard," he said simply. His voice was deep, slightly gravelly, like someone who didn't waste words.

Nia nodded back. "Nice to meet you."

Danielle pulled out a chair for her at the long wooden table. "Go ahead and sit. I'll fix you a plate."

Claire returned to her seat, picking up her fork, while Richard took a slow sip from his glass, watching Nia with mild curiosity, but nothing too pointed.

"You have a long trip?" Claire asked, her tone even, not overly warm but not cold either.

"Yeah," Nia said, sliding into the chair. "It wasn't bad, though."

Claire nodded, as if that was all the small talk required.

Danielle placed a plate in front of Nia—braised meat, roasted potatoes, cornbread, and greens. It smelled rich, comforting, like something that had been cooking for hours.

"Hope you like it," Danielle said, sitting across from her. "We eat simple here, but it's good."

Nia picked up her fork. "Smells amazing."

Richard let out a small grunt, amused. "It's real food, not that takeout stuff."

Claire shot him a look. "Richard."

He shrugged. "Just sayin'. Kids these days eat like they're afraid of a stove."

Nia smirked slightly but didn't respond, just took a bite of the meat. It was tender, well-seasoned, falling apart the second she pressed her fork into it. The cornbread was soft, slightly sweet, the kind that didn't need butter to be good but would probably be even better with it.

Danielle grinned as she watched her eat. "Told you."

"It's good," Nia admitted.

Richard nodded in approval before returning to his plate.

The conversation was minimal as they ate. The Mercers weren't the type to fill silence just for the sake of it, but it didn't feel awkward. It felt normal. Like they were used to sitting together, eating in the comfort of their own space, not performing politeness for guests.

Claire finally broke the quiet. "So, Nia," she said, setting her fork down. "What do you do?"

"I'm a geneticist," Nia said, wiping her mouth with her napkin. "I specialize in ancestry research."

Richard huffed. "So that's how you found Danielle?"

"Pretty much. Well, techinically she found me."

Claire gave a slow nod, eyes sharp but unreadable. "Interesting work."

Nia nodded, waiting for the next question, but Claire didn't press further.

Richard finished the last of his food, leaned back in his chair, and stretched. "Well," he said, pushing his plate aside, "guess we'll see what comes of all this."

Nia wasn't entirely sure what he meant by that, but she didn't ask.

Danielle, sensing the shift in conversation, smiled at Nia. "Want a drink? We've got sweet tea, lemonade, or I can grab you a beer."

"Tea's fine," Nia said, still processing the dynamic in the room. The Mercers weren't unfriendly, but there was something carefully measured about them.

They weren't overwhelmed by her presence, weren't fawning over her like some long-lost relative.

They were simply... waiting.

For what, she wasn't sure.

Nia set down her fork, her appetite dimming beneath the weight of the question that had been lingering in the back of her mind since she arrived. She glanced at

Richard, who was leaning back in his chair, arms crossed loosely over his broad chest, watching her with that same quiet, unreadable expression.

"So, just to be clear," she said, keeping her voice even, "are you Danielle's biological dad?"

Danielle stilled slightly, though her expression remained neutral. Claire's fingers tapped once against the table, a subtle motion, but otherwise, she didn't react.

Richard exhaled through his nose, the faintest smirk tugging at the corner of his mouth, like he'd been expecting the question. "No," he said simply.

Nia felt something cold settle in her stomach.

Richard shifted, resting his forearm against the table. "I met Claire when Danielle was just a baby. She was already here, already part of this place. I came later."

Nia studied him, trying to read between the lines. His answer wasn't evasive, but it was deliberate, like he had measured every word before saying it.

Claire sat perfectly still beside him, her expression composed, but there was something solid, unwavering in the way she held herself.

Nia turned toward Danielle. "So… your biological dad?"

Danielle offered a small, knowing smile. "That's what we're going to talk about. But not tonight."

Nia frowned. "Why not?"

Claire finally spoke, her voice even. "Because this is your first night here. There's no rush."

There was something final in her tone, not unkind, but firm, like she had already decided how this was going to go.

Nia clenched her jaw but nodded slowly. She could press, but what would that get her? She had already committed to this trip, to playing by their rules, at least for now.

Richard stood, stretching slightly, then picked up his plate and carried it to the sink without another word.

Danielle gave Nia an easy smile, but there was something else behind it, something careful. "You're tired," she said. "We can get into all the heavy stuff later."

Nia wanted to argue that she wasn't tired, that she had spent the last week waiting for answers only to now be told she needed to wait longer. But she could already tell that pushing wasn't going to get her anywhere.

So, she forced herself to relax, leaning back in her chair. "Fine. I'll wait."

Danielle grinned. "Good. Now let's get you that tea."

Nia exhaled slowly, watching as Danielle stood and moved toward the kitchen counter, pulling a glass from the cupboard.

The questions would have to wait. But something told her the answers were going to be more complicated than she was prepared for.

Nia finished her sweet tea, the cool liquid settling in her stomach as the last of dinner wrapped up. The conversation had shifted to nothing in particular—Danielle mentioning something about the town's recent harvest festival, Claire commenting on the weather, Richard not saying much at all. It wasn't unfriendly, but it also wasn't the cozy, long-lost-family reunion vibe that might've come with a situation like this.

She wasn't sure if that made her more comfortable or more uneasy.

After helping Danielle clear the dishes, she excused herself, making her way back down the hall to her room. The house had grown quieter, the warm glow of oil lamps flickering against the wooden walls, casting long, uneven shadows. It wasn't eerie, exactly—but it did feel insulated, as if the house itself existed separately from the rest of the world.

Inside the guest room, she shut the door softly behind her and exhaled.

She wasn't tired, not really. The day had been long, but her mind was still too wired, too full to even think about sleep.

Unzipping her suitcase, she began unpacking—folding clothes into the dresser, setting her toiletries in the small washroom attached to the room. As she moved, she let her thoughts untangle.

Richard wasn't Danielle's biological dad. That meant he wasn't her dad either. Which left the biggest question of all—who was?

Danielle had danced around the topic, and Claire had shut it down altogether. Not yet. Not tonight. Like there was a right time for that kind of information.

Nia frowned as she tucked her empty suitcase beside the dresser.

They knew something.

Something they weren't telling her.

Sitting on the edge of the bed, she pulled out her phone and dialed Malcolm. The call rang twice before his familiar voice came through the speaker.

"Hey, babe," he said, sounding both relieved and amused. "You're still alive. That's a good start."

Nia rolled her eyes, smirking. "Yes, Malcolm. I haven't been sacrificed to a small-town ritual. Yet."

"*Yet*," he repeated. "I don't like that you had to add that word."

She sighed, shifting against the bed. "It's... different here."

"Different how?"

She glanced around the room, as if the walls might have something to say about it. "The town's small—way smaller than I imagined. There's no Walmart, no gas stations, nothing you'd expect to find in a place that actually has people living in it. It's like they don't want to be connected to the outside world."

Malcolm was quiet for a second. "You sure you don't want to get a hotel in the next town over?"

She huffed. "You think I didn't look? There's nowhere to stay outside of Darbonne. Nowhere close enough to make it work. And besides... I already agreed to stay here."

"Of course you did," he muttered.

She smirked. "You're enjoying this, aren't you?"

"Oh yeah. I *love* knowing my girlfriend is staying in a place that doesn't show up on GPS with people who don't believe in giving straight answers."

She rubbed her temple. "They're not *weird* exactly. Just… reserved. Like they're waiting for the right moment to tell me things. And Richard—Danielle's dad? He's not actually her dad. Which means he's not mine either."

Malcolm let out a low breath. "So that leaves…?"

"No one," Nia said, frustration creeping into her voice. "At least no one they want to talk about yet."

Malcolm didn't like that. She could tell by the way his tone sharpened. "You think they're hiding something?"

"I don't know." She exhaled. "I just know there's something *off* about this place."

"Then be careful," he said, voice firm. "Promise me, Nia."

She softened slightly. He knew her too well, knew how easy it was for her to get wrapped up in something once she set her mind to it.

"I promise," she said.

A pause, then, lighter, "So, how's the food?"

She chuckled. "Actually? Damn good."

Malcolm groaned. "Now I'm jealous."

"You should be. The cornbread was perfect."

"Alright, you're just being mean now."

She smiled, letting the moment settle between them.

"Get some rest," Malcolm said after a beat. "And keep me updated. Every few hours, if possible."

"Yes, sir."

"Damn right."

She laughed, shaking her head. "Goodnight, Malcolm."

"Night, babe."

Hanging up, she stared at the phone for a moment before setting it on the nightstand. The house around her was quiet again, the low hum of the night outside filtering through the thin walls.

Nia pulled the blanket over her legs, leaning back against the pillows. She wasn't tired, but eventually, she'd have to sleep.

And something told her that when she did, she'd wake up feeling even deeper in this than she already was.

CHAPTER EIGHT:

Knowing

Nia woke up feeling surprisingly refreshed, the kind of rest that settled deep into her bones, smoothing out the exhaustion of travel. The air in the room was cool but not cold, the weight of the thick quilt making it easy to sink into the mattress.

For a moment, she just lay there, listening.

No car horns. No distant hum of traffic. No city noise pressing against the edges of her thoughts.

Just quiet.

And then, the scent hit her.

Breakfast.

It drifted through the air, warm and rich, something undeniably Southern—buttery, savory, the kind of scent that made you want to abandon all pretense of eating light. There was a hint of bacon, something fluffy and sweet—maybe biscuits or pancakes—and the unmistakable smell of coffee, deep and roasted.

Okay, she could get used to this part.

Stretching, she sat up, running a hand over her scalp, fingers catching slightly at the new growth near the roots of her locs. She made a mental note—*retwist. Soon.*

But before she got sucked into the promise of breakfast, she reached for her laptop. She needed to check in.

Flipping it open, she logged into her work account, scanning through her inbox. Lena had things under control, as expected. A few flagged emails, a couple of questions from the grad students, but nothing urgent.

Satisfied, she clicked to open a video call.

Lena picked up after a couple of rings, her face filling the screen, already sipping from a large coffee mug, her dark curls piled into a loose bun.

"Well, well, well," Lena said, smirking. "She lives."

Nia scoffed. "Barely. But yeah, still here."

Lena took another sip of coffee, studying her. "You look… well-rested. That's suspicious."

"Blame the quiet," Nia said, leaning back slightly. "And the food. I haven't even eaten yet, but I can already tell I'm about to be fed like someone's grandma has claimed me."

Lena grinned. "I mean, if you *had* to go get yourself tangled in some weird family mystery, at least you're doing it with good food."

"Silver lining," Nia muttered, rubbing her temple.

"So?" Lena asked, setting her mug down. "What's the verdict so far? Super cult-y or just mildly unsettling?"

Nia sighed. "Honestly? Still figuring that out. The town is… weird, but not in an obvious way. No big red flags, just a *lot* of little things that don't add up."

Lena tilted her head. "Like?"

Nia hesitated, drumming her fingers against the edge of her laptop. "For one, there's no outside industry. No hotels, no grocery chains, no *reason* for this town to be as self-sustaining as it is. Everything just *functions* without anyone questioning it."

"That *is* weird," Lena admitted.

"And then there's the people. Everyone here looks… related. Not just in the 'small town, we all know each other' way, but actually related. The same bone structure, the same facial similarities."

Lena frowned. "Like, *inbreeding-level* similarities?"

"No, nothing that extreme," Nia said quickly. "But enough that I noticed it almost immediately. Like there's a shared genetic foundation across the whole town."

Lena sat back, processing that. "And they still won't tell you anything about your dad?"

"Nope," Nia muttered. "Richard isn't Danielle's biological dad. He came here later, after she was born. And when I asked about who *was* her dad—our dad—they basically shut it down. Said we'd 'talk about it later.'"

Lena gave her a long look. "Yeah, that's suspicious as hell."

Nia sighed, rubbing her eyes. "Tell me about it."

"So what's the plan?"

"For now?" Nia exhaled, closing her laptop. "Breakfast."

Lena laughed. "That's probably the smartest thing you've said since you got there."

"Shut up."

They smirked at each other before Lena shook her head. "Alright, go eat. But keep checking in. I don't trust this."

"Neither do I," Nia admitted.

And with that, she ended the call, standing to stretch before heading toward the kitchen, the smell of breakfast growing stronger with every step.

The smell of breakfast still clung to the air long after they had finished eating—buttery biscuits, crisp bacon, eggs soft and creamy in a way that only came from experience. Nia had to admit, she wasn't used to this kind of home-cooked meal every morning. It was dangerously easy to enjoy.

After clearing the table and rinsing her plate, she turned to find Danielle leaning against the kitchen counter, a mischievous glint in her eyes.

"So," Danielle said, wiping her hands on a dish towel. "How do you feel about a little tour?"

Nia raised a brow. "A tour?"

Danielle grinned. "Yeah. You came all this way—you might as well see the town for yourself."

Nia hesitated. "I mean… I kind of got a good look yesterday when we drove in."

"Trust me," Danielle said, pushing off the counter. "There's more to Darbonne than what you saw from the car."

That gave Nia pause.

More.

Like what?

Danielle was already heading toward the front door, clearly expecting her to follow. Nia sighed, glancing toward Claire and Richard, who were still seated at the table, sipping their coffee. Neither of them said anything, but Claire gave a slow, knowing smile.

Something about that made Nia uneasy.

Still, she grabbed her light jacket from the chair and followed Danielle out onto the wide wraparound porch, stepping into the bright morning air.

It was warmer than she expected, but not oppressive, the kind of humid Southern heat that settled in slowly, creeping along your skin. The town was already alive—people walking along the dirt roads, stopping to chat, moving through their morning routines with an ease that suggested they had been doing the same thing for generations.

Danielle started down the steps, motioning for Nia to follow. "Come on, we'll start with the market."

Nia fell into step beside her, the road beneath them a mix of packed dirt and gravel, smoothed by years of foot traffic and the occasional car.

She had questions—so many questions—but something about the way Danielle carried herself, so casual and at ease, made her hesitate. Like this wasn't just about showing her the town.

Like it was about easing her into something bigger.

Still, she walked.

For now, she would just observe.

And if something felt off, she would figure out exactly why.

The deeper they walked into town, the more Nia noticed.

It wasn't just the way the town looked—old-fashioned but well-maintained, frozen in time like an antique carefully polished for display. It was the way the people moved, the way they interacted, the way their eyes lingered just a second too long.

They weren't unfriendly.

But they weren't exactly welcoming either.

Everyone acknowledged Danielle with familiarity—small nods, murmured greetings, knowing smiles that carried a weight she couldn't quite define. But when their gazes flickered to Nia, something in their expressions would shift. Not suspicion, not outright wariness, but something... measured. Like she was something to be examined, not embraced.

She kept her face neutral, scanning the buildings as they passed.

Everything had an unmistakable uniformity—not in structure, but in preservation. The wooden storefronts were old but not decayed, aged but not neglected. Hand-painted signs hung above each shop, lettering in the same traditional script, as if every sign in town had been designed by the same hand.

There were no modern logos, no bright colors, no digital displays.

Even the windows seemed different—no neon signs, no posters advertising sales or promotions. Just curtains drawn back enough to reveal carefully arranged goods inside.

And the people?

It was subtle, but now that she was walking among them, she could see it even more clearly.

The resemblance.

It wasn't just one or two people who looked alike—it was almost everyone.

Same high cheekbones, same striking eyes, variations of the same nose, the same sharp jawlines. Even their hair, though differing in shades from blonde to deep brown, had a similar texture, a certain natural wave that repeated itself from one face to another.

In any other town, you'd expect some variety—some genetic mixing, some clear sign of outside influence.

But here?

It was too uniform.

Too intentional.

The sound of a bell chiming softly drew her attention, and she realized they were standing in front of Mercer's Market—the same one she had seen in old photos, the one with the faded wooden sign.

Danielle turned to her with a smile. "Come on, I'll show you around."

Nia hesitated for just a second, then followed her inside.

The scent of wood, herbs, and something vaguely sweet—molasses, maybe—filled the air. The interior was exactly what she expected—no automatic doors, no glossy tiled floors, just wooden shelves stacked neatly with goods, baskets of fresh produce arranged with care.

But the oddities continued.

The products lining the shelves were… strange.

No brand names. No logos.

Jars of preserved vegetables, dried herbs, handmade candles, all labeled in the same careful handwriting.

Even the bags of flour, the sacks of grain, the bottled honey—all without commercial labels.

Everything here was produced in Darbonne.

Everything was kept in Darbonne.

And still, no one acknowledged her outright.

The woman behind the counter, a thin, older woman with silver-threaded dark hair, smiled at Danielle warmly but barely spared Nia more than a glance. A man stacking apples in a wooden crate glanced her way, his gaze sliding over her like he was assessing something unspoken.

And yet, no one questioned her presence.

No one asked who she was, or why she was here.

Because, somehow, they already knew.

Nia's stomach tightened, but she kept her expression unreadable as Danielle led her toward the back of the store.

"Most of what we sell here is made by people in town," Danielle explained, running a hand along a shelf of hand-labeled jars of jam. "We don't really rely on outside shipments much."

Nia nodded slowly. "Yeah, I can see that."

She wanted to ask more, to push, to dig at the logic of it all—how could a town this small sustain itself so completely? How did people survive with no external trade, no outside industry?

But she held back.

For now.

Instead, she let Danielle lead her through the shop, nodding at the right moments, keeping her thoughts to herself.

Because as much as she had expected answers, she was only finding more questions.

And the biggest one of all was pressing harder and harder against the edges of her mind.

What exactly was Darbonne hiding?

Nia followed Danielle through the narrow aisles of Mercer's Market, taking in the way the store was curated more like a living artifact than a place of commerce. Every item seemed intentional, every placement deliberate, like someone had taken great care to ensure nothing looked out of place.

Danielle chatted easily, pointing out little things about the store—where they sourced their vegetables, how the town had a system of bartering that made traditional currency almost unnecessary—but Nia only half-listened.

She was too busy studying the people.

They moved through the shop with a quiet purpose, their interactions smooth, almost rehearsed. The way they greeted each other, the way their conversations paused just long enough when she passed—it was as if they were aware of her without acknowledging her outright.

She had never been in a place that felt so closed in, so self-sustained, so... insular.

And then the murmur of voices near the entrance shifted.

A ripple of something subtle, almost imperceptible, passed through the store. It wasn't alarm, but it was awareness.

Nia turned just as a man stepped inside.

Mayor Harris Grayson.

She knew it was him before Danielle even said a word.

He carried himself with the kind of self-assurance that came from years of power, but it wasn't the overbearing kind. It was smooth, calculated, easy. His tall frame, neatly pressed button-down, and rolled-up sleeves gave him an approachable air, but Nia recognized the control in his movements.

Everything about him was polished but not extravagant. His hair was streaked lightly with gray at the temples, his smile perfectly practiced, the kind that made people trust him without even realizing they were doing it.

As he approached, everyone subtly shifted, not out of fear, but out of deference.

It was an instinct, woven into the air like muscle memory.

"Well, well," he said, voice wrapped in honey but weighted with something heavier. His eyes flickered over Nia, assessing, like he had already formed an opinion before she spoke. "So, this is the one we've been waiting for."

Danielle smiled, stepping aside slightly. "Mayor Grayson, this is Nia Wallace. Nia, this is—"

"Harris, please," he interrupted, offering a hand. "No need for formality."

Nia hesitated, but only for a second before shaking his hand. His grip was firm but not overbearing, his expression friendly but watchful.

"Welcome to Darbonne," he said, tilting his head slightly, studying her in a way that felt… measured.

"Thanks," Nia said, keeping her voice even. "It's definitely different from what I'm used to."

Harris chuckled. "I imagine so. The outside world moves fast. But here? We like to keep things simple."

Simple.

That word sat strangely in her chest.

His smile widened. "I'm sure Danielle's been showing you around, but if you ever have any questions, my door is always open."

That felt like a lie.

But Nia just nodded. "Appreciate that."

Harris studied her for a moment longer before looking toward Danielle. "You'll bring her by the hall, won't you? No visit is complete without a proper welcome."

"Of course," Danielle said easily, as if that had always been part of the plan.

Nia wanted to ask what exactly a 'proper welcome' entailed, but something told her now wasn't the time.

Harris gave her one last assessing look before smiling again. "Enjoy your tour, Ms. Wallace. I have a feeling you'll find Darbonne has a way of growing on people."

And with that, he turned, engaging someone else in conversation as if the exchange had never happened.

Nia exhaled slowly, glancing at Danielle. "He runs things around here, huh?"

Danielle nodded, leading her toward the back exit of the shop. "You could say that."

And that, Nia thought, was probably an understatement.

Danielle led Nia out of Mercer's Market, stepping into the warm, humid air as the door creaked shut behind them. The scent of fresh earth and slow-burning wood lingered in the streets, mixing with the faint sweetness of something being baked nearby—maybe pies, maybe bread, something rich enough to make Nia's stomach stir despite her full breakfast.

But her mind was elsewhere.

"Okay," she said, lowering her voice slightly as they walked along the main road. "That guy. Harris Grayson. He's got the whole friendly small-town mayor thing down to a science, but something about him feels…"

Danielle gave her a knowing look. "Controlled?"

"Yeah," Nia admitted. "Like everything he says is precisely calculated, but in a way that makes it seem natural."

Danielle exhaled through her nose, amused. "That's Harris. He's been mayor for as long as I can remember. Keeps the town running, keeps the peace."

"Right," Nia said slowly, glancing back over her shoulder at the market's entrance, where Harris was now speaking to a small group of people, his smile easy, his body language effortless—but there was something in the way people listened to him that made her stomach tighten.

It wasn't just respect.

It was obedience.

She turned back to Danielle. "And when you say 'keeps the peace'…?"

Danielle shrugged, stepping around a puddle in the uneven dirt road. "I just mean people trust him. He knows how to make things work. If there's a dispute, he settles it. If something needs fixing, he finds a way. He's good at keeping Darbonne…" She hesitated, choosing her words carefully. "*The way it's supposed to be.*"

Nia caught the phrasing immediately. "And how exactly is it supposed to be?"

Danielle smiled, but there was a flicker of something underneath it. "You'll see."

That was quickly becoming a theme in Darbonne.

Nia let the silence sit between them for a moment, watching as they passed more weathered wooden buildings, each one meticulously preserved in a way that didn't feel like restoration, but rather deliberate maintenance. The town wasn't frozen in time.

It was being held there.

They passed Langley's Café & Bakery, where a few people sat on the shaded porch, sipping from ceramic mugs. A small chalkboard sign near the entrance read:

TODAY'S SPECIAL: Sweet cream biscuits & fig preserves.

It looked homey, inviting. But when one of the women at the table noticed Nia, her gaze lingered just a second too long, and she leaned toward the man sitting across from her, whispering something.

Nia clenched her jaw. She was being watched.

Not directly. Not in a way she could call out.

But in a way that told her people had already decided what they thought about her.

Danielle must have noticed because she gave Nia's shoulder a small nudge. "Ignore that."

"That's a little hard to do."

"They're just curious," Danielle said lightly, leading her down another narrow street. "New faces don't come through here often."

"That much is obvious."

Danielle didn't argue. Instead, she gestured toward a two-story brick building at the end of the street, its white shutters freshly painted, its large oak doors polished to a soft gleam. A sign above the entrance read:

DARBONNE PARISH HALL.

It looked part town hall, part church, part something else entirely.

"We'll stop by later," Danielle said, noticing Nia's lingering stare. "Harris will want to do the formal introduction thing."

Nia tore her eyes away from the building. "That seems... unnecessary."

Danielle smirked. "Like I said, you'll see."

The conversation left her with more questions than answers, but for now, she absorbed the details, cataloged the strangeness, let the town settle into her bones in a way that made her both uneasy and intrigued.

Because one thing was clear.

Darbonne wasn't just a place. It was a system. A carefully balanced structure. A town that had somehow evaded change, evaded time itself. And she had a feeling she was walking straight into the center of whatever was keeping it that way.

CHAPTER NINE:

CRYPTIC

Back at the Mercer house, Nia finally had a moment to herself. Danielle had excused herself to help her mother with something in the kitchen, and Richard had disappeared somewhere, leaving Nia in the quiet of the guest room with nothing but her thoughts—and her growing list of questions.

She had spent the day absorbing everything—the market, the people, the way the town seemed to move as one collective entity. There were no outsiders, no lingering visitors, no evidence of the modern world creeping in at all.

And then there was Harris Grayson.

The way people reacted to him, the way his presence seemed to shift the air in a room without him having to do much at all. He wasn't just a mayor. He was something else here.

There were too many gaps in what she knew, too many details that didn't make sense.

So, she would do what she did best—dig.

Pulling her laptop from her bag, she powered it on, waiting for the screen to glow to life. She adjusted her position on the bed, fingers hovering over the keyboard before typing:

Darbonne, Louisiana – History.

The first results were useless—basic snippets, census data, outdated town directories. There was no official town website, no archive of public records she could access. Darbonne had existed since 1852, according to the faded welcome sign, but where was its history?

She refined her search.

Darbonne, Louisiana – Archives.

Darbonne, Louisiana – Founding Families.

Darbonne, Louisiana – Mayor Harris Grayson.

Nothing.

She frowned, shifting against the pillows. That was odd. Even small, rural towns had some sort of historical documentation. There should have been something—an old newspaper article, a local historian's blog, anything.

She clicked through another page of results, frustration growing.

Then, one link caught her eye.

A buried forum thread, deep in an old genealogy site. The title read:

DARONNE, LA – ANYONE HAVE FAMILY FROM THERE? CAN'T FIND MUCH INFO.

She clicked.

The post was old—more than a decade. A user had written:

"I've been researching my family tree and found records linking some of my ancestors to a place called Darbonne, Louisiana. But there's hardly anything about it online. My great-great-grandmother's birth certificate lists it as her place of origin, but I can't find any records of her after 1893. It's like she just disappeared. Anyone else have relatives from there?"

A few replies followed.

One person mentioned hearing similar stories from an older relative—ancestors from Darbonne who had seemingly vanished from the historical record.

Another claimed their family had once lived near the area but left abruptly in the early 1900s, never speaking of it again.

And then, at the bottom, the last response sent a chill down Nia's spine.

"Darbonne doesn't like being found. And people who leave don't talk about it. Be careful where you start digging."

Nia swallowed, staring at the words, heart thudding just slightly harder. She scrolled down, but the thread had been locked. No more replies. No more information.

Her fingers tightened around the laptop. This place wasn't just small or self-sustained—it had been deliberately erased. And now, she was starting to understand why.

A sound outside made Nia pause, fingers hovering over the laptop keys. A soft creak—not from the house settling, but from the porch.

She frowned, pushing the computer aside and moving toward the window. Pulling the lace curtain back slightly, she scanned the view beyond the porch.

There, just beyond the steps, stood an elderly woman.

Her frame was thin but upright, her skin dark and weathered like polished mahogany, lined with years of knowing. She wore a simple cotton dress and a worn shawl draped over her shoulders, but it was her eyes that struck Nia the hardest.

Sharp. Piercing.

And unlike the other people in town, she was looking directly at her.

Not in passing. Not measuring her the way the others did.

But seeing her.

Nia's breath caught slightly, her heart knocking against her ribs.

Before she could move, before she could even decide what to do, the woman lifted a hand and curled her fingers in a slow, deliberate motion.

Come here.

Nia hesitated.

She had spent her entire time in Darbonne being observed, treated like an outsider without being openly rejected. But this? This was different.

This woman wanted something from her.

Anywhere But Here

Grabbing her phone, she slipped out of the room, making her way down the hall. The house was quiet, only the faint clinking of dishes from the kitchen breaking the silence. Danielle was still with her mother, nowhere in sight.

Nia reached the front door, hesitating for just a second before pushing it open.

The woman—Aunt Celeste, something in her gut told her that was the name—stood still, watching as Nia stepped onto the porch.

"You're the one," Aunt Celeste said, her voice low but firm, like she wasn't asking.

Nia frowned. "Excuse me?"

Aunt Celeste tilted her head slightly, looking her over. Not with curiosity, but with recognition.

"You shouldn't be here," she murmured.

Nia's spine stiffened. "And why's that?"

Aunt Celeste let out a slow breath, glancing toward the house behind her before stepping closer. "Because they've been waiting for you. And that ain't a good thing, baby."

The words sent a ripple through Nia's chest. Not fear, exactly. But something close.

Before she could ask anything else, the sound of a door swinging open behind her made her turn.

Danielle stepped onto the porch, her expression carefully blank, but her body language tight. "Aunt Celeste."

The way she said it wasn't warm.

It wasn't affectionate.

It was an acknowledgment.

Aunt Celeste didn't turn around. Her eyes stayed locked on Nia. "You listen to me," she murmured, just low enough that only Nia could hear. "Before you let this place make you forget who you are, come find me."

Nia's fingers curled slightly at her sides.

Before she could respond, Aunt Celeste turned, moving with slow, measured steps down the gravel path leading away from the house.

Danielle let out a small sigh, folding her arms. "She's harmless," she said, but there was something forced about it.

Nia narrowed her eyes. "Doesn't seem like you believe that."

Danielle's mouth twitched into a tight smile. "She… keeps to herself. Lives on the outskirts of town. People don't really go out there."

"Why not?"

Danielle hesitated, then shrugged. "She just likes stirring the pot."

That was a deflection.

Nia knew one when she heard it.

Her gaze flickered toward the direction Aunt Celeste had walked, watching the old woman's figure disappear into the thick trees beyond the road.

She didn't know what exactly she had just been warned about.

Anywhere But Here

But she knew one thing for certain—Aunt Celeste wasn't the one she needed to be afraid of.

Dinner that evening was another well-cooked, heavy Southern meal—braised chicken, rice and gravy, slow-cooked greens, and cornbread so soft it practically melted in her mouth. The food was unquestionably good, but the conversation?

The same polite, surface-level talk.

Nia sat at the large wooden dining table, pushing her rice around her plate as Danielle talked about something that happened at the market earlier that day, and Claire nodded along, occasionally adding her own thoughts. Richard barely spoke, as usual, eating steadily and drinking from a glass of tea, his expression unreadable.

And Nia was tired of it.

They had all gone out of their way to bring her here, welcomed her, fed her, given her a place to stay—but not one of them had sat her down and actually said why.

She had met the mayor. She had walked the town. She had seen the way people watched her—not with hostility, but with expectation.

And then there was Aunt Celeste.

The only person in this town who had spoken to her directly, honestly.

You shouldn't be here.

That ain't a good thing, baby.

Before you let this place make you forget who you are, come find me.

Nia set down her fork and exhaled, patience finally snapping.

"So, when exactly are we going to talk about the real reason I'm here?"

The conversation at the table halted.

Danielle's fork stilled against her plate. Claire and Richard exchanged one of those glances, quick but full of meaning, the kind only long-married people knew how to have without words.

Finally, Claire dabbed her mouth with a napkin and looked at Nia carefully. "I was wondering when you were going to ask that."

Nia leaned back slightly, folding her arms. "I've been asking. Just not getting a lot of answers."

Danielle sighed. "It's not that we don't want to tell you—"

"Then tell me."

Claire let out a slow breath, setting her utensils down with careful precision. "It's complicated."

Nia scoffed. "It's always complicated."

A long pause settled over the table.

Then, Claire tilted her head slightly. "Are you really thinking about leaving?"

That caught Nia off guard for a second. "Excuse me?"

"You said earlier, you'd just go home," Claire clarified, her voice even. "That you'd leave."

"I mean, yeah," Nia said. "I came here for answers. And so far, all I've gotten is weird stares and vague half-truths. So why stay?"

Danielle shifted uncomfortably, but Claire studied her carefully.

Then, her expression softened, and when she spoke again, her voice carried something different. Not secrecy. Not avoidance. Something close to honesty.

"I knew your father," Claire said.

Nia stilled.

Claire folded her hands neatly in front of her, looking down at them for a moment, as if gathering her words. "Not just in passing. Not just as some name on a piece of paper. I knew him. Loved him, in my own way."

Nia's throat tightened.

For all her digging, all her questions, she had never expected to hear something like that so plainly.

Claire looked up at her again, and for the first time since Nia had arrived, her expression didn't seem careful or rehearsed. It just looked… sad.

"He was good," she said. "Good in ways that are hard to explain. But also troubled. He… had choices to make. And some of those choices meant that he couldn't be here. That he couldn't stay."

The words hung between them, weighty and vague all at once.

Nia's mind raced with follow-up questions, but something about Claire's tone—the way she said couldn't stay instead of didn't stay—made her hesitate.

"He didn't abandon you, Nia," Claire continued. "I know it might have felt that way, growing up. But he didn't. Not in the way you think."

Nia's fingers curled slightly against her arms. "Then what way?"

Claire gave her a small, sad smile. "That's something I can't tell you all at once."

Nia exhaled, looking away, staring down at her untouched food. She felt like she was standing at the edge of something, close enough to see the outline of the truth but not close enough to touch it.

Finally, Claire spoke again. "I just need you to trust that what I'm telling you is real. That there's more to this than I can explain in one conversation."

Richard, silent until now, let out a quiet breath and muttered, "Ain't nothing simple 'bout it."

Nia flicked her gaze toward him. "But you know."

His jaw tightened slightly, but he nodded once.

Danielle reached for Nia's hand, squeezing it gently. "Just stay a little longer. If you go now, you're leaving with only half the story."

Nia stared at her, then at Claire, then at Richard.

Everything in her told her this was the moment to make a choice. She could leave, pack her bags and go home, put all of this behind her. Or she could stay.

Stay, and let the rest of the story unfold.

She sighed, running a hand down her face. "Fine."

Danielle let out a breath she had clearly been holding.

Claire nodded approvingly. "Good."

Richard just grunted and returned to his food.

And Nia? She still didn't know if she had just made the right choice.

Or the worst one yet.

Dinner wrapped up in a slow, measured rhythm, the way everything in Darbonne seemed to move. Claire and Richard continued eating at their own pace, their silverware clinking softly against the ceramic plates. Danielle made light conversation to keep the atmosphere from settling into something too tense, but Nia wasn't really listening.

Her mind was still turning over Claire's words, trying to dissect them, analyze them for truth, for omission.

Her father didn't abandon her.

He had choices to make.

He couldn't stay.

None of it told her who he was, what kind of man he had been, or why his name was such a carefully avoided subject.

By the time she set down her fork, her appetite was gone.

She helped clear the table out of politeness, rinsing her plate before setting it in the sink. Claire and Richard remained seated, still finishing their drinks, while Danielle leaned against the counter, watching her.

"You okay?" she asked softly as Nia dried her hands on a dish towel.

Nia nodded, but it wasn't a real answer. She was somewhere between uneasy and restless, and she didn't know how to explain it.

"I think I'm just going to turn in early," she said instead, setting the towel aside.

Danielle gave a small nod. "Alright. Sleep well."

Nia wasn't sure she would.

She made her way back to the guest room, the house quieter now, the air thick with the scent of the meal they had just eaten. A part of her still couldn't believe she was staying here, in this house, in this town that seemed to be holding its secrets just out of her reach.

Once inside, she shut the door, locking it out of habit before leaning against it with a sigh.

She kicked off her shoes, peeled off her jeans, and swapped her top for a soft oversized tee, something she always packed for comfort when traveling. Her body felt exhausted, but her mind wouldn't stop running.

So she grabbed her phone from the nightstand and dialed Malcolm.

He answered almost immediately.

"Hey, babe." His voice was warm, familiar, grounding.

"Hey," she exhaled, sinking onto the bed.

"You good?" There was an edge to his voice—he could always tell when something was off with her.

"Define 'good,'" she muttered.

"That bad, huh?"

She let out a tired laugh. "I don't even know where to start."

"Try me."

She shifted onto her side, staring at the ceiling. "Claire—Danielle's mom—she told me she *knew* my dad. But she still wouldn't tell me everything. Just gave me some cryptic, half-answer bullshit about how he 'couldn't stay' and how he 'didn't abandon me the way I thought.'"

Malcolm was silent for a second, processing. "Okay... so what does that mean?"

"Exactly my question," she sighed. "And of course, she wouldn't give me anything else. Just told me to trust her and stay longer if I wanted the whole story."

"You're still staying?"

"For now."

Malcolm let out a slow breath. "I don't like this, Nia."

She closed her eyes. "I know."

"It's too many people controlling how much you're allowed to know. That's not normal. If they really just wanted to tell you about your dad, why the secrecy?"

She swallowed. "I don't know."

"Then promise me you'll be careful," he said, voice firm now. "Seriously, Nia. If something feels wrong, leave. I don't care if it's the middle of the night, I'll book you a flight out of there myself."

She smiled slightly. "My hero."

"Damn right."

The warmth in his voice made her feel a little steadier, even if her mind was still racing.

They talked for a few more minutes—not about Darbonne, just about home, about work, about normal things—before Malcolm finally yawned and told her to get some rest.

"I'll check in with you tomorrow," she promised.

"You better."

Hanging up, she sighed, running a hand over her face before unlocking her phone again.

Text to Lena:

Nia: *Still alive. Still in Darbonne.*

Lena's reply came almost instantly.

Lena: *Good to know. Did you uncover the town's dark secrets yet, or are they still playing the long con?*

Nia: *Oh, they're conning me, alright. Whole town is one big mystery wrapped in Southern charm and excellent food.*

Lena: *Not the worst way to go, tbh.*

Nia: *Malcolm is ready to book me a flight back. He's convinced I'm about to get sacrificed.*

Lena: *Smart man. You should listen to him.*

Nia smirked.

Nia: *Not yet. But if I end up missing, you know where to start looking.*

Lena: *Oh, don't worry. I'd be in that town within 24 hours, kicking down doors.*

That made Nia chuckle.

Nia: *Appreciate the backup.*

Lena: *Always.*

Setting her phone down, she exhaled, stretching out under the blanket.

The house was completely silent now. Not even the soft creaks of settling wood.

Just… stillness.

She pulled the blanket up to her shoulders, staring at the ceiling. Tomorrow, she needed answers—one way or another.

CHAPTER TEN:

Lapse

The town square was buzzing with activity by the time Nia arrived with Danielle. The morning heat had settled into a humid weight, the sun bright but slightly diffused through the canopy of towering oak and cypress trees that lined the main road.

The event—some kind of community gathering, a mix of a market, social gathering, and town meeting—had transformed the usually quiet square into a carefully arranged celebration. Long wooden tables were set up, covered in homemade goods, hand-sewn crafts, fresh produce from local farms. Children ran barefoot through the grass, laughter punctuating the air, while adults stood in small clusters, chatting in the way people did when they'd known each other their entire lives.

Everything about it felt quaint, charming—even picturesque.

And yet, Nia couldn't shake the feeling that it was all curated.

Anywhere But Here

The way people interacted, the way they moved—smooth, practiced, like they were performing a well-rehearsed play.

Danielle, of course, was completely at ease. She greeted people with familiarity, hugged some, exchanged warm smiles with others. No one asked Nia who she was. They already knew.

It was a subtle but deeply unnerving detail.

Danielle turned to her as they walked past a table of handwoven baskets and jars of honey, flashing an encouraging smile. "Just enjoy yourself," she said. "Eat something, talk to people. Let them get to know you."

Nia nodded, but her mind was elsewhere.

If there was ever an opportunity to dig deeper, this was it.

She started moving through the crowd, observing, listening, picking up pieces of conversation.

She passed Mercer's Market's stall, where Claire was selling jars of preserves and bundles of dried herbs.

She passed Langley's Café's table, where someone had stacked warm biscuits and freshly baked pies, the scent thick in the humid air.

And then, near the far end of the square, she saw it.

A small historical display.

There were old photographs, framed newspaper clippings, a carefully printed timeline of Darbonne's history—the kind of exhibit meant to celebrate the town's roots.

It was exactly what she needed.

Danielle was still distracted, caught in a conversation with an older woman near one of the produce tables, so Nia took her chance.

She stepped toward the display, scanning the timeline first.

Founded in 1852.

Prospered as a farming settlement.

Population remained steady for generations.

Her gaze flickered to the photographs.

There were sepia-toned images of early settlers, a black-and-white photo of the town square from the early 1900s, a faded picture of a community gathering that looked eerily similar to the one happening right now.

Something about the photos felt off.

She leaned in, studying them closer.

It wasn't just that the town had barely changed—it was that the people looked eerily familiar.

Same features. Same genetic similarities.

The resemblance between past and present was too strong to be coincidence.

Her eyes darted to a framed newspaper clipping—an article from the 1950s. She read the first few lines, brow furrowing.

It was a celebratory piece about Darbonne's continued prosperity, about how the town had remained virtually unchanged despite outside pressures to modernize.

Her stomach tightened.

No mention of economic shifts.
No mention of how the town survived with no outside commerce.
No mention of why no one ever seemed to leave.

She moved to another clipping.

A missing persons report.

But something was wrong with it.

The name of the missing individual had been carefully scratched out. The article itself was yellowed with age, the ink faded, but the redaction wasn't old.

Someone had altered it recently.

Her pulse quickened.

She flipped through a small leather-bound book sitting at the edge of the table—a record of town leadership, dating back over a century.

Her finger traced the list of names.

There—Harris Grayson.

She blinked.

Harris Grayson, listed as mayor in 1953.

That was impossible.

She quickly skimmed further. The name repeated every few decades. Harris Grayson, 1978. Harris Grayson, 1995.

Her throat went dry.

This wasn't a lineage of men named Harris Grayson.

It was the same man.

The same Harris Grayson who had shaken her hand yesterday, smiling like he wasn't listed in a historical record from over fifty years ago.

A chill crawled up her spine.

She looked around, suddenly hyperaware of how many people were near her, how many pairs of eyes had drifted toward her, watching.

Danielle was still talking, unaware of what Nia had just uncovered.

Nia exhaled slowly, her pulse steady but racing underneath.

Darbonne's history hadn't just been rewritten.

It had been deliberately erased and rebuilt.

And the man running it had been here a lot longer than he should have.

The weight of the revelation pressed against Nia's chest as she slowly closed the leather-bound record, her fingers lingering over the cover as if the book itself might offer more answers. The sounds of the town event carried on around her—the murmur of voices, the distant laughter of children, the rhythmic creak of a wooden rocking chair nearby. Someone walked past carrying a tray of hand-poured lemonade, the scent of fresh citrus mingling with the richer, earthier aroma of burning hickory from a smoker at the far end of the square. The air was thick, damp from the lingering heat of the day, but the tension running through Nia's body left her feeling cool beneath the surface.

She forced herself to take a slow breath, steadying the rush of thoughts circling in her head. If Harris Grayson had been recorded as mayor for the past fifty years or more, that meant one of two things—either the records were intentionally false, or Harris wasn't just some charming small-town politician.

The thought unsettled her in a way she couldn't yet name.

Before she could dwell on it further, a voice behind her broke her focus.

"You're Nia Wallace."

She turned sharply, her pulse still too high from what she had just uncovered. The man standing in front of her was older, probably in his sixties, with dark brown skin, deep-set eyes, and a thin frame that carried a quiet energy beneath it. His salt-and-pepper hair was cropped close, his mustache neatly trimmed. He wore a pressed white linen shirt and lightweight slacks, his posture relaxed but attentive.

Nia eyed him warily. "That depends on who's asking."

His mouth curved slightly, though it wasn't quite a smile. "Dr. Samuel Baines." He extended a hand, his grip firm, steady, but not forceful. "I've been following your work for a while."

Nia frowned. "You're familiar with my research?"

His expression didn't change. "More than you'd think."

There was something in the way he said it—pointed, intentional.

She studied him, searching for any sign that he was another town official, another part of whatever well-rehearsed, carefully controlled system was in place here.

But he didn't have the same unnerving calm as Harris, or the controlled warmth of Claire.

He looked like someone who knew more than he was supposed to.

"I wasn't expecting to meet another scientist here," she admitted, keeping her tone neutral.

Baines chuckled lightly, glancing around the square before stepping closer, lowering his voice just enough that only she could hear. "There's a lot you probably weren't expecting to find in Darbonne."

Her jaw tightened. "That much is clear."

He nodded toward the historical records on the table, his gaze flickering over them briefly before returning to her. "Finding anything interesting?"

Nia hesitated. It was a test—she could feel it.

She chose her words carefully. "Just trying to get a better sense of this place."

He tilted his head slightly, his expression unreadable. "And?"

She exhaled. "And… something doesn't add up."

A slow, knowing look crossed his face. "It rarely does."

Nia felt another small pulse of unease, the weight of the conversation shifting from small talk to something heavier. He wasn't just being friendly. He was feeling her out—gauging how much she had figured out on her own.

"So what is it you do here, Dr. Baines?" she asked, keeping her voice light, conversational.

"Used to be research," he said simply. "Biology, genetics. But now?" He glanced around the square. "Now I mostly keep to myself."

Genetics.

Her stomach tightened. "You used to study genetics?"

He gave a slow nod. "Years ago." He hesitated just briefly, then added, "Darbonne has an... interesting history, scientifically speaking."

She knew an open door when she saw one.

"And what does that mean?"

His expression remained carefully neutral. "Let's just say there's a reason this town is the way it is."

Nia felt her pulse tick up again.

He knew something. Something big.

Before she could press further, a voice called out from across the square.

"Dr. Baines."

They both turned toward the source.

Harris Grayson stood near the main gathering space, smiling—but not at Nia. His attention was on Baines, his expression calm, pleasant, but unmistakably firm.

Baines met his gaze, his jaw tightening almost imperceptibly.

Harris gestured lightly toward a group of men standing near the Parish Hall. "You're needed for something."

It wasn't a request.

Nia didn't miss the way Baines' fingers flexed at his sides before he finally nodded. "Of course."

He glanced at Nia one last time before turning and walking away, his shoulders just slightly stiffer than before.

Nia's gaze followed him, her skin prickling with a sudden certainty. Dr. Samuel Baines had just given her more than anyone else in this town. And Harris Grayson knew it.

Nia stood in the square, watching as Dr. Baines walked away, Harris Grayson's quiet presence looming just behind him. The exchange had been brief, but it had confirmed something she had already suspected.

The answers she was looking for weren't going to be found on the internet.

She had spent years relying on research, on records, archives, digitized databases—facts that could be cross-checked, documented, analyzed. But Darbonne didn't exist in those spaces. It had been scrubbed clean, deliberately erased from history in a way that made it clear:

The truth wasn't written down.

It lived here, inside the town itself.

In the way people moved, in the words they didn't say, in the tight-lipped stories passed between generations.

And now, she understood something else—there were people who knew.

Claire.

Richard.

Harris.

Danielle, to some degree.

Dr. Baines, definitely.

Probably Aunt Celeste, though she was being kept at a distance from the rest of them.

Nia exhaled slowly, watching the town move around her with fresh eyes.

The families gathered at the stalls weren't just shopping, they were reinforcing something. The people talking in small groups weren't just catching up, they were maintaining something.

This town wasn't just small and tight-knit—it was controlled.

Not by laws, not by outside influences, but by an understanding.

A system.

A structure.

And Harris Grayson was at the center of it.

The afternoon heat pressed against her skin, making the fabric of her shirt stick lightly to her back. The scent of grilled meats and spiced cider drifted from a nearby stall, blending with the faint, earthy dampness that seemed to settle in the air no matter where she went.

The sounds of the event swirled around her—laughter, low conversations, the occasional bark of a dog in the distance.

On the surface, it was all so normal. But she had spent her career studying what people don't say. This town was screaming in silence.

She needed to stop thinking like a researcher trying to find a paper trail.

She needed to start thinking like a journalist, an investigator, someone who found the truth by listening to the right people, asking the right questions, pressing the right buttons.

She needed to figure out who, in this town, was willing to talk.

Her gaze flickered toward where Dr. Baines had disappeared.

He had told her *just enough* to get her attention. Now, she had to figure out how to get the rest.

The weight of the afternoon sun had begun to shift, casting longer shadows over the town square, cooling the air just slightly. People were still gathered in clusters, talking, laughing, exchanging goods at the market stalls. The atmosphere was lively, warm, practiced—but Nia couldn't shake the feeling that it was all just a carefully preserved illusion.

She needed space.

She needed to clear her head, to step away from the staged normalcy of Darbonne and find something real.

So, when she saw a small, overgrown path veering off from the main square, partially hidden behind the Parish Hall, her curiosity pushed her forward. It wasn't marked, no signs pointing to where it led, but she didn't hesitate. She wasn't going to find answers standing in the middle of the crowd.

The deeper she walked, the quieter the world became. The footsteps of the townspeople faded behind her, replaced by the sound of her own breathing, the rustling of wind through the moss-covered trees. The path narrowed, weaving between ancient cypress and oak, the damp earth beneath her feet thick with fallen leaves.

Then, just beyond the next turn, she saw it. An abandoned building, hidden in the trees.

It was small, single-story, with a sagging roof and faded wooden siding, half-covered by creeping vines. The windows were boarded up, the front door slightly ajar, its frame warped from time and neglect.

But what struck her most was the symbol carved into the door. A familiar spiral-like pattern, etched deep into the wood.

She had seen it before.

Somewhere—in the town, on the market jars, maybe even in Mercer's home.

Her heart thumped harder as she stepped forward, the floorboards creaking under her weight. The air inside was thick with dust, aged paper, the faintest trace of something chemical.

The room was cluttered—tables covered in old books, stacks of yellowed paper, jars filled with unidentifiable substances. The walls were lined with shelves of worn leather-bound journals, the spines cracked with age.

Her pulse quickened.

This wasn't just an abandoned space. This was a research room. A lab, of sorts.

She moved further inside, her fingers brushing over a stack of handwritten notes, the pages curling at the edges. The handwriting was small, precise, almost clinical.

She scanned the notes quickly, her breath catching.

Subject 14 – Increased genetic stability observed. Traits remain consistent through generational replication. No degradation. Further study required.

Another entry, written in a different hand:

Results indicate controlled variation within isolated population. Lineage intact. History must be maintained.

Her fingers trembled slightly as she picked up a small metal tin, its lid rusted. Inside were photographs—old black-and-white portraits, some faded, others more recent.

One of them made her stomach drop.

It was a picture of Harris Grayson.

The same man she had seen just hours ago, standing beside a group of people dressed in clothing from at least a century ago.

The inked date at the bottom read:

1896.

Her breathing shallowed.

She needed to leave. Now.

But just as she turned, her eyes caught on something else.

A large, hand-drawn family tree pinned to the far wall.

It was intricate, lines weaving together, generations stretching backward in careful, deliberate branches. Names, some familiar—Mercer, Grayson, Langley.

And then, at the very bottom, freshly written, unmistakable, in dark ink.

Nia Wallace.

A chill crawled down her spine, coiling in her gut.

Her name.

Here.

She stepped back, heart hammering.

Someone had known she was coming. Long before she ever took the DNA test. Long before she ever stepped foot in Darbonne.

This wasn't just a discovery.

It was a warning.

Nia could barely breathe.

Her name—written on that family tree, ink still dark and fresh, standing out among generations of carefully recorded names. Someone had been waiting for her, anticipating her presence here before she even knew this town existed.

Her pulse thundered in her ears as she stepped away from the wall, her mind scrambling for an explanation. The research notes, the altered town records, the photo of Harris Grayson from over a century ago—everything about this place had felt carefully preserved, but this? This felt orchestrated.

Like the town had been expecting her.

A floorboard creaked outside.

Nia's breath caught as she spun toward the open door, heart pounding, expecting to see Harris, or Claire, or some unseen figure watching from the shadows.

But it was Danielle.

She stood in the doorway, arms crossed, watching her with a mix of curiosity and something else— something measured.

"You shouldn't be in here," she said, her voice soft but firm.

Nia swallowed, her throat dry. "Why does my name—" She motioned toward the family tree, struggling to form the words. "Why does my name *already* exist in your history?"

Danielle exhaled, stepping inside, letting the old door creak shut behind her. "I told you," she said, voice gentle, like she was explaining something to a skittish animal. "Everything will make sense soon."

Nia let out a hollow laugh. "Yeah? Because right now, nothing makes sense, Danielle. Your mayor has apparently been alive for a hundred years, there are missing person reports that have been altered, and someone's been tracking my existence before I even knew you people existed."

Danielle flinched slightly at the word *you people*, but she didn't argue. Instead, she glanced around the room, her expression shifting into something less defensive, more cautious.

"I didn't want you to find all this yet," she admitted.

Nia's breath hitched. "Yet?"

Danielle sighed, running a hand through her hair. "I was going to explain things when you were ready."

Nia let out a sharp exhale. "I think I passed *ready* a long time ago."

Danielle studied her, then walked slowly to the family tree. Her fingers brushed against the parchment, following the lines of ancestry, the carefully preserved names.

"I know this looks strange," she said, eyes lingering on the spot where Nia's name had been written. "But I promise you, it's not what you think."

"Then tell me what it is."

Danielle hesitated. "You're part of this place, Nia. Whether you knew it or not."

"That doesn't answer anything."

Danielle turned to her, expression unreadable. "Then let me answer it in the right way. Give me time."

Nia shook her head, frustration knotting in her chest. "Why does everything in this town require *waiting*?"

Danielle exhaled, stepping closer. "Because you're not ready to hear it yet."

Nia clenched her jaw. She hated this. Hated being led in circles, hated feeling like she was on the outside of a story that she was somehow written into.

But pushing Danielle wouldn't work.

Not yet.

So instead, she let out a slow breath and nodded stiffly. "Fine."

Danielle studied her, as if trying to decipher whether she really meant it. Then, after a moment, she motioned toward the door.

"Come on," she said softly. "Let's get out of here."

Nia hesitated for just a second longer before following her, casting one last glance at the family tree, at the old books, at the knowledge that had been deliberately hidden away.

She might have agreed to wait for answers. But she wouldn't stop looking for them.

CHAPTER ELEVEN:

BLOODLINE

The shift in Danielle was subtle at first.

One moment, she was warm, familiar, the sister Nia had started to accept—the one who had welcomed her with open arms, who had promised answers, who had looked so genuinely happy to have her here. But then, just as quickly, she would pull away, her voice carefully neutral, her gaze distant, her movements measured.

Nia noticed it the morning after she had stumbled upon the abandoned research building.

At breakfast, Danielle had been herself, laughing easily as she helped Claire slice fresh fruit, nudging Nia playfully when she sat down. She had poured Nia coffee before she even asked, had teased her about looking exhausted, had leaned in close like they had been doing this their whole lives.

But by the afternoon, when they had gone for a walk along the outskirts of town, she had changed.

She was quieter. Watching. Answering Nia's questions with half-truths and clipped responses.

It wasn't just mood swings. It was something deeper.

Like she was constantly shifting between two versions of herself—the sister Nia was meant to trust, and the stranger she didn't quite recognize.

And now, as they sat on the Mercer's front porch in the late evening, the sky a soft wash of deep blues and grays, Nia could feel it again.

The distance. The pullback.

"You've been weird all day," Nia said finally, breaking the silence.

Danielle exhaled, tucking her legs beneath her on the porch swing. "I've been tired."

"Not buying it."

Danielle gave a small, tired smile. "Maybe I'm just not used to someone paying this much attention to me."

Nia narrowed her eyes. "That's not it, either."

Danielle tensed, just slightly, before forcing herself to relax.

There it was. The shift.

The way she kept catching herself.

Like she was trying to remember which version of herself she was supposed to be.

Nia studied her, trying to map the inconsistencies, trying to figure out why Danielle had been so eager to bring her here, only to keep her at arm's length now that she was.

"You're pulling away," Nia said.

Danielle's fingers tightened around the edge of the porch swing, her gaze flickering toward the dark stretch of road beyond the yard.

"I don't mean to."

"Then stop doing it."

Danielle let out a slow breath, her expression flickering between guilt and something unreadable.

"It's just... hard to explain," she said finally.

"Try me."

Danielle's mouth pressed into a thin line.

The silence stretched between them, heavy and weighted, before Danielle finally spoke.

"I want you to be here," she said, voice soft, careful. "But there are things about this place that you don't understand yet."

"Then explain them to me."

Danielle hesitated.

And there it was again—the flicker of hesitation, the silent decision not to tell her something.

Nia clenched her jaw. "Danielle."

Danielle stood abruptly, brushing imaginary dust from her jeans. "I'm going inside."

Nia stared up at her, frustration bubbling in her chest. "That's it? You're just gonna walk away?"

Danielle's eyes softened, but there was something haunted in them, something restless.

"You'll understand soon," she murmured, more to herself than to Nia.

And then, she was gone.

Leaving Nia on the porch, feeling like she was grasping at something that kept slipping through her fingers.

Danielle's retreat into the house left Nia simmering with frustration, staring out into the darkened stretch of road beyond the Mercer home. The air was thick and still, the deep hum of crickets and distant rustling of tree branches the only sounds breaking the silence.

She had waited long enough.

She had played along, followed Danielle's lead, sat through vague explanations and half-truths. And now, she was done waiting for someone to hand her the answers.

She needed to find them herself.

Grabbing her light jacket from the back of her chair, she stepped off the porch and into the night.

The dirt road beneath her feet was uneven but familiar by now. The town, so vibrant earlier in the day, was eerily quiet at night—not empty, but muted. There were still a few porch lights glowing, still shadows shifting behind drawn curtains, but there was no traffic, no distant murmur of televisions or radios, no dogs barking at unseen movement.

It was a quiet that didn't feel natural.

It felt enforced.

Nia pulled out her phone, tapping the screen, but as expected—no signal.

Just like every other time she had tried to reach beyond Darbonne's invisible boundaries.

Her feet carried her past the town square, past the darkened market, past the shuttered windows of Langley's Café. She had spent days trying to piece together the gaps in the town's history, but tonight, she wasn't looking for clues in old documents or controlled conversations.

She needed to find something that hadn't been filtered for her consumption.

Her mind drifted back to Dr. Baines.

He had mentioned genetics—not just casually, but with meaning. He had given her a breadcrumb, a sliver of acknowledgment that Darbonne wasn't just a town frozen in time—it was an experiment.

And she had a feeling the answers were hidden somewhere the town didn't want her to look.

She followed the path toward the outskirts, away from the town's carefully preserved center.

The buildings here were older, more neglected, their edges softened by time and overgrowth. Houses sat at odd distances, some long abandoned, their wooden frames sagging, roofs caved in from years of neglect.

And then she saw it.

Another faded marker, nearly swallowed by the thick brush, its carved lettering barely visible beneath the layers of dirt and moss.

DARBONNE ARCHIVES – ESTABLISHED 1863

Her pulse quickened.

An archives building.

She stepped closer, running her fingers along the old wood of the doorframe. The structure was modest, a single-room building with no exterior lights, no signs of recent maintenance. But the lock on the door was new—not rusted like the rest of the place.

Someone had been inside. Recently.

She crouched, inspecting the base of the door. The ground had been disturbed, footprints barely visible in the soft earth.

This place wasn't forgotten.

It was hidden.

Nia reached into her pocket, pulled out a hairpin, and worked it into the lock. She had learned how to pick locks in college—a skill gained more out of curiosity than necessity—but now, she was grateful for it.

With a soft click, the door swung open.

The air inside was stale, heavy with dust and something deeper—aged paper, ink, decay.

She stepped inside, pulling her phone's flashlight from her pocket and scanning the room.

Shelves lined the walls, stacked with brittle books, aging ledgers, and unfiled records. A long wooden table sat in the center, its surface covered in loose pages, old maps, hand-written notes.

But what caught her eye was the journal lying open in the middle of it all.

She stepped forward, her breath catching as she read the first few lines.

June 3rd, 1857 – The trials continue. The subjects remain stable, but long-term effects are yet to be seen. If the hypothesis is correct, we may have found the key to controlled generational traits.

Her stomach turned.

She flipped forward.

November 12th, 1861 – The Council has approved the expansion. More subjects will be needed. Volunteers are preferred, but selection may be required if compliance is low.

She flipped faster.

March 8th, 1865 – The population remains genetically consistent. The system works. We have ensured the purity of Darbonne's lineage.

Her hands shook as she reached the final entry.

July 2nd, 1871 – The bloodline is intact. The town will remain as it was intended. Selection will continue. Deviation will not be tolerated.

Nia staggered back from the table, her breath sharp and uneven.

They hadn't just built a town.

They had engineered it.

And she—a geneticist, a scientist who had spent years tracing lineage and ancestry—was standing in the middle of a living experiment.

She heard the soft creak of the door behind her—and she wasn't alone.

Nia's breath caught, her heart pounding as the creaking door sent a cold rush of adrenaline through her veins. She spun around, her flashlight beam slicing through the darkness.

A pair of glowing yellow eyes stared back at her from the doorway.

Her pulse slowed just slightly when she realized what it was—a cat, scruffy and lean, its dark fur dusted with bits of leaves. It blinked at her lazily before stepping inside, tail flicking as it began to inspect the room.

Nia let out a shaky breath, hand pressing against her chest.

"Jesus," she muttered, running a hand down her face.

The cat ignored her, hopping onto one of the lower shelves, weaving between stacks of forgotten papers.

Her heart was still hammering, but she forced herself to turn back to the journal, to the brittle pages that contained the real horror of what she had just uncovered.

She skimmed backward, searching for the beginning—some kind of context for what she had just read.

The first pages weren't scientific in nature. They were personal accounts, written by one of the town's founders, someone deeply involved in the "selection process."

Her fingers trembled slightly as she traced over the ink, reading in silence.

August 4th, 1852 – The first generation has been chosen. The Council agrees that the best way forward is controlled breeding—intelligence, endurance, obedience. We will refine them. They will become something greater.

Her throat tightened. Refine?

She flipped ahead.

January 17th, 1854 – The subjects have been paired strategically. Generations will pass before we see the full results, but already, the children show promise. Stronger, healthier, more resistant to illness. If we are careful, if we maintain control, the purity of the lineage will ensure Darbonne's prosperity.

March 3rd, 1855 – Deviations have begun to appear. Certain offspring do not exhibit the desired traits. We will take corrective measures. Compliance is paramount. The Council will not tolerate failure.

Her stomach turned violently as the pieces snapped together in her mind.

This wasn't just a project.

This wasn't about legacy.

This was eugenics.

The "subjects" they had been refining, controlling, breeding—they had been enslaved people.

She pressed a hand against the table, nausea rising in her throat.

Darbonne had never just been a town. It had been an experiment in forced genetic selection, a carefully maintained breeding ground designed to engineer "perfection."

She flipped to another entry, unable to stop reading despite the horror curling inside her.

July 9th, 1860 – The results are undeniable. The strongest bloodlines have been identified. We must ensure their continuation. To allow intermingling with outsiders would dilute the progress we have made. Selection must continue. Unfit subjects will be removed.

Her vision blurred with disgust.

They had isolated themselves, cut themselves off from the outside world—not out of preservation, but out of a desire to maintain the lineage they had created.

And now, over a century and a half later, she was standing in the middle of it.

She let out a slow, shaking breath, her hands gripping the edge of the table to steady herself.

The air in the abandoned archive felt thicker now, like the walls had absorbed the weight of history, like the shadows themselves carried whispers of the past.

The cat let out a soft chirp from the shelf, batting at something—a loose scrap of paper.

Nia swallowed hard and stepped back, forcing herself to take in the full terrible truth.

This place—this town—was not a mistake.

It was by design.

Nia's hands were trembling as she carefully closed the leather-bound journal, pressing it back onto the cluttered table exactly where she had found it. The words still clung to her, thick as humidity, soaking into her skin like something she'd never be able to wash off.

This town—its entire existence, its closed-off, self-sustaining nature—wasn't just some Southern quirk. It had been engineered. Maintained. And she had walked right into it.

She swallowed hard, forcing herself to take slow, steady breaths. Panicking wouldn't help.

She needed to get out of here. Now.

Turning back to the door, she stepped lightly, making sure not to disturb anything as she moved. The cat flicked its tail at her as if bored by the horror she had just uncovered, but Nia barely glanced at it.

She crept out into the night, pulling the door shut behind her. The air outside felt heavier than before, thick with the weight of her discovery.

The walk back into town stretched before her, the trees casting long, skeletal shadows under the moonlight. The quiet of Darbonne wasn't peaceful anymore—it was suffocating.

She made it a few steps down the path when a sudden rustling in the underbrush made her pulse spike.

Nia froze.

She turned sharply, scanning the darkness beyond the tree line, heart hammering in her chest.

And then, from the shadows, a low voice murmured—so soft, so deliberate. "They think they made this place. But they ain't never been the ones in control."

A figure stepped forward, emerging from the tree line—Aunt Celeste.

Her shawl was wrapped tightly around her thin shoulders, her dark, lined face partially illuminated by the moonlight. Her eyes—sharp, knowing—pierced right through Nia like she had seen everything she had just uncovered without Nia needing to say a word.

Nia let out the breath she hadn't realized she was holding. "Jesus, you scared the hell out of me."

Aunt Celeste didn't smile. Didn't soften.

"You went looking," she murmured, her voice low but certain.

Nia's throat tightened. "Yeah."

A slow nod. "And now you know."

A chill wrapped itself around Nia's spine.

The way she said it—not like a question, not like a warning.

Like a fact.

Like Celeste had been waiting for her to figure it out.

"They did things here," Nia said, barely recognizing her own voice. "Things to people. My people."

Celeste's eyes flickered, something shifting in her face—something that looked like a deeply buried, long-weathered grief.

"Oh, baby," she murmured, stepping closer. "It's worse than you think."

Nia's pulse thrummed in her ears. "What do you mean?"

Celeste tilted her head slightly. "You think they stopped?"

The words hit Nia like ice to the chest.

Her stomach turned. "What?"

"They never stopped." Celeste's voice was softer now, but weighted. "They just got better at hiding it."

Nia's breath came quicker, her hands curling into fists at her sides. The research, the erased records, the rigid control over the town's population—it had never been about history.

It had been about continuation.

Before she could speak, before she could even process what Celeste was telling her, the sound of approaching footsteps made them both turn.

Danielle.

Her silhouette cut through the moonlight, her stance rigid, unreadable.

Nia couldn't tell if she had overheard anything.

But her voice, when she spoke, was tight, urgent.

"Nia," she called out, stepping closer. "What are you doing out here?"

Aunt Celeste didn't move. Didn't speak.

She just watched.

Nia's heartbeat slammed against her ribs as she took a slow step back.

She was caught between two worlds now.

One that wanted to keep her blind.

And one that wanted her to see.

Nia's mind raced, calculating her next move.

She couldn't let Danielle know she knew. Not yet.

If what Aunt Celeste had just told her was true—if Darbonne's so-called *experiment* never stopped—then there was so much more happening beneath the surface than she could even begin to understand. And if Danielle was in on it, if she was a part of whatever structure was keeping this town locked into its twisted past, then Nia had to be careful.

So, she did the only thing she could.

She faked it.

"I got turned around," she said, forcing frustration into her voice, making her body sag just a little like she was exhausted instead of buzzing with adrenaline. "I was trying to get back to the house and must've taken the wrong road."

Danielle slowed as she reached them, her eyes scanning Nia's face, searching. "You got lost?"

Nia let out a breath, pushing out an awkward laugh. "Yeah. I should've just stayed on the main road, but I thought I saw a shortcut." She glanced toward Aunt Celeste, subtly waiting for backup.

Aunt Celeste held her gaze for a long moment, something unreadable in her expression. Then, she exhaled slowly and nodded.

"She wandered down the wrong path," Celeste murmured, playing along. "Happens more often than you'd think. Roads here all start lookin' the same at night."

Danielle studied them both, her posture still stiff, still guarded. But then, after a beat, she let out a small chuckle.

"Well," she sighed, shaking her head. "At least you didn't end up in the bayou. Come on, I'll walk you back."

Nia forced a grateful smile, pretending like her pulse wasn't thundering in her ears.

She turned toward Aunt Celeste, giving her a quick, unspoken look of thanks.

Celeste's expression remained unreadable, but the small flicker in her eyes told Nia she understood.

They walked back in silence.

The weight of the night pressed around them, the town's unnatural stillness settling over Nia like a thick second skin. The only sounds were the faint rustling of wind through the trees and the rhythmic crunch of gravel beneath their feet.

Danielle walked beside her, close but not too close, and Nia could feel her watching.

Like she was trying to read something beneath the surface.

Nia kept her face neutral.

When they reached the Mercer house, the porch light glowed softly in the dark, casting long shadows across the worn wooden steps. Danielle opened the door, stepping inside first, and Nia followed, forcing herself to act like she wasn't unraveling on the inside.

"You sure you're okay?" Danielle asked, tilting her head slightly, still assessing.

Nia nodded, rubbing her forehead. "Yeah. Just tired. I think I need to sleep."

Danielle hummed softly, then turned toward the kitchen.

"I was about to make some tea," she said, voice casual. "You want some?"

Nia's stomach tightened.

Something about the offer felt wrong.

Maybe it was nothing—just Danielle trying to take care of her, like she had since she got here. But maybe it was something.

She couldn't be sure.

So she shook her head. "No, thanks. I just need rest."

Danielle didn't push. Just nodded and gave her a small, almost absentminded smile.

"Well," she said lightly, "you still planning on sticking around?"

It was a test.

Nia felt it immediately.

She met Danielle's gaze, letting just enough hesitation creep into her voice to sound natural.

"I don't know," she admitted. "I came here for answers. And I'm starting to think I might not get them."

Danielle's smile faltered for a fraction of a second.

Then, just as quickly, she recovered.

"Give it time," she said softly.

Nia nodded, pretending to consider it.

She turned toward the hallway, toward the guest room, hoping Danielle couldn't hear how hard her heart was pounding.

Because now, she knew that she couldn't trust anyone. Not until she knew who was really in control.

CHAPTER TWELVE:

APPEARED

Nia was somewhere else.

She knew it was a dream—had to be—but it felt too real, too sharp, like she had stepped into someone else's memory.

The air was thick, humid, alive, pressing against her skin like a second layer. The scent of cypress, wet earth, and something faintly metallic filled her nose. She was standing in a field—or maybe a clearing—surrounded by towering trees that stretched endlessly into the dark. A fire flickered nearby, its glow casting dancing shadows against the thick trunks, illuminating figures that stood just beyond the light.

She tried to move, but her body didn't belong to her.

She wasn't just watching this dream.

She was inside it.

A voice—deep, steady—cut through the warm night air.

"This is the only way to keep it pure."

Nia turned, her breath catching in her throat.

A group of men stood in a circle, their faces partially obscured by the low-burning firelight. They wore old-fashioned clothes—high-collared shirts, suspenders, long coats that brushed against the ground. Their expressions were grim, resolute.

And then, in the center of them, a woman.

She was tall, proud, her dark skin glistening in the firelight, her eyes burning with something fierce. She looked afraid, but not defeated.

"You can't stop what's coming," she spat. "No matter how deep you bury the truth, it'll find its way to the surface."

One of the men stepped forward.

Harris Grayson.

But not as she had seen him before.

Younger. Or at least, a version of him that belonged to another time.

His hair was dark, his features sharp in the flickering firelight, his expression unreadable.

"Then we will control the surface."

The fire flared suddenly, a gust of heat rushing toward her, and Nia gasped—

And bolted upright in bed.

Her chest was heaving, sweat clinging to her skin despite the cool air in the room. Her head throbbed, a sharp, pulsing ache sitting right behind her temples.

She swallowed hard, blinking against the darkness, trying to steady herself.

The dream was already slipping away, like sand through her fingers. But the faces remained.

The woman's defiance.

The men's determination.

The sound of Harris Grayson's voice echoing in her skull.

"Then we will control the surface."

Nia pressed her palms against her forehead, squeezing her eyes shut. This wasn't just a nightmare. It was something else. And it wasn't the first time.

The headaches had started the day before, dull at first, just a small pressure behind her eyes. Then, the memory lapses—gaps where she couldn't remember how she got from one place to another, conversations that felt fractured, incomplete. And now, this.

Dreams that felt like memories.

Dreams that felt like warnings.

She took a slow breath and reached for her phone. No new messages. No signal.

Of course.

Her fingers hovered over the screen, hesitating. She needed to tell someone.

Malcolm.

Lena.

Aunt Celeste.

But no. Not yet.

Not until she understood what was happening to her.

Because this? This wasn't normal. And somehow, she knew—deep in her gut, deep in her bones—that Darbonne was the reason for it.

Nia's phone buzzed violently against the nightstand, the sound making her flinch. She grabbed it with shaky fingers, heart still pounding from the dream. The screen flashed Malcolm's name.

She swiped to answer.

"Hello?" Her voice was rough, still tangled in sleep and confusion.

"Nia?" Malcolm's voice was sharp, urgent. Tense.

She sat up straighter. "Yeah, it's me. What's wrong?"

"What's wrong?" He let out a sharp breath. "I haven't heard from you in three days, Nia."

Her stomach dropped.

"What?" she whispered.

"I called, I texted—nothing. I was about to book a flight to Louisiana to come drag your ass out of there."

Nia clutched the phone tighter, the pounding in her skull intensifying. "That's not possible," she said firmly. "We talked yesterday."

Malcolm went silent for a moment. When he spoke again, his voice was low, careful.

"Nia," he said slowly, "we last talked on Sunday. It's Wednesday."

A cold chill raced up her spine.

She shook her head. "No, I—no, Malcolm, I know we talked yesterday. You called, we joked about you being jealous of the food here."

"Nia, that was days ago."

Her breathing hitched, her pulse hammering erratically. That couldn't be right. She would know if she had lost time.

Wouldn't she?

"I—I think you're just confused," she said, her voice coming out weaker than she intended. "Maybe your calls didn't go through."

Malcolm cursed under his breath. "Listen to me. You're the one who's confused. You're acting like this is normal, but it's not. Something is happening to you, and I don't know if it's stress or that damn town or—"

"It's not the town," she snapped, suddenly defensive.

"The hell it isn't," Malcolm shot back. "Nia, ever since you got there, you've been acting off. I can hear it in your voice. And now you're telling me you lost three whole days without realizing it? That's not you."

She squeezed her eyes shut, rubbing her forehead. The headache was pulsing harder now, like something was trying to force its way into her skull.

"I don't—I don't know what's happening," she admitted, hating the way her voice wavered.

Malcolm sighed heavily. "Then get out, babe. Leave. Whatever's happening there, it's messing with you."

She opened her mouth to respond, but then—

The call dropped.

Dead silence.

She pulled the phone away from her ear, staring at the blank screen.

No service.

Her stomach twisted.

That wasn't a coincidence.

Something—or someone—had cut the call off.

Her fingers trembled as she set the phone down, pressing the heels of her hands into her temples, forcing herself to breathe, to stay calm.

But then—

A soft knock at her door.

Nia snapped her head up just as the door creaked open.

Danielle peeked inside, her expression carefully neutral, but her eyes scanning Nia's face. "Everything okay? I heard you talking."

Nia forced herself to relax, unclenching her jaw, loosening her shoulders.

"Yeah," she muttered, rubbing her temples as she swung her legs over the side of the bed. "Just man problems."

Danielle leaned against the doorframe, tilting her head slightly. "Malcolm?"

Nia nodded, keeping her face carefully unreadable. "Yeah. He's mad I haven't been checking in enough."

Danielle's eyes flickered with something—sympathy, concern… relief?

"You know how men are," she said lightly, offering a small smile. "They always think they know what's best."

Nia forced a laugh that sounded too hollow to be convincing. "Yeah."

Danielle stepped a little closer. "You sure you're okay?"

Nia waved a dismissive hand. "I'm fine. Just tired. I think I should probably start making plans to head home soon anyway."

Danielle stilled.

It was subtle—a barely-there pause, a flicker of something behind her eyes.

But Nia caught it.

Just for a second, Danielle's mask slipped.

Then, just as quickly, she smiled again. "Of course," she said easily. "Whenever you're ready."

Nia nodded, swallowing the sudden dryness in her throat.

She wanted to believe her.

But after everything she had seen—the altered history, the experiments, the family tree, the missing time—she knew one thing for certain.

Danielle didn't want her to leave.

Morning came slowly in Darbonne, the kind of slow that felt intentional, as if the town itself dictated the pace of time. The mist hung low over the fields beyond the Mercer house, swirling in lazy tendrils across the dirt roads. The air smelled of damp earth and old wood, the faintest trace of something sweet—honeysuckle, maybe—clinging to the air as the sun began its slow crawl upward.

Nia sat on the front porch, gripping a cup of coffee she wasn't drinking. The ceramic was warm against her palms, grounding her, though nothing felt quite real anymore. Her mind was still snared in the tangled weight of her dream, the missing days, the words Malcolm had barely managed to say before the call was cut short.

Everything about this place was calculated. Preserved. Maintained.

Across the yard, an older man in overalls made his way down the road, moving at a measured, familiar pace, like he had walked the same stretch of land every morning for the past fifty years. He nodded at a neighbor—a woman who had been sweeping the same spot on her porch for the past ten minutes, moving dust that didn't exist. She looked up briefly, acknowledging the man with a small, practiced smile before returning to her motions.

Nia's stomach tightened.

Nothing in this town felt spontaneous.

She had spent her life in cities where people moved with urgency, with distraction, with personal ambition pulling them forward. Here, in Darbonne, everything was synchronized.

The people moved in a rhythm she wasn't part of, a rhythm she could almost hear beneath the stillness.

A few feet away, Danielle sat on the porch swing, one leg tucked beneath her, rocking slowly as she scrolled through her phone. Not speaking. Not prying.

But watching.

Not directly. Not in an obvious way. But Nia could feel it, the subtle awareness, the way Danielle's gaze flickered toward her every now and then.

She had spent the past few days believing that Danielle's warmth was genuine, that her excitement over having a sister was real. And maybe it had been.

But now, Nia couldn't tell if Danielle wanted her here because she was family… or because she was part of the system.

Something deep in her gut told her the answer was more complicated than she was ready for.

From the far side of the square, the town began its slow waking.

A bell rang from Mercer's Market, signaling the first deliveries of the day. A few of the townspeople made their way toward the center of town, moving with the same quiet precision as always, their conversations hushed, their smiles measured.

The Parish Hall stood in the distance, its white shutters gleaming in the morning light, its doors closed but never quite locked. Nia's gaze drifted toward it, toward the tall, stately building that sat at the very center of Darbonne's existence.

Everything here led back to that place.

The town's secrets were woven into its walls, tucked into its foundations.

And if she wanted to understand what was happening to her—the memory gaps, the dreams, the unraveling of time itself—that was where she had to start.

She just had to figure out how to get inside.

The air shifted.

It was subtle at first—a small tremor in the town's perfect rhythm. A bird, perched lazily on the wooden railing of the porch, suddenly took off in a frantic burst of wings, disappearing into the mist.

Then, the wind changed.

Nia felt it before she understood it—a sudden drop in pressure, a shift in the weight of the atmosphere. The porch swing creaked, Danielle's scrolling fingers pausing, her entire body tensing in a way that wasn't obvious but wasn't normal, either.

Something was wrong.

A shout echoed from down the road—not the casual call of neighbors greeting one another, not the soft murmur of people exchanging morning pleasantries. It was sharp, panicked.

And then—

The siren.

A deep, unnatural wail cut through the stillness, rolling across the town like a tremor beneath the earth. It wasn't the high-pitched scream of a modern emergency system—it was older, mechanical, a guttural groan of rusted metal that had been waiting, unused, for something inevitable.

The moment it rang out, Darbonne changed.

The people in the streets reacted instantly, moving without hesitation, without confusion, as if they had always known exactly what to do. Storefronts shut their doors, curtains snapped closed in windows. A man grabbed his small child from the steps of the bakery, hurrying inside without looking back.

It was a drill. A practiced, conditioned response.

Danielle was already on her feet.

"Inside," she said, her voice too calm for what was happening.

"What the hell is that?" Nia demanded, still gripping the railing, her breath coming quicker now.

Danielle's expression didn't change. "Just come inside."

No.

Every instinct in Nia's body screamed against it.

She wasn't part of the system. She didn't move with their rhythm. And right now, her body knew something she hadn't caught up to yet. This wasn't just a storm alarm.

This was a warning.

Aunt Celeste's voice from the night before ripped through her memory.

"You think they stopped? They never stopped."

Her feet were moving before she had made the conscious choice to run. Not into the house. Not toward shelter. But toward the Parish Hall.

If this was a drill, a protocol, a planned event—then she needed to see what happened when the town thought it wasn't being watched.

Danielle called her name, but Nia was already down the steps, already sprinting toward the town square. She cut through the mist, past the now-locked doors, past the windows where people stood just behind the curtains, waiting.

The siren groaned again. The air hummed with something electric, something old, something deep. Then, she saw it.

A group of men—five, maybe six—moving toward the Parish Hall with intention. And at the center of them, walking calmly, untouched by the tension in the air—

Harris Grayson.

His face was unreadable, his pace steady. The men flanking him were dressed in dark clothes, moving like shadows, like enforcers.

They weren't rushing, weren't panicked.

They were escorting something.

Someone.

Nia skidded to a stop, her breath caught in her throat. The figure stumbled between them, wrists bound, head low. His clothes—torn, dust-covered—looked out of place, too modern for Darbonne's neatly preserved world. His eyes darted wildly, searching. Then—he saw her. Even from a distance, she could see it—the terror in his eyes.

Then, a sudden, violent burst of energy—something unseen, something forceful—rippled through the square. The air seemed to distort, like heat rising off pavement, but faster, sharper.

Nia felt it in her skull first, a pressure, a pull—like something inside her was being stretched, yanked toward something unseen.

Her vision blurred, doubled, twisted. Then—blackness.

Nothing.

Darkness pressed in.

Not the absence of light, not a simple closing of her eyes, but something denser, something suffocating. A void that swallowed thought, space, and time. Then—

A gasp. A rush of sensation slamming back into her body.

Nia jolted awake, her breath catching as she sucked in air too sharply, too fast. The pressure in her skull pulsed like a living thing, a slow, rhythmic pounding that made her stomach turn. She clenched her jaw against the nausea, forcing herself to focus on something, anything.

Her phone.

It was still in her hand, slick with sweat. The screen glowed harshly in the dark, making her head throb as she tried to read the numbers. The numbers on her phone blurred, shifting, wrong.

March 4th.

That couldn't be. That *wasn't* right.

Her fingers shook as she swiped through her call log—empty. No outgoing calls. No messages from Malcolm. Nothing to prove she had existed in those missing two days. A sharp, nauseating pressure gripped her skull, and suddenly, she was terrified to close her eyes. Her breathing started coming in sharp, shallow bursts. She turned her head, slow, careful, bracing for the wave of dizziness that followed. Her muscles ached as if she had run for miles, as if she had fought something she couldn't remember.

Where was she?

Not outside. Not in the square.

Her surroundings were wrong.

A room. Unfamiliar.

Lamplight spilled from a single source in the corner, casting warped shadows along the walls. The furniture was old, heavy, and the air carried the scent of something faintly metallic, something stale.

Her fingers curled against fabric. A bed.

Not hers. Not Danielle's.

She swallowed, forcing her sluggish thoughts into order. She needed to move.

The moment she pushed herself upright, a sharp pain lanced through her skull, sending her reeling. The world tilted, blurred. A cold sweat broke across her skin as she forced her body to stillness, gripping the edge of the mattress.

Slow. Steady.

The walls weren't shifting. That was just her head.

The phone in her hand buzzed. A message.

Her fingers shook as she swiped at the screen. The brightness cut into her vision, but she forced herself to read it.

One word.

STAY.

No name. No sender.

The breath left her lungs.

She looked up, pulse hammering, ears straining for any sign that she wasn't alone.

Footsteps.

Soft. Controlled. Just beyond the door.

She sucked in a slow, steady breath, muscles coiling beneath the weight of uncertainty.

The handle turned.

A slow, deliberate movement. Not rushed. Not tentative. Whoever was on the other side knew they belonged here.

Nia's breath came too fast, too loud. Her body felt too small in the vast, pulsing dark. The pressure in her skull twisted, a hook lodged behind her eyes, tugging, stretching something loose.

The door creaked open.

A sliver of shadow slipped through the gap.

No—not shadow. Not absence. A shape. A figure. It stood in the doorway, tall, its head tilted at an unnatural angle, watching her.

The lamp flickered. Nia pressed back against the headboard, the room folding in on itself.

The figure moved.

Not walked—moved. A shift of presence, a slithering displacement of space. And then she saw its face.

Her own.

Distorted, slack-jawed, eyes black pits of nothing.

A mirror of herself. A wrong version.

It opened its mouth, and her own voice poured out.

"You're unraveling."

The words shuddered through the walls, through the air, through her bones.

Her phone screen lit up again.

A new message.

RUN.

Her heart jerked, stuttering against her ribs.

The figure in the doorway took a step forward, the floorboards not creaking beneath its weight. Because it had none.

Nia moved.

Or tried to.

Her body wasn't responding.

Her limbs were there but weren't hers.

The figure's head tilted again, a jagged, mechanical snap, its mouth stretching wider—too wide, unhinged like a snake's. And then—

A scream.

Not hers.

From outside.

From the streets. From Darbonne. A shrill, animal sound, something caught, something breaking, something splitting apart—

The walls buckled. The room folded in. And then—

Nothing.

A breath. A gasp. A jolt.

Nia snapped upright, her lungs clawing for air. The room was still. The lamp burned steadily in the corner, a warm, flickering glow. The wooden furniture was solid, unmoving. The walls stood firm, no longer breathing, no longer collapsing in on her. Her hands were fisted in the sheets. Her legs were trembling.

She wasn't in a stranger's house. She was still in Danielle's parents' home. The same room she had been given when she arrived. Nothing had changed. Except—

The time.

Her phone lay beside her, the screen still glowing.

March 4th.

Two days missing.

Her skin prickled, cold despite the heat pooling at the base of her spine. She looked at the screen again, her breath catching as she scrolled through her messages.

No messages.

No STAY.

No RUN.

Just a black void where they should have been.

Had she dreamed it?

Had any of it been real?

Her heart was still racing, her body still humming with leftover terror, her mind struggling to close the distance between what she had seen and where she was now.

She swallowed hard, pressing her hands against her face. The headaches were worse. The gaps in time were growing. And now—hallucinations.

If that's what they were.

Because it hadn't felt like her mind turning against her. It had felt like something else entirely.

CHAPTER THIRTEEN:
ARCHIVES

Nia sat on the edge of the bed, her breath still uneven, her skin cold despite the thick humidity pressing in from the barely cracked window. The weight of exhaustion sat heavy on her chest, but sleep wasn't an option. She had lost two days—two whole days that had slipped away like sand through her fingers, and now, her own mind had turned against her. The hallucination still clung to her, its shape lingering in the edges of her vision.

Her reflection—wrong, twisted, watching.

She shuddered and stood, her legs unsteady beneath her, her pulse still rabbiting in her throat. Whatever was happening here—whatever Darbonne was doing to her—she couldn't stay.

She had to go. Now.

Digging through her bag, she pulled out her jeans, her shirt, her shoes, dressing quickly, hands fumbling as she shoved her phone into her pocket. The numbers on the screen didn't shift, didn't change. March 4th. Still a reality she didn't recognize.

She pushed the door open carefully, stepping into the dark hallway. The house was quiet. Danielle's parents were either asleep or just gone, their presence in this place always strangely thin, like ghosts occupying the space rather than living people. Danielle's room was shut, no sound coming from behind it.

Good. She didn't want a conversation. She didn't want explanations.

She wanted out.

The front door opened without resistance. The air outside was thick, heavy, pressing against her skin like damp wool. The mist hadn't lifted—it never really did. It curled around the houses, slithered through the trees, moved like something alive.

The street was empty.

Her shoes made no sound against the wooden porch as she stepped down, moving quickly, her breath shallow in her chest. She just had to make it to her car. She would drive, keep going, put miles between herself and this place before the hallucinations swallowed her whole.

But when she turned the corner, the car wasn't there.

Her breath hitched. She spun, scanning the road, the curb, the small patch of gravel where she had parked just yesterday—or was it three days ago?

Nothing.

It was gone.

Panic coiled tight in her ribs. Had Danielle moved it? Had someone taken it? She tried to steady her thoughts, tried to push down the rising wave of nausea creeping up her throat.

Walk. Just walk.

The town square wasn't far. Someone would have seen it. She could call a tow, get a ride out of here, figure it out once she was gone.

The mist thickened around her ankles as she moved, the buildings looming taller, the space between them stretching wider.

The street wasn't empty anymore.

She stopped, breath stalling as she scanned the road ahead. Figures stood in the fog, half-obscured. Still. Watching.

Her stomach turned, her skin prickling as she forced herself to move forward, past them, through them. They didn't speak. Didn't move. Their faces—blurred, indistinct, shifting in a way her mind couldn't process.

She pressed forward, faster now, pushing toward the main road that led out of Darbonne. She could see the break in the trees, the curve of the highway stretching beyond it. She just had to keep moving.

Her feet hit pavement. The road felt strange beneath her, softer than it should be, like damp earth instead of asphalt. She didn't look down. She just kept walking. Then, she was back in front of the house.

She turned, looking down the street, looking at the path she had just taken—but it wasn't there.

The town square, the highway—gone.

It was just the house again, Danielle's parents' house, the front porch light buzzing dimly against the thickening dark.

A hand clamped over her mouth before she could scream. She twisted, thrashing, but the grip was iron. The air pulsed, the world tilted, and then—

A voice, low, urgent, right against her ear.

"Stop trying to leave."

Nia froze, heart hammering against her ribs. The hand loosened, and she spun, stumbling back.

Danielle stood in front of her, eyes dark, face unreadable. "You can't leave," she said, her voice steady, almost sympathetic.

Nia's pulse roared in her ears. She wanted to argue, to scream, to demand an explanation. But the street behind Danielle stretched wrong, warping at the edges, bending in on itself like a loop folding over and over.

She tried to take a step back, but the house was there again, right behind her, pressing against her spine.

Her body wasn't hers anymore.

The air hummed, thrummed, pulsed with something unseen, something deep, something ancient.

Danielle took a slow step forward. "You're not the first to try," she said softly. "But you can't leave, Nia. Not until they let you."

The words sank into her bones. Nia looked past her, at the street, at the figures watching from the mist, at the road that was no longer a road. Finally, she understood.

She wasn't trapped in Darbonne.

Darbonne was trapped in her.

She woke up gasping, her body lurching upright before she even understood why.

The room spun, a slow, dragging tilt that made her stomach lurch. The sheets beneath her palms were damp, clinging to her skin. Her pulse hammered against her ribs. Her mouth was dry, her head aching—no, splitting.

She pressed a hand to her forehead. Was she awake?

She had been outside. Running. Fleeing. The town had twisted, curled in on itself like a living thing. Danielle had been there, whispering, "You can't leave."

Now—she was here again.

The room was the same as before—wood-paneled walls, the single lamp casting its soft glow, her bag still half-zipped where she had left it. No mist. No figures in the fog. Just stillness.

A dream.

A hallucination.

But it had felt real.

She curled her fingers against the blanket, grounding herself in the rough texture, in the cool air against her damp skin. If this was another trick of her mind, it was a cruel one. Then, a scent. Warm, familiar, normal.

Breakfast.

The smell drifted through the door, thick with butter, eggs, something sizzling in a pan. Something real.

She exhaled slowly, swinging her legs over the side of the bed. Her body still ached, her head still pounded, but she moved. Because no hallucination—not after what she had seen—would offer her breakfast.

She shoved her phone into her pocket without looking at it, unwilling to confirm the date or time, unwilling to fall back into another spiral. She just needed to get up, to move, to breathe.

The floor was cool beneath her bare feet as she stepped into the hallway. The air in the house was thick, but not oppressive—not charged with whatever energy had swallowed her whole in the last dream, or vision, or whatever the hell that had been.

As she neared the kitchen, voices drifted toward her, low and familiar.

Danielle. Her mother. Someone else.

Normal.

She clung to that word as she stepped into the doorway.

Danielle sat at the table, picking at a plate of eggs with lazy disinterest. Across from her, her mother moved between the stove and counter, scraping fresh bacon onto a plate, the smell of coffee curling through the air.

A quiet morning.

No sirens. No figures in the fog. No distorted faces peering back at her from a warped world.

This day felt different.

More real.

Danielle looked up, meeting Nia's gaze with something unreadable before gesturing toward an empty chair. "You're up."

It wasn't a question.

Nia hesitated, scanning the room again for any strange gaps, anything misplaced. But nothing flickered, nothing shifted.

Her stomach tightened. She wanted to ask if anything had happened the night before, if Danielle remembered standing outside telling her she couldn't leave.

But she didn't.

She stepped forward instead, lowering herself into the chair, fingers curling around the mug already waiting for her.

Warm. Solid.

She lifted it, sipped. The coffee wasn't bitter. Wasn't burning or ice-cold or any other strange, unnatural thing.

It was just coffee.

Danielle watched her carefully, her fork scraping against the plate. "How's your head?"

Nia swallowed, feeling the dull throb pulsing beneath her skull. There. Always there. "I'm fine."

A pause.

Danielle's mother set a fresh plate in front of her without a word, then moved toward the sink.

Nia stared down at the food.

Eggs. Toast. Bacon.

Ordinary.

Her stomach clenched, uneasy.

If this was another hallucination, why did it feel like the most grounded thing she'd experienced in days?

Anywhere But Here

The kitchen's warmth contrasted sharply with the chill that had settled in Nia's bones over the past days. The mundane clatter of breakfast preparations, the soft hum of conversation—it all felt disconcertingly normal. She forced herself to take a bite of toast, the crunch grounding her, even as her mind swirled with unanswered questions.

A knock echoed through the house, abrupt and authoritative. Danielle's mother paused, wiping her hands on a dish towel, a fleeting shadow crossing her face before she moved to answer the door. Nia's senses sharpened, a prickle of unease crawling up her spine.

Mayor Harris Grayson stepped into the room, his presence commanding, eyes scanning the occupants with practiced ease. He wore a congenial smile, but there was an edge to it, a sharpness that didn't reach his eyes.

"Good morning," he greeted, his voice smooth. "I hope I'm not intruding."

Danielle's mother shook her head, though her posture remained stiff. "Not at all, Mayor. Can we offer you some breakfast?"

He waved a dismissive hand. "No, thank you. I'm here on a bit of business." His gaze settled on Nia, and the air seemed to thicken. "Dr. Wallace, may we have a word?"

Nia's pulse quickened, but she met his gaze evenly, nodding. "Of course."

He gestured toward the adjoining room, and she followed, acutely aware of Danielle's watchful eyes tracking their movement. The living room felt cooler, shadows lingering in the corners despite the morning light filtering through the curtains.

"I understand you've had some... concerns about our town," Harris began, clasping his hands behind his back, his stance relaxed yet imposing.

Nia straightened, choosing her words carefully. "I've noticed certain anomalies, yes. Unexplained occurrences, gaps in my memory. And I can't ignore the uniformity among the residents—the similarities in appearance."

Harris chuckled softly, a sound devoid of genuine amusement. "Darbonne is a close-knit community, Dr. Wallace. Families have intermarried for generations. Resemblances are bound to occur."

She narrowed her eyes, unwilling to be placated. "That doesn't explain the missing time or the hallucinations."

His smile tightened. "Perhaps the stress of your work is taking its toll. It's not uncommon for the mind to play tricks under duress."

Frustration bubbled within her. "Don't patronize me. I know what I've experienced."

Harris's expression remained calm, but his eyes hardened, a flicker of something dangerous lurking beneath the surface. "Be careful, Dr. Wallace. Sometimes, digging into the past can unearth things best left buried. And in Darbonne, we value our privacy."

The subtle threat hung in the air, chilling in its implication. Nia held his gaze, refusing to be intimidated. "Are you warning me, Mayor?"

"Simply offering friendly advice," he replied smoothly. "We wouldn't want a guest to feel unwelcome or... unsafe."

The room seemed to constrict around her, the walls pressing in as the weight of his words settled. She forced a tight smile. "I appreciate your concern."

Harris nodded, the genial mask slipping back into place. "Enjoy the rest of your breakfast, Dr. Wallace. And remember, some questions are better left unanswered."

With that, he turned and exited the room, leaving Nia standing amidst the suffocating tension, her mind racing with the unspoken threats veiled beneath his cordial demeanor.

The door clicked shut behind Mayor Harris, but the weight of his presence lingered in the air. Nia stood motionless, her breath shallow, every nerve in her body still coiled tight.

That was real. This is real.

She wasn't hallucinating anymore.

The momentary doubt—the lingering fear that her mind was playing tricks on her—vanished in the wake of his carefully veiled threat. Harris wasn't just dismissing her concerns. He was warning her.

And that meant she was right.

The town wasn't just strange. It was dangerous.

She had to get out.

Her hands curled into fists at her sides as she walked back into the kitchen. Danielle was staring at her, her posture stiff, unreadable. Her mother pretended to busy herself at the stove, but there was no mistaking the tension that had settled in the room like an unwanted guest.

Nia didn't sit back down. "I need to go," she said simply.

Danielle's fork clinked against her plate. "Go where?"

"Back home. I've been here long enough. I've got… work to get back to."

She expected Danielle to argue, to at least try to convince her to stay. But her friend just looked at her, something shuttered in her expression.

"I'll take you to the bus station," she said.

That wasn't the answer Nia expected. The casual way she said it sent a fresh wave of unease down Nia's spine.

She didn't press further. She just nodded, grabbing her bag from the chair and slinging it over her shoulder. "Let's go."

Danielle didn't say another word as she stood, grabbed her keys, and led Nia out the door.

The ride to the bus station was quiet. Too quiet.

Danielle didn't turn on the radio. Didn't make conversation. She just drove, her hands tight around the wheel, her knuckles pale against the sun-warmed leather.

Nia stared out the window, watching the town slip by in eerie silence. No one was outside. The shops were open, but their windows were dark, curtains drawn.

Even the houses seemed... off, their porches empty, their doors closed tight.

A chill crawled up her spine.

She kept expecting to see those figures in the mist, standing still, watching. But there was nothing. Just the unnatural stillness.

Danielle pulled up in front of the bus station—a squat, worn-down building that looked like it hadn't been renovated since the 70s.

Nia exhaled, gripping the strap of her bag.

This was it.

The bus station was exactly as she'd expected it—aged, stagnant, caught in time.

Its once-white brick exterior was dulled to an uneven beige, the letters on the faded sign hanging at an awkward tilt. A thick layer of dust coated the rows of plastic seats inside, their surfaces cracked from years of heat and humidity. The schedule board flickered intermittently, some letters missing entirely, others frozen mid-update.

For a place meant to be a hub of movement, it felt like it hadn't seen real life in years.

Nia swallowed back the unease curling in her stomach.

Danielle didn't walk her inside, didn't say much at all—just dropped her off with a curt, "Be safe," before driving off.

The departure times listed on the board didn't make sense.

She frowned, staring at the numbers. No buses until tomorrow.

That couldn't be right. There had been a morning schedule listed online, a departure that should have been arriving any minute.

She checked her phone, refreshing the page.

"Service unavailable."

Nia exhaled sharply. Of course.

Her fingers hovered over her contacts. She could call an Uber, but she already knew what would happen. She had tried it the night before, staring at the spinning "searching for a driver" message for nearly an hour before finally giving up.

This town didn't want people leaving.

She shoved her phone back into her pocket, pushing down the flicker of paranoia, and turned toward the counter. A small bell sat on the scratched wood, tarnished and dented like it had been there longer than the building itself.

She pressed it.

A hollow chime rang out, the sound swallowed by the stillness of the station.

Nothing.

No movement from the back office, no weary employee dragging themselves forward to help.

She rang it again.

Still nothing.

Her pulse quickened, a familiar unease settling into her bones. It felt like she was being watched, but when she turned, the station was just as empty as before.

Maybe she could find a rental car. Even if she had to go to the next town over, she needed to move. Sitting here wasn't an option.

Nia strode back outside, scanning the nearly deserted parking lot. The only cars belonged to a couple of rusted-out pickups and a single, battered sedan.

The sun pressed down on her, thick and oppressive.

Something about Darbonne's heat felt different from anywhere else. It wasn't just the humidity, wasn't just the way the air clung to her skin—it was weighty, as if it pressed into her bones rather than just against her skin.

She started walking.

The road stretched ahead, a cracked ribbon of pavement cutting through a landscape of endless trees and silent buildings.

The town didn't have the usual roadside sprawl—no fast food chains, no gas stations littering the highway exits. Just old brick structures, heavy with time, their windows covered in film, their doors still.

A single signpost jutted out near the edge of the station's parking lot, its paint peeling, its text sun-faded:

"Next Gas: 42 Miles."

Her stomach dropped.

That couldn't be right. That wasn't what she saw on the drive in.

She clenched her teeth, ignoring the gnawing sensation creeping through her chest.

She kept walking.

The first car to pass her was an old pickup, its driver hidden behind dark-tinted windows. It didn't slow down. Didn't acknowledge her. Just rumbled past, the heat from the pavement shimmering in its wake.

She walked for nearly ten minutes before she heard another car approaching from behind.

Nia turned, sticking out a hand to flag it down.

The sleek black sedan slowed as it neared, rolling to a stop just beside her.

She took a step closer, relief washing over her—until she saw who was behind the wheel.

Mayor Harris.

The window slid down with a smooth mechanical hum, revealing his too-polished smile, his unnervingly even gaze.

"Dr. Wallace," he greeted. "Taking the scenic route?"

Her fingers curled into her palms.

"I was just heading out," she said, forcing her voice to stay level. "The bus wasn't running."

He hummed, as if unsurprised. "Ah, yes. The schedules can be a bit... inconsistent. A quirk of small-town life, I'm afraid."

She stared at him, searching his expression for something—mockery, malice, a hint of anything beneath his placid demeanor.

"Would you like a ride back?" he asked.

Back. Not forward. Not out.

She shook her head. "No, thanks. I'll figure something out."

The smile never wavered, but something shifted in his gaze, something small but unmistakable.

"You should be careful wandering alone, Dr. Wallace," he said, his voice light, conversational. "The roads can be unpredictable."

Before she could respond, he rolled the window back up and drove away, the car's engine a low, steady hum that faded into the thick air.

She stood there, skin prickling, heart pounding.

The roads can be unpredictable.

It wasn't just a warning.

It was a promise.

Nia turned and kept walking.

Five minutes later, a vehicle crested the horizon—an old, blue sedan, heading in the opposite direction.

Her hand shot up.

The driver—a woman in her forties, curly hair piled high on her head—slowed, her expression wary as she rolled the window down.

"You lost?" she asked.

Nia exhaled, pushing down her unease. "Not lost. Just trying to get out of town."

The woman hesitated.

Then, in a lower voice, she said, "Get in."

Nia didn't hesitate. She yanked the door open, slid into the passenger seat, and shut it behind her.

The woman didn't ask questions. She just pulled onto the road, fingers tight on the wheel.

For the first time in days, Nia felt hope.

Until the car jerked.

A sickening lurch, a violent shudder.

The steering wheel wrenched sideways.

The woman cursed, gripping it tightly, struggling to keep control.

A harsh, grinding sound split the air, metal scraping against metal, rubber dragging over asphalt.

Then—

A final, wheezing jolt.

The car died.

Nia's breath came sharp and fast as silence swallowed the road around them.

The woman slammed her palm against the dashboard.

"You have got to be kidding me," she muttered, twisting the key in the ignition.

Nothing.

Just dead air.

Nia's pulse thundered as she turned, looking back down the road.

In the distance, just barely visible through the shimmer of heat and dust—

A black sedan.

Parked.

Waiting.

Mayor Harris wasn't inside. But he didn't need to be. Darbonne had already made its choice—and Nia wasn't going anywhere.

CHAPTER FOURTEEN:

CENTENNIAL

Nia had never known what it felt like to truly break.

She had known exhaustion. She had known stress, even grief, had felt the jagged edges of loss scraping at the softest parts of her. But she had never known what it meant to have her mind—her one certainty, her one truth—betray her.

Until now.

Because this wasn't just stress. This wasn't exhaustion. This wasn't even trauma unraveling her at the seams.

This was something deeper.

Something wrong.

She sat in the passenger seat of the dead car, fingers curled against her thighs, breath coming in short, sharp bursts. The woman beside her—who was she? Had she given a name? Did she even exist?—kept turning the key, each dry click of the ignition sounding less and less real.

Anywhere But Here

There was no reason for the car to have died. No warning signs. No overheating engine, no sputtering gas line. Just—a sudden stop, a mechanical failure that made no sense, perfectly timed to kill any chance of her leaving.

Another glitch.

That was the only word she had for it.

She turned her head, staring down the long stretch of road, her vision bending at the edges, warping like heat off pavement.

Something was happening to her. Something that had started long before she had arrived in Darbonne.

The truth was here, just beyond the veil of her own memory, tangled in the years she had spent thinking she was normal.

A name pressed against the back of her skull, burning like an old wound.

Her father.

She thought of him rarely, and when she did, it was in the abstract—the distant, half-faded figure who had never quite belonged to her life the way her mother had. A quiet man, a researcher, always somewhere else, always engaged in something too important to explain.

He had been involved.

No.

Not just involved.

He had been part of it.

Her hands clenched against her jeans.

A flash of memory—sharp, unbidden, rising like bile.

A cold room. The smell of antiseptic. Bright white light flooding her vision, so intense it burned.

And his voice.

"Hold still, sweetheart. I just need a little more time."

Her lungs seized.

This isn't real. This isn't real.

Except it was.

Because she could still feel the press of leather straps against her arms. The cold bite of metal against her skin. The hum of machines, the rhythmic beep-beep-beep of something tracking—what? Her vitals? Her brain activity? Her DNA?

The woman in the driver's seat swore under her breath, slamming a fist against the wheel.

Nia barely heard her.

Her mind was folding in on itself, peeling back layers she had never realized were there.

Her father had been experimenting on her.

Not a patient. Not a subject. Her.

She pressed a trembling hand to her temple, breath shuddering as the world shifted.

The road ahead was gone.

Instead, she saw—

A lab. Hidden beneath a house she barely remembered, a childhood home she hadn't thought of in years.

The walls lined with file cabinets, with old research notes, with things that should never have been written down.

Darbonne wasn't just a place.

It was a design.

A controlled experiment. A genetic ecosystem carefully crafted, its bloodlines monitored, altered, perfected.

And she—

She had been made for it.

That was why she had been drawn here. Why she couldn't leave.

Her body knew this place.

Her blood knew this place.

And the town knew her.

A wave of nausea surged through her, bile rising at the back of her throat. She shoved open the car door, stumbled out into the thick, humid air, and bent over, dry-heaving onto the cracked pavement.

The woman—her would-be savior, her escape plan—was speaking, her voice sharp, worried.

"Nia, what's wrong? Hey—hey, look at me."

But she couldn't.

Because the world was splitting apart.

The road wasn't real. The trees weren't real.

Everything around her rippled, flickered, bent at impossible angles.

And then—

A new sound.

The slow creak of a door.

Nia lifted her head.

The car was gone.

The woman was gone.

She was standing in front of a house she recognized but had never seen before.

Her father's house.

No.

Not his.

Theirs.

Because his research, his experiments—they had never been just his.

Darbonne had owned him.

Just like they owned her.

Her breath came shallow, her skin crawling with the certainty of what was inside.

This was where the truth was kept. And for the first time in her life, she wasn't sure if she wanted to know.

Nia's feet moved before her mind caught up.

The choice had been made.

She followed Baines down the cracked pavement, past the dead car, past the skeletal outlines of Darbonne's oldest buildings, their wooden facades sun-bleached and silent. The air felt heavier the farther they walked, pressing against her skin like something alive, like the town itself was trying to pull her back.

Baines kept a brisk pace, his posture tight, shoulders squared. He wasn't talking, and Nia didn't press him—not yet. Her own thoughts were unraveling too fast to keep up with.

Her father. The research. The engineering.

She had been made for Darbonne.

The realization had settled in her bones like an old sickness, something inherited, something passed down through generations, waiting for her to return.

She swallowed hard, staring at the back of Baines' head as they walked. He had known all along. Maybe not everything, maybe not every detail, but enough.

"Where are we going?" she finally asked.

Baines didn't answer right away. He cut across an alley between two old shopfronts, leading her into the shadowed space between the buildings. The temperature dropped immediately, the air thick with the scent of damp wood and something metallic.

When he finally spoke, his voice was quieter. "Somewhere safe."

Nia scoffed. "Safe doesn't exist here."

Baines glanced at her over his shoulder, his mouth set in a grim line. "No, it doesn't."

That was the most honest thing he had said to her so far.

He led her through a back entrance of what looked like an abandoned pharmacy. The windows were boarded up, the old DARBY'S DRUGS sign hanging crooked above the door, its paint peeling.

Inside, the air smelled of dust and old paper. Shelves still lined the walls, though most of them had been stripped bare, save for a few discarded pill bottles and faded labels.

Baines locked the door behind them.

"Sit," he ordered, gesturing to a stool near the old counter.

Nia didn't.

She folded her arms instead, watching him with sharp, untrusting eyes. "Start talking."

Baines exhaled through his nose, rubbing his temple like he was nursing his own headache. "You really want the whole story right now?"

"I don't think I have time for anything else."

Something flickered across his face—an agreement he didn't voice.

"Darbonne was never just a town," he said finally. "It was a test site. Generations of selective breeding, controlled lineage. Your father was part of the last phase—refinement. He didn't just study what came before. He altered what came after."

Nia's breath came slow and uneven. Refinement.

"Meaning what?"

Baines hesitated. Then:

"Meaning you."

The word landed like a blow, but she didn't flinch.

"How?" Her voice was steel now, all the fear burned away by the firestorm raging beneath her ribs.

Baines shook his head. "I don't know every detail. I wasn't in the program when you were a child. But I know he was working on something with your mother—in utero modifications. Enhancements. He was trying to accelerate something."

The word enhancements made her stomach turn.

"My mother," she said, voice barely above a whisper. "Was she—did she know?"

Baines' expression didn't change.

And that told her everything.

A hollow feeling spread through her chest, the kind of grief that didn't settle but sank, deep and permanent.

Her mother had known.

And she had never told her.

Nia's legs felt unsteady, but she forced herself to stay upright. "So what does that make me?"

Baines met her gaze, his eyes unreadable. "An anomaly."

The word made something in her pulse stutter.

"You mean an experiment."

Baines didn't confirm or deny. He just kept watching her.

"Why are you helping me?" she pressed.

"Because I don't think you understand what they're planning to do to you now that you're back."

A slow, sick feeling slithered through her stomach.

She thought of Harris, his too-smooth voice, his veiled threats. *We value our privacy.*

She thought of Danielle, how her demeanor had shifted, how she had grown colder, distant.

She thought of the town itself, the way the roads warped, the way Darbonne swallowed time, the way it refused to let her go.

"What do they want from me?" she whispered.

Baines took a breath like he was about to say something, but then—

The back door rattled.

Nia tensed.

Baines moved quickly, pressing a hand to her arm, forcing her behind the counter.

"Stay down," he muttered.

Nia's heart slammed against her ribs.

Something was out there.

The door creaked, the knob twisting too slowly, deliberately.

Baines reached into his coat, pulled something out—a syringe.

Nia barely had time to react.

"What the—"

The door burst open.

A figure stepped inside.

Black boots. A heavy coat. And then—a mask.

A mask covering the lower half of their face, obscuring everything but their piercing, familiar eyes.

Danielle.

Nia's brain barely processed the recognition before she felt a sharp prick at her neck.

Baines.

Her limbs seized, her body locking up as her vision tilted.

No. No, no, no.

She tried to move, tried to fight, but her body wasn't responding. Her arms felt too heavy, her legs distant, detached. Baines was still gripping her arm, lowering her too gently to the floor.

His voice was distant, muffled. *"I told you to trust me."*

The last thing she saw before darkness swallowed her whole—Danielle, standing over her. Expression blank. Eyes unreadable. And then—nothing.

CHAPTER FIFTEEN:

SELECTION

Nia woke to the sensation of being watched.

The air was thick—too still, too sterile. The kind of air that belonged in hospitals or laboratories, scrubbed of anything natural, anything human. The scent of antiseptic burned the inside of her nose, mixing with something sharper, something chemical.

Her body felt wrong. Weighted. Detached.

She tried to move. Her limbs resisted.

A slow, creeping fear uncoiled in her chest.

Not again.

Her eyes fluttered open, and for a brief moment, she thought she was still dreaming.

The room around her was… wrong.

The walls weren't made of wood or concrete but a smooth, seamless white surface. No corners, no clear distinction between where one wall ended and another began. Like the space had been molded instead of built.

Anywhere But Here

A single, dim light source glowed from the ceiling—soft, artificial, casting no shadows.

She blinked, and for a moment, she felt like she wasn't fully inside her own body.

Like the room had absorbed her, was holding her in place.

Slowly, sluggishly, she tried to sit up. The movement sent a slow ripple of nausea rolling through her stomach.

She felt drugged.

The last thing she remembered—

Baines. The pharmacy. The door swinging open. Danielle's masked face. The needle.

Her pulse spiked.

She looked down at her arms.

Thin, silver electrodes clung to her skin—three on her left forearm, two more on the inside of her wrist. They were smooth, almost metallic, but warm to the touch. Like they had been designed to blend into her.

A fresh wave of nausea swelled in her gut.

She tore at them.

A sharp, electrical pulse raced up her arm, locking her muscles in place.

She gasped, eyes watering.

The electrodes didn't budge.

Her chest tightened as she forced herself to focus, scanning the room for any details, any weak points.

The walls were lined with faint, vertical lines—doors? Panels? There was no visible handle, no hinges, no windows.

No way out.

Her breath quickened.

This wasn't just a room.

It was a holding cell.

Her throat felt tight, the raw edge of panic creeping in, pressing at the edges of her fraying control.

"I told you to trust me."

Baines' voice rang in her head, but there was no comfort in it. Only betrayal.

She clenched her fists, forcing herself to breathe.

Then—

A sound.

A soft hiss, like air releasing from a sealed container.

The farthest wall shifted.

A panel slid open with a slow, seamless glide, revealing a doorway that hadn't been there before.

A man stepped inside.

Not Harris. Not Baines.

Someone else.

His presence commanded the space instantly.

Tall. Pale suit. Silver-gray hair combed back with meticulous care. He looked like a man who had never misplaced a single thing in his life.

His expression was unreadable, but his eyes—deep-set, sharp, too light—studied her with clinical interest.

Nia's skin crawled.

"You're awake," he said, as if stating a mild observation.

Her mouth was dry, her thoughts sluggish, but she forced herself to sit straighter, to hold his gaze.

"Where am I?"

The man didn't answer immediately. He stepped closer, the fabric of his suit pristine, uncreased, as if he hadn't been touched by the same laws of movement as everything else.

"You are where you belong," he said smoothly.

The words sent ice through her spine.

She gritted her teeth. "What does that mean?"

For the first time, the faintest hint of amusement flickered across his face.

"It means, Dr. Wallace, that you should start asking the right questions."

She hated the way he said her name. Like he had always known it. Like he had been waiting.

Her heart pounded, but she refused to let him see her fear.

"So let me ask again," she said, her voice steadier now. "Where am I?"

His head tilted slightly, as if considering whether she deserved an answer.

Then:

"The Institute," he said simply.

The name sent something cold and familiar skittering through her skull.

The Institute.

She knew that name.

Not from the town. Not from the stories she had heard growing up.

From her father's files.

Her stomach flipped.

She remembered the old research notes, the fragmented documents she had found on his laptop as a teenager—files marked INSTITUTE ARCHIVES, PROJECT: BLOODLINE.

She had never understood what they meant. Until now.

"Your father laid the foundation for everything we've built," the man continued, his voice smooth, deliberate. "And you—"

His gaze sharpened.

"—are his legacy."

Her body went cold.

The room seemed to shrink around her.

The humming in her skull—the pulsing, electric weight of Darbonne pressing in on her mind—grew sharper, stronger.

They had done something to her.

She felt it now. In her blood, in her skin, in the unnatural weight pressing against the back of her eyes.

They had changed her.

She wasn't just here for observation.

She was here for activation.

Her vision swam, the drug still dragging her down, dulling the edges of her thoughts. But one thing was clear. She had never been a visitor in Darbonne. She had never been an outsider. She was part of it, and now, they were claiming her.

The words settled over Nia like a suffocating fog, thick and inescapable.

"You are his legacy."

She tried to process them, but the meaning slithered through her like something slick, something she couldn't grasp. The Institute. The name alone sent waves of unease through her, unlocking memories she hadn't realized she had buried. Files on her father's laptop, documents she had skimmed as a teenager, dismissing them as unrelated to her life, unrelated to her. But now, those words, those half-forgotten phrases, burned in the back of her skull like a brand. Project: Bloodline.

She swallowed against the nausea clawing its way up her throat. The room remained unnervingly still, the air too sterile, too controlled. There were no visible vents, no camera lenses tucked into the corners, but she knew she was being watched. The man in the pale suit remained standing, poised and unaffected, his expression unreadable. He was studying her, waiting, his posture betraying no urgency.

A scientist. A handler. Someone who had spent years in power, never needing to rush.

Nia forced herself to sit up straighter, ignoring the sluggish weight in her limbs, the chemical fog still dulling her edges. "My father had nothing to do with this," she said, but even as she said it, the words tasted like a lie.

The man smiled—not with warmth, not with arrogance, but with patience. Like he was waiting for her to catch up. "I think you already know that isn't true," he said, his voice even, smooth as glass. "Otherwise, you wouldn't be here. And you certainly wouldn't be alive."

The hairs on the back of her neck lifted.

He took a slow step forward, clasping his hands behind his back. "Your father was instrumental in what we've achieved. You were his proof of concept, his most promising success. Though, of course, you were never meant to remember."

A sharp pulse of pressure pressed against her skull, a migraine blooming behind her eyes, as if something inside her recoiled at the words. "You're lying," she said, but her voice lacked the force she wanted. She hated how small it sounded in this room, how hollow.

"Lying would be unnecessary," he replied, tilting his head slightly. "You'll see the records soon enough."

Her stomach twisted violently. "Records?"

"Everything. His work. His notes. The monitoring of your progress. Your entire life has been documented, Dr. Wallace. You are—" he exhaled slowly, almost reverently "—the key."

Her mind refused to accept it, but her body already knew. The sensation in her bones, the unnatural way her presence seemed to sync with the air in this town, the way Darbonne itself had bent around her, trapping her. The gaps in her memory. The hallucinations. The unshakeable sense that she had never truly left, that she had always been part of something bigger, something unseen.

She had spent years studying genetics, mapping lineages, tracing the hidden threads of inheritance, believing she was untangling history. But now she understood—she was the thread.

"Why?" The word scraped out of her throat, raw and unsteady.

The man's gaze flickered, just for a moment. "Because you are the culmination of generations of work. A controlled lineage. A perfect design."

She thought of the people in Darbonne—the unsettling sameness in their features, their movements, the way they seemed synchronized. She thought of Danielle, the way she had changed, become distant, colder, less human. A practiced response, an ingrained role. A system.

"You've been refining the bloodlines," she said, the words forming before she even understood them. "This town—this entire town is—"

"An ecosystem," the man finished for her. "A closed system, perfected through careful engineering. A community built to sustain its own evolution." He studied her for a long moment, then took another slow step closer. "And now, thanks to your father's work, it's ready to enter its next phase."

The headache behind her eyes sharpened, her vision pulsing at the edges. Something was wrong—more wrong than before. The air felt thicker, pressing in around her, a sensation that wasn't just physical but something deeper, something she couldn't shake. Her skin prickled as she noticed it—a change, subtle but suffocating.

The room was shifting. Not moving, not changing shape, but something in the air, something in the pressure, had altered.

She sucked in a breath, but it didn't feel the same in her lungs. The edges of her vision blurred again, the nausea rolling back through her stomach with twice the force.

"What did you—"

Her words slurred, her body swaying against her will.

The man didn't look surprised.

Her pulse spiked.

Not again.

Her fingers curled weakly against her thigh, but the strength was already draining from her muscles, her limbs unraveling beneath her like silk slipping through fingers.

"You were already injected before you woke up," the man said, as if reading her thoughts. "We needed you stable before the transfer process."

Her heart slammed against her ribs, a sluggish, too-late panic.

"You—" Her tongue felt thick, heavy, her vision tunneling.

"Shh," he murmured, almost gentle. "It'll be over soon."

The last thing she saw before darkness took her was his pale suit, pristine and unmoving, standing against the stark white walls of her prison.

And then—oblivion.

Darkness wrapped around Nia, thick and suffocating, but inside it—beneath it—something stirred.

Memories, fractured and unfurling, not like dreams, but like something waking up.

She was small—five, maybe six—sitting in a cold room that smelled like clean metal and something faintly sweet. Her feet dangled from a padded examination table, her fingers tracing the stitches on the hem of her dress.

"Be still, sweetheart," her father's voice murmured, gentle but firm.

She couldn't see his face—only the silhouette of his hands, moving quickly, adjusting machines that blinked softly in the dim light.

The beeping sound was steady, rhythmic, keeping time with something inside her.

A pressure cuff tightened around her arm, too tight, making her fingers tingle.

"This is just to measure," he said, but he wasn't speaking to her.

Someone else was in the room.

She turned her head, but the memory blurred at the edges, the details slipping away like ink in water.

She saw the outline of another figure—not her mother.

Someone taller, thinner. A woman.

"She's responding faster than expected," the stranger said, her voice clipped, professional.

"She was designed to."

Her father's voice was different now. Distant. Not unkind, but not the voice of a father. The voice of a man explaining his work.

The beeping quickened.

A sharp, pinching pain in her arm.

She looked down. A thin, silver electrode lay against the inside of her wrist, pulsing faintly beneath her skin. She didn't remember it being attached.

Her small fingers reached for it, but before she could touch it—the memory fractured. Everything twisted, folded, collapsed, and Nia fell through the dark. A dull pressure in her skull pulled her back toward consciousness.

She drifted at the edges of waking, still caught between past and present, reality and whatever came before it.

She wasn't alone.

The presence in the room wasn't cold like the man in the pale suit, wasn't stiff with clinical indifference. It was heavier, more tangled—warm and conflicted, tense with something unsaid.

Danielle.

Even before she opened her eyes, she knew.

There was a silence, stretched taut between them, like Danielle had been sitting there for a long time, waiting for Nia to wake, but not wanting her to.

Finally, her voice cut through the stillness, quiet, uneven. "I thought you'd be different."

Nia forced her eyes open, the effort making her stomach twist, her limbs still thick with whatever drug they had used on her. The ceiling above her was smooth, sterile white—the same as the holding room. But this wasn't the same space.

Softer lighting. A real bed, not a cot.

Not a prison.

But not freedom, either.

Her gaze shifted, landing on Danielle.

She sat stiffly in a chair against the far wall, her body wound tight, arms crossed over her chest like she was trying to keep herself from unraveling.

She looked different.

Not just tired, not just worn down—but changed.

Not the Danielle who had been her eager, overexcited sibling just days ago. Not the one who had dragged her through Darbonne's history, talking about their shared lineage like it was a gift.

This Danielle was someone else.

"You drugged me," Nia croaked, her throat raw.

Danielle flinched, just barely. "I didn't do it."

"But you let them."

Silence.

Nia forced herself to sit up, the motion sluggish, every part of her body still rebelling. "Tell me the truth," she said, her voice steadier now. "How long have you known?"

Danielle didn't answer immediately. She ran a hand over her face, her fingers shaking slightly.

"All my life," she admitted finally. "I just didn't know what it meant. Not really."

Nia swallowed against the nausea rising in her throat.

Danielle had always known.

She had always been part of this.

The betrayal settled deep, not sharp but dull and heavy, like something long overdue.

Danielle exhaled shakily, her eyes flickering to the floor. "I wanted you to stay."

Nia's jaw clenched. "So, you helped them trap me."

"You don't understand," Danielle snapped, looking up now, something raw flashing across her face. "This place—it's bigger than you, Nia. Bigger than me. It's...it's been built for generations. It's not just history, it's survival."

"Survival?" Nia scoffed, her anger bubbling past the fear. "You call this survival?" She gestured weakly to the electrodes still attached to her skin, to the thin, pulsing wires beneath them, connected to something unseen. "This isn't living, Danielle. This is control."

Danielle's fingers curled into fists. "You don't know what it was like. You got to leave. You got to live outside this place. The rest of us? We didn't have a choice. We had to trust them. We had to be part of the system, or we'd be—" She cut herself off, biting down hard on whatever she had been about to say.

But Nia had already heard enough. "You were afraid."

Danielle's throat bobbed as she swallowed hard.

"You're still afraid," Nia murmured.

Danielle looked away.

For a long time, neither of them spoke. The truth had already been laid between them, thick and unmovable.

Finally, Danielle exhaled shakily, rubbing her temples. "I tried to make it easy for you," she admitted, softer now. "I thought if you saw what Darbonne really was—if you understood—you'd stay. You'd *want* to stay."

Nia let the silence stretch again, let the weight of those words settle.

It should have made her angrier. It should have deepened the betrayal.

But more than anything, it terrified her.

Because part of her understood what Danielle had meant.

Part of her felt it too—that pull, that sick sense of belonging, that itch in her blood that told her she wasn't supposed to leave.

Not because of the town itself. Because of whatever had been done to her before she was even born.

Danielle stood abruptly, rubbing her hands over her arms like she was cold. "They'll come for you soon. To tell you everything. Or at least, everything they think you need to know."

Nia's stomach twisted. "And then what?"

Danielle hesitated. "You'll have a choice."

Nia didn't believe her.

Danielle walked toward the door, her movements sharp, practiced. She paused before opening it, her hand gripping the frame.

"I wanted you to stay," she said again. "But I didn't want it to be like this."

Then she left, the door sliding shut behind her.

Nia let out a slow, shaking breath, her head still pounding. She wasn't sure how much of her past had been stolen from her, how much had been built, engineered, manipulated.

But she knew one thing—she was done being their experiment.

Nia pressed the heels of her hands against her forehead, trying to push back the pounding inside her skull. The weight of everything—the town, the betrayal, the realization that she wasn't just connected to this place but made for it—was settling into her bones in a way she couldn't shake.

But this—this was something else.

The missing time.

The gap.

She had always assumed her childhood had been ordinary, if somewhat distant. Her mother had raised her, her father had been busy with his research, and she had never questioned it.

But now that she was staring down the truth—really staring at it—it was impossible to ignore.

The absence wasn't just a lack of memories. It was a hole. A void where an entire piece of her life should have been.

She had no childhood friends. No strong attachments to any school, any neighborhood. When she tried to think back—really think back—there was no one moment that defined her before college.

She had always been focused.

Driven.

Buried in her work.

And that, more than anything, was what made her stomach churn. Because why?

How had she ended up following in the exact same field as her father, walking the exact same path, without ever feeling like she had chosen it?

A shudder ran through her.

This wasn't just missing memories. It was missing control.

How much of her life had ever really been hers?

She exhaled shakily, forcing herself to peel back the layers of the past, searching for the moment when things had changed, when the edges of her memory had started to blur.

And then—

A flicker.

Not a memory exactly, but a sensation.

Cold metal pressed against her skin.

A voice, calm and clinical: *"We'll just make a small adjustment."*

The smell of something sterile, sharp, something that didn't belong in a home but in a lab.

She flinched, her breath catching as the memory tried to surface, like something pushing up from the depths of deep water.

No. Not a memory. Something buried.

The pressure in her skull deepened.

She saw herself—younger, smaller—standing in front of a mirror. She couldn't have been more than eight, maybe nine.

She looked normal. But something was off.

Her own face—blank, distant. Not sad, not afraid.

Just empty.

A woman—not her mother, but someone else, someone with a crisp white coat and a clipboard—stood behind her.

"You won't feel any different," the woman had said, smiling. *"This will help you."*

Help her.

Help her forget?

Nia gritted her teeth, her pulse skipping.

What had they done?

Her fingers pressed against her temple, feeling something deep beneath her skin. A knowledge she wasn't supposed to have, a truth she wasn't supposed to reach.

The gaps in her memory—they weren't natural.

They were placed.

Replaced.

Her father. His research.

What if the work hadn't just been about altering genetic structures but about controlling something deeper? Behavior. Memory. Obedience.

She sucked in a sharp breath, nausea curling in her stomach.

How many times had they wiped her clean?

The answer pulsed inside her, a slow, sick realization.

More than once.

Again.

And again.

Until she had become exactly what they had needed her to be.

A scientist. A researcher. Someone who would chase answers without realizing she was only ever retracing her own father's steps.

The air in the room felt thinner now, the walls pressing in, the silence too perfect.

She had been controlled, molded, directed back to this place like a moth drawn to a flame, because she had never really left.

Not in the way that mattered. Now, she wasn't sure if she had ever been herself at all.

CHAPTER SIXTEEN:

PROGRESS

The room they brought her to was different from the first. Larger, more open, with sleek walls that curved seamlessly into the ceiling, giving it an unsettling, cocoon-like effect. A long glass table stretched through the center, its surface so pristine it looked untouched. The chairs surrounding it were a soft, near-clinical shade of gray, arranged with careful precision. It wasn't an interrogation room.

It was a boardroom.

Two men sat at the far end, waiting.

Mayor Harris—poised, deliberate, the same man who had welcomed her to Darbonne with his too-smooth charm. And beside him, Dr. Baines, his expression as unreadable as ever.

The sight of them together sent a fresh wave of nausea through her. There was no pretense anymore. No illusion of help, no veil of concern. They were two sides of the same equation, different tools for the same purpose.

"You look well, Dr. Wallace," Mayor Harris said, gesturing toward the chair across from them. "Please, sit."

Nia stayed standing.

Her body was still sluggish from the drugs, her head heavy with the remnants of fragmented memories. But she had enough clarity now to know one thing: they were about to tell her exactly what they wanted from her. And she needed to hear it.

So, she took a slow breath, forcing her feet forward, and sat.

Harris folded his hands together, his ring catching the light. "I imagine you have many questions."

Nia didn't bother responding.

He continued, voice smooth, measured. "Darbonne is not just a town, Dr. Wallace. It is an achievement. A living success story of human potential, built on generations of careful, intentional progress."

Progress.

The word sent an icy shudder through her.

"We are standing on the foundation of something greater than ourselves," he went on. "Your father understood that. He helped lay the groundwork for the future we are building here."

She forced herself to keep her expression neutral. "A future built on what?"

Harris exchanged a glance with Baines. It was brief, but there was something in it. A silent agreement.

Baines leaned forward. "Genetic refinement."

The words landed like lead in her stomach.

She should have known. She *had* known. But hearing them say it out loud was something else entirely.

"Darbonne was designed to be self-sustaining," Baines continued, his tone clinical, detached. "Not just economically, not just socially—but biologically. Evolution is slow, chaotic, prone to failure. We have removed those inefficiencies."

"You mean you've been controlling people," Nia said, her voice sharp, cutting through the stale air.

Harris barely reacted. "Guiding," he corrected. "We have simply removed variables. Ensured that the next generation is stronger, smarter, healthier. Free of genetic predispositions to disease, mental instability, physical limitations."

Nia's stomach twisted. They weren't just selecting for traits. They were erasing what they saw as defects. And that meant—

Her fingers curled against the armrest of the chair.

"What happens to the ones who don't fit your blueprint?"

The silence stretched just long enough for her to know she wouldn't like the answer.

"We don't waste potential," Baines said finally.

Cold. Practical. Like culling livestock.

"Darbonne has always been a controlled ecosystem," Harris added, watching her carefully. "The families here are part of a lineage that stretches back centuries. Your own bloodline is one of the most important."

Nia's pulse pounded in her ears.

They weren't just telling her this to make her understand. They were telling her because they needed something from her.

"You are the key to the next phase," Baines said, confirming her fears. "Your father's research into hereditary intelligence, cellular regeneration, cognitive resilience—it all began with you."

Her breath stalled. "You mean it began *on* me," she said, her voice low, shaking with controlled fury.

Baines didn't deny it.

Her childhood, her missing years, the memories she hadn't questioned—she had been part of their data. Not a participant, not a subject who had volunteered.

A prototype.

She felt sick.

"This is why you wanted me back." She looked at Harris now, at his infuriatingly calm expression. "You're trying to move into another phase of your experiment, and you think I'm going to help you?"

Harris smiled, slow and measured. "We think you'll come to see that this is not an experiment. It's the future. A future your father fought to protect."

A fresh chill slid down her spine.

"He didn't protect me," she said, her voice sharp. "He used me."

Harris tilted his head slightly, considering. "Perhaps. But in the end, he still made sure you were kept safe. You were allowed to leave, weren't you?"

The words hit her harder than they should have.

Allowed.

Not escaped.

Her father had let her go. Had erased something, buried something in her mind, given her the illusion of freedom—but he had never truly let her leave. She had never been outside their reach. Never truly beyond their control.

She clenched her jaw, every nerve in her body coiled tight. "And if I refuse?"

Harris sighed, as if disappointed.

"You misunderstand, Dr. Wallace. There is no refusal. There is only acceptance. Whether you choose to resist or embrace what you are, your role in this will not change."

The calm finality in his voice sent ice through her veins.

This wasn't just a town. It was a machine. A living construct, built and refined over generations, designed for one singular purpose: to perfect itself. And now, she was part of its final design.

Her hands clenched into fists. They had spent years shaping this place, these people. They had spent her entire life shaping her. But they had made one mistake.

They had let her remember.

And that meant she could still break the pattern. She would find a way—even if it killed her.

Nia let the silence stretch, thick and suffocating, pressing against the walls of the pristine room. She stared at the two men across from her, their suits crisp, their postures perfect, so assured of their righteousness.

The weight of their words churned in her stomach. They had framed Darbonne's evolution as inevitable, as something greater than simple control, but that was the oldest lie in the world, wasn't it?

Call it refinement, call it efficiency, call it progress—it was all the same.

Oppression, polished and rebranded.

She exhaled slowly, gripping the arms of the chair until her nails bit into the material.

"You think you're different," she said, her voice measured but laced with anger. "You think because you use words like 'optimization' and 'progress,' you've risen above what came before. But this is just eugenics with better PR."

Baines' jaw twitched slightly, but Harris? Harris smiled.

"You misunderstand," the mayor said, his voice gentle, almost pitying. "This is not about superiority. It is about balance. Sustainability. A future without suffering."

Nia barked out a sharp, bitter laugh. "Without suffering? That's funny, considering I was strapped to a table as a child, having my brain rewired for whatever utopia you think you're creating."

Baines exhaled sharply, adjusting his cuffs, his expression darkening. "You were not harmed."

Nia's stomach twisted, revulsion curling inside her. "Oh? And you get to decide that, do you?"

Baines didn't respond.

She leaned forward now, something reckless, something defiant burning in her chest.

"You talk about this place like it's some paradise, but tell me—what happens to the ones who don't conform? The ones who don't fit your perfect vision?" She let the question hang for a second before pressing harder. "Because that's the part you're not saying, isn't it? A closed system like this? It doesn't allow for error. And what you see as an error—" she let her gaze flick to Baines "—is just a human being who doesn't fit into your equations."

Baines' expression remained neutral, but his silence said everything.

It was Harris who finally spoke, voice as even as ever. "Those who are unable to integrate—who reject our way of life—do not belong here."

The casual way he said it, as if the answer was obvious, as if people could simply be discarded like defective machinery, sent a wave of cold rage through her.

"And what does that mean?" she pressed, her voice sharp now. "Where do they go?"

Again, that pause.

Baines folded his hands together. "Darbonne is self-sustaining," he repeated, as if that was an answer.

Nia's breath stalled.

She thought of the silence in the streets, the synchronized responses of the townspeople, the eerie sameness of their faces, their expressions, their compliance.

She thought of the siren, the drill, the way everyone knew exactly what to do.

She thought of the man being escorted into the Parish Hall.

The terror in his eyes.

And she realized—she had already seen what happened to those who didn't belong.

The truth curled, heavy and sick, in her gut.

"This isn't a town," she said, voice quieter now. "It's a lab."

Harris nodded, almost pleased.

"A thriving one," he said. "A system that works."

She stared at him, at his perfectly composed face, his even tone, the careful cadence of every word.

And for the first time, she understood exactly what he was.

Not just a mayor.

Not just an enforcer.

He was a product. A creation of this place, just as much as she was.

That was why he spoke with such certainty, such conviction.

He had been designed for this.

And they wanted to shape her into the same thing.

She clenched her jaw, her pulse thudding in her ears. "You're not building a better world," she said, barely keeping her voice steady. "You're just repeating history. But this time, you're the ones holding the scalpel."

Harris's expression didn't flicker. "History only repeats itself when we fail to learn from it."

Her stomach twisted at the calm finality in his voice.

This was never about choice.

She could resist. She could fight. She could scream the truth to anyone who would listen.

But as far as they were concerned, her fate was already written. And she was running out of time to prove them wrong.

Nia let the weight of their stares settle, let the silence stretch just long enough for it to shift from expectant to uneasy.

They thought they had the upper hand.

They thought because they had taken her, because they had pulled her into this carefully built machine of theirs, she would accept her role.

But they had forgotten something.

She was not just another variable in their equation.

She was Dr. Nia Wallace.

A name that carried weight. A name that had been spoken in lecture halls, in research institutions, in places far beyond the reach of Darbonne.

A name that meant something.

She leaned forward, slow and deliberate, letting her words slice through the sterile air like a scalpel.

"You talk about inevitability like I don't have an entire world outside of this place."

Harris didn't move, but Baines shifted slightly, his fingers pressing against the table in a near-imperceptible movement.

Good.

They weren't used to people pushing back.

"You think you can just erase me?" she continued, her voice steady, controlled. "Like I don't have colleagues? Like I don't have people watching my work, expecting results? Like my sudden disappearance wouldn't raise every possible red flag?"

She saw the flicker of calculation in Harris's eyes, the slight adjustment in his posture.

"You're not dealing with some nobody who can vanish into the ether," she said, her pulse quick but controlled. "I've spent years building my career, building my name, building my life. And just like this town, that life was carefully crafted. Not by you. Not by whatever twisted vision you have for the future. But by me."

She saw it now—the slight, fractional change in their expressions. The momentary shift in the air.

For the briefest moment, they believed her.

And then—

A phone slid across the table.

The glass screen caught the dim overhead light, reflecting back at her like a taunt.

Harris gestured toward it, his movement smooth, almost amused.

"Go ahead," he said. "See for yourself."

Nia hesitated, but only for a second. She grabbed the phone, her fingers gripping it harder than necessary as she turned the screen toward her.

Her breath stalled.

Her own face stared back at her, smiling, radiant, against the backdrop of what looked like a seaside resort. Sun-drenched beaches, elegant cafés, candid shots that looked effortlessly curated.

A soft laugh, like she was on the best vacation of her life.

The caption beneath it made her stomach twist violently.

"Much-needed time away from the lab. Finally getting to breathe, to rest, to explore. I'll be back when I'm ready 🖤."

Her pulse slammed in her ears.

She scrolled.

More photos. More updates. A stream of carefully manufactured moments, posts that sounded like her but were just off enough to make her blood run cold.

"Needed this escape. Sometimes you have to disconnect to reconnect."

"The ocean is a cure for everything. I could stay here forever."

And worst of all—comments.

Colleagues. Friends. Even old classmates.

Believing it.

"So glad you're taking time for yourself!"

"You deserve it, doc. Don't rush back!"

"Ugh, jealous. Enjoy paradise!"

Her stomach dropped into freefall.

The edges of her vision blurred as she kept scrolling, as post after post cemented an alternate reality—one where she had left on her own, where she was safe, happy, untouched.

No one was looking for her.

Because as far as they were concerned, she was exactly where she wanted to be.

Her fingers clenched around the phone, her breath shallow, heart hammering against her ribs like it was trying to escape her chest.

She finally tore her eyes away from the screen, looking up at them.

Harris's expression was infuriatingly calm.

Baines, for once, actually looked interested.

"This is what progress looks like," Harris said, folding his hands neatly in front of him. "Seamless integration. No one is asking where you are because, as far as they know, you never left."

Nia's mind reeled.

They had planned this.

Not just for her, but for anyone who resisted.

For anyone who thought they could escape.

"How?" she asked, her voice barely above a whisper.

Harris gestured toward the phone. "Your digital footprint, your voice patterns, your language style—all of it can be replicated. Social media is a tool, Dr. Wallace. One we've mastered. And we understand human psychology just as well as we understand genetics. If a lie looks good enough, people won't question it. They'll believe it because they want to."

Baines spoke this time, voice quiet but firm. "No one is coming for you, Nia."

Her grip on the phone tightened.

Harris leaned forward slightly, his voice dropping to something almost reassuring. "You belong here. And the sooner you accept that, the easier this will be for you."

Nia forced herself to breathe.

Forced herself to think.

They wanted her to feel hopeless. Wanted her to believe there was no one left to save her.

But she wasn't broken yet.

She hadn't lost.

They were good at constructing lies.

But so was she.

Slowly, carefully, she set the phone back down on the table. Her expression was unreadable, her face smoothing into something almost passive.

"Then I guess I'm exactly where I need to be," she said softly.

The lie slipped effortlessly from her lips, and for the first time, she saw something flicker in Harris's expression.

Doubt.

She had given them what they wanted. And now, she would wait for the moment to take everything back.

The lie sat heavy on her tongue, bitter and suffocating, but she let it settle. She had to.

She had to keep them from seeing the wildfire beneath her skin, from realizing that their carefully curated world had only made her more determined to burn it down.

But then she made the mistake of looking at the phone again.

The images stared back at her, each one a mockery of her real life. A digital ghost built to replace her. Her identity reduced to algorithms and fabrications, feeding the world a version of herself that wasn't real.

A world that believed it.

A world that wouldn't come looking.

And that was when something inside her snapped.

The chair beneath her scraped violently against the floor as she shoved herself up, the movement so sudden that Baines stiffened, his fingers twitching toward something unseen.

Nia didn't care.

Her hands found the nearest chair—solid, heavy, cold steel.

She lifted it before she had even made the conscious decision, her pulse slamming against her ribs.

And then she threw it.

The sound it made as it crashed against the glass wall was a sharp, splitting crack, not quite shattering but damaging.

The impact sent vibrations rippling through the room.

For the first time since she had been in this town, the silence was hers.

It only lasted a second.

"That was unnecessary," Harris said, voice maddeningly calm.

Nia spun on him.

"Unnecessary?" Her voice was raw, her chest rising and falling too fast, too sharp. She wanted to tear something apart. "You think this is unnecessary? You think you can just sit there and tell me that my life—my entire existence—is nothing more than a carefully controlled project, and I'm just supposed to nod and accept it?"

Harris didn't even blink. "Yes."

That was the moment her body betrayed her.

Her hands trembled, her breath came in quick, short bursts, her mind spinning so fast that she felt lightheaded. The rage coursing through her was a physical force, clawing at the inside of her ribs, demanding release.

"Fuck you," she snarled, the words ripping out of her.

Baines sighed, rubbing his temple. "This is what we meant when we said you'd need time to adjust."

She laughed then. A sound so sharp, so bitter, that it didn't even feel like her own voice. "Adjust? You think I need time to adjust?" She took a step closer, the floor vibrating beneath her feet, or maybe that was just the sheer force of her rage. "I am not some stray you picked up off the street, some lost soul grateful for your twisted sense of salvation. I am Dr. Nia Wallace. You think you can erase me? You think I'll just disappear?"

Harris watched her with something almost like amusement. Like he was indulging her. Like she was just another variable they had accounted for. And that made her rage turn to something else entirely.

She lunged.

A hand caught her wrist before she could reach him, tight and unyielding.

Baines.

His grip was like steel, his expression colder than before. "Enough," he said, voice even.

Her pulse roared in her ears. She wanted to break free. She wanted to claw at him, at all of this, tear it apart with her bare hands.

But her body was still sluggish, still fighting off whatever lingering poison they had pumped into her.

Harris exhaled, adjusting his cuff like this had been nothing more than a minor inconvenience.

"You'll tire yourself out," he said, his voice as smooth as ever. "They always do."

They.

The word lodged itself in her throat like a blade.

They had done this before.

They had taken people before.

She was just another iteration of their perfect little plan.

A wave of nausea rolled through her.

Baines' grip loosened slightly, enough for her to yank away, stumbling back.

Her chest ached, her breath coming too fast, her hands still trembling.

But she refused to let them see her break.

Not now.

Not yet.

She swallowed the scream that still clawed at her throat, shoved down the raw, shaking rage still coursing through every nerve in her body.

And she smiled.

Slow. Cold.

"Enjoy your fucking utopia," she said, her voice shaking just enough to sound dangerous.

Then she turned her back on them, on the shattered chair, on the phone still glowing with its manufactured version of her life.

She walked out. She didn't know where they would take her next. But she knew one thing—she was never going to be one of them.

CHAPTER SEVENTEEN:
WAITING

The walls of the corridor pulsed faintly, or maybe that was just Nia's vision warping again.

Her body still hummed with adrenaline, her nerves raw, her skin too hot, too tight. Her breath came uneven as she forced herself forward, away from that room, away from their calm certainty that she would break.

She wouldn't break.

But something inside her was shifting.

The memory hit her before she had the chance to brace herself.

—A hallway. Not this one. Brighter, whiter, endless.

She was small. Barefoot. The floor beneath her was cold, humming faintly with unseen machines.

"Come along, sweetheart."

Her father's voice.

She turned, but he wasn't looking at her. He was speaking to someone else.

A door hissed open ahead of them, and she followed—not because she wanted to, but because something in her had been trained to obey.

The room beyond it was filled with rows of chairs, reclining like hospital beds.

And in one of them—

Her stomach lurched.

She saw a man.

Or what used to be a man.

His skin was too smooth, too perfect, as if time had been erased from it. His hair silvered, but his face—ageless. His eyes open, staring, his breath slow and measured.

She knew that face.

Mayor Harris Grayson.

But in this memory, he wasn't the mayor. He was something else.

A subject.

An experiment.

She gasped as the memory fractured, splitting apart like cracked glass, shards stabbing into her brain. The hallway around her reeled back into place, the sterile walls pressing in again.

Her hands shook.

Harris wasn't just old.

He was unnaturally old.

How many times had he reset? How many times had they pulled him back from the brink?

The realization settled in her stomach like a stone. Darbonne wasn't just selecting for traits. It was preserving them. Refining them. Erasing the expiration date of its most valuable assets. And at some point, her father had been part of that process.

Nia braced herself against the wall, her breath coming in short, sharp bursts.

They had taken Harris' body and rewritten it. Repaired it. Restored it. If they had done that to him—

What had they done to her?

A sharp, stabbing pain lanced through her skull, another memory forcing its way to the surface. This time, she was younger. No more than six. Her father's hands, steady, careful, clinical.

A syringe.

A soft hum of approval from someone standing just out of sight.

"She's responding faster than expected."

Faster than expected.

Like she was something to be tested.

Not a child.

A product.

She gasped, stumbling, nearly collapsing as the memory wrenched itself free and vanished. What the hell had they done to her? How many times had they altered her? Had her father ever loved her? Or had she only ever been his greatest success?

A rush of nausea burned the back of her throat. She pressed a hand to her chest, steady, steady, stay upright, stay in control.

They thought she didn't remember. But the memories were coming back now, faster, sharper, louder. And with every piece that surfaced, she understood. She was never meant to be free.

She was meant to be perfected.

She clenched her fists, grounding herself, swallowing the bile that threatened to rise. They thought she was still playing their game. But she was about to end it.

The corridor stretched long and empty, its stark white walls curving inward as if the space itself had been grown rather than built. The lighting was soft and indirect, humming at a frequency just beneath her awareness, an artificial warmth that never flickered, never dimmed. Too perfect. Too controlled.

The air here was sterile, thick with something more than just oxygen—something engineered, something faintly metallic. It clung to her tongue, settled in her lungs, made her pulse too steady, too measured, as if the environment itself was syncing with her body.

They had thought of everything.

She pressed her palm against the wall, half-expecting it to pulse beneath her touch. It didn't. But she could feel it. Something humming within the structure, faint and distant, like the slow exhale of a sleeping beast.

This place was alive in a way that had nothing to do with biology.

It was designed.

A perfectly sealed ecosystem, self-sustaining, self-correcting. She had seen clean labs before, containment chambers, research facilities, but this was different.

This wasn't just a lab. It was a living blueprint.

And she was part of its design.

A sharp chill coiled in her spine.

She walked forward, slow and steady, her pulse loud in her ears. The floor beneath her was smooth but not slick, a material that absorbed sound rather than reflected it. No echoes, no disruption—everything here was meant to exist in harmony.

Even the silence was manufactured.

She ran her fingers along the seams of the wall, searching for anything out of place. But there was nothing—no panels, no bolts, no visible entry points. As if everything had been seamlessly merged into one continuous surface.

She had no doubt that there were doors, but they wouldn't be opened by force.

They would open when the system allowed them to.

A sense of claustrophobia pressed against her ribs.

She was inside something. Not just a building—a machine.

A memory stirred, half-formed, rising like mist in the back of her mind.

She was small again, walking barefoot down another corridor just like this one.

She remembered the quiet hum of something beneath her feet, a sensation she had found oddly comforting at the time.

"This place is special, Nia."

Her father's voice.

"It will take care of us, if we take care of it."

At six years old, she had believed him.

Now, standing in the same kind of engineered silence, she felt the lie wrapped around those words.

Darbonne wasn't taking care of its people.

It was preserving them, containing them, controlling them.

Her father had understood that. He had been part of it.

And yet—

Harris was older than her father should have been.

If he had worked with her father, if he had been part of the project from the beginning, then how—

Another ripple of nausea twisted in her gut.

They weren't just refining genetics. They were extending them.

They were cheating death.

Harris wasn't just a leader.

He was proof of concept.

The realization sank its claws into her mind, heavy and sharp.

They had erased the natural expiration date, manipulated the sequence of decay, built something that could outlive itself.

If they had done that to Harris—if they had tested longevity on him—then what had they done to her?

She stumbled forward, pressing a hand against the wall to steady herself.

The hum of the space pressed against her skin, vibrating at the base of her skull, as if something inside her was reacting, syncing, adjusting.

She swallowed hard.

They had built Darbonne to be self-sustaining.

But what if it wasn't just the town?

What if it was the people themselves?

What if they weren't just refining bloodlines for intelligence, for disease resistance, for strength—but for permanence?

The thought sent a pulse of cold through her limbs.

What if she wasn't meant to just stay?

What if she was meant to never leave?

Not just physically.

Not just now.

Ever.

Her hands curled into fists, her nails pressing into her palms.

No.

They hadn't won.

They hadn't erased her yet.

Her memories were coming back, her mind was fighting to reassemble the truth.

And if she could remember—if she could trace the fault lines back to their source—

She could break them.

She just had to find the right fracture point.

She straightened, her breath steadying, the storm inside her settling not into fear, but into clarity.

They wanted her to believe she had no control.

But she wasn't their machine.

And she would find the weak spot.

Every system had one.

Even this.

Nia inhaled deeply, forcing herself to think.

If there was one thing she could rely on, it was her mind.

They had altered her, shaped her, manipulated her memories. But they hadn't taken away her intelligence.

They had made a mistake.

They had brought back a geneticist.

She closed her eyes for a moment, shutting out the sterile walls, the engineered silence, the quiet hum beneath her feet. She needed to focus—break this down the way she would a problem in the lab.

The human brain is plastic.

That was the first truth.

Memories weren't fixed. They could be rewritten, reshaped, molded through repetition. Trauma could bury them, and external forces could rewire the way they surfaced.

She knew this.

She had studied this.

Neuroplasticity was the foundation of memory manipulation. It was why PTSD survivors struggled with flashbacks. Why childhood trauma could alter the way a brain developed. Why false memories could be implanted through suggestion.

So if her memories had been tampered with, blocked, or suppressed—

How?

And more importantly—how could she undo it?

She started listing the possibilities, her mind clicking through hypotheses as if she were back in her office, working through a particularly complex genetic sequence.

1. Chemical interference.

Drugs. Hormonal regulation. Cortisol suppression. If they had used pharmaceuticals, it would have dampened neural pathways related to recall. Some memory-erasure drugs were already being tested in neuroscience trials—beta-blockers like propranolol had been shown to reduce the emotional impact of traumatic memories.

But this felt deeper. More precise.

2. Direct electrical stimulation.

Deep brain stimulation, TMS, or something more advanced.

The hippocampus was the storage vault of memory, while the amygdala dictated how memories were emotionally weighted. If they had been targeted—if the town had the kind of technology that could disrupt or rewrite neural encoding—then they could have selectively erased moments of her past without damaging anything else.

The thought made her struggle to catch her breath.

Had they reprogrammed her?

Had they gone into her mind and edited her the way she edited gene sequences in a lab?

She swallowed hard and pressed forward.

3. Long-term environmental reinforcement.

This one scared her the most.

Because if her father had been involved—if she had been part of this since birth—then what if it wasn't just drugs?

What if it wasn't just stimulation?

What if she had been conditioned?

Neural networks adapt to repetition. The more a lie is told, the more the brain accepts it as truth. Children's memories were malleable—it was why childhood amnesia existed, why memories before the age of three were often inaccessible.

If Darbonne had raised her in a controlled environment, monitored her, reinforced certain patterns over and over again—

Then what parts of her life had ever truly belonged to her?

Her fingers dug into the skin of her palm.

There had to be a way to undo it.

Her brain had started fighting back the moment she entered Darbonne, flashing suppressed memories like warnings, like emergency alarms in the dark.

That meant her neural pathways weren't completely severed.

She could rebuild them.

Her breath steadied as she began mapping out what she needed.

How to recover suppressed memories:

    1. Trigger neuroplasticity. She had to reawaken the neural pathways that had been shut down, force her brain to reconnect its old circuits.

    2. Access the original emotional weight. The amygdala stored the emotional context of memories—fear, grief, pain. If she could push herself into situations that mimicked those original emotions, it could reawaken the connections that had been lost.

    3. Disrupt the interference. If they had used a drug, she needed an antagonist. If they had used electrical interference, she needed to overwhelm the system with new sensory input.

    4. Re-expose herself to triggers. If her body and mind were already reacting to Darbonne,

then being here was the key. This town was the trigger.

They thought they had buried the past.

But all they had done was leave her inside the burial site long enough to dig herself out.

She exhaled sharply, her hands still shaking but now with clarity, not fear.

The problem with controlling people was that it never lasted forever.

Their methods might be advanced, their science might be years ahead of the outside world, but in the end, human nature couldn't be programmed indefinitely.

Memories were fluid.

And so was resistance.

Her time in Darbonne had already started the unraveling process. She just had to keep pulling the thread.

Nia's thoughts moved fast, snapping through possibilities, arranging information into something actionable. But a question burned at the back of her mind, something just as important as unraveling her own memory.

Why had they let her leave in the first place?

Everything she had uncovered so far pointed to control—absolute, unshakable control over every bloodline in Darbonne.

They didn't let variables walk away.

So why her?

She pressed her fingers to her temple, trying to push through the static hum in her brain.

She had always assumed she left for college because she had worked hard, because her mother had encouraged her, because it had been her choice.

But that was a lie, wasn't it?

She had never been in control.

Her fingers curled into fists as she forced herself to follow the logic.

She wasn't just a product of Darbonne—she was one of their most valuable assets.

And yet, she had gone.

Either they had let her, or—she had escaped.

No, not escape. That wasn't right. She had been allowed to leave.

Which meant—

She wasn't useful to them then.

Her bloodline mattered, her father's work mattered, but she had still been unfinished. An experiment still in progress.

Had they been waiting for something?

A chill crawled down her spine.

Maybe they had needed more time. Maybe they had been watching her from a distance, tracking her, waiting for the right moment.

Had her whole life outside Darbonne just been a test phase?

The thought made her stomach lurch.

She thought back to the phone, the curated posts, the version of herself they had manufactured.

They had been planning this.

For years.

The timing wasn't a coincidence.

She gritted her teeth. What changed? What made them call her back now?

Then, a flicker of memory. A moment she had dismissed when she first arrived.

Danielle, on the porch, scrolling through her phone. Danielle, watching her too carefully.

"I was waiting for you to figure it out."

Nia's pulse quickened. Danielle hadn't just invited her here. She had known she would come. The realization slammed into her.

The DNA-matching app.

That was the variable.

She had spent years tracking lineages, mapping ancestral histories, reconstructing genetic blueprints. And then, suddenly, a match appeared. Danielle had reached out, drawing her in.

Nia clenched her fists.

The app had been the bait. But who had set the trap?

Had it been Harris? Baines? Or—her father?

Her heart pounded.

She had spent her whole life studying the past. And now, she was caught in it. Whatever they had been waiting for, whatever final stage they had needed her to reach—she had reached it.

That was why she was here.

Her presence in Darbonne hadn't been a choice. It had been the last step in a process that had started before she was even born.

Her breath slowed, her mind sharpening into something cold, calculating.

Fine.

They had spent years planning for her return. They thought she was just a piece of their grand design. But they had underestimated her.

Because now that she knew, she could use it. She wasn't just going to uncover the truth. She was going to burn their entire system to the ground.

CHAPTER EIGHTEEN:

Return

The walls whispered around her. Not with sound, but with pressure—a hum beneath the surface, like the entire space was alive, waiting, watching.

Nia sat motionless on the edge of the bed, staring at the seamless walls, at the absence of doors, handles, exits. They had designed this space to be impossible to leave. But nothing was impossible.

She had mapped it all out in her mind—the security patterns, the way the walls pulsed with unseen energy, the way the air circulated in regular, mechanical cycles. The details were subtle, but they were there.

Every system had a weak point.

She wasn't alone.

She could feel someone on the other side of the wall. Not watching her—waiting.

Aunt Celeste.

The thought sent a pulse of something strange through her, something too raw to name.

Celeste had been the first to warn her. The first to hint that everything wasn't as it seemed.

"You think they stopped? They never stopped."

Had Celeste always been on the outskirts, playing a dangerous game, waiting for someone—waiting for her—to wake up?

A sharp, metallic hiss broke the silence.

The wall shifted, just slightly.

A seam split open near the base, so subtle it could have been an illusion. But it wasn't.

A sound—a hand tapping lightly, just once.

Nia moved.

She pressed her fingers against the seam, feeling the hidden edge of a panel. It was thin, too thin for a normal door, and yet—her fingers found the latch.

She pulled.

The panel slid open, revealing a narrow passage, the space dimly lit, filled with old, heavy air. The veins of Darbonne were hidden in places like this.

Celeste stood just inside, a figure of quiet urgency, her sharp eyes glinting in the dim light.

"Come on," she whispered. "Before they realize you're gone."

Nia didn't hesitate.

She stepped through the threshold, leaving captivity behind.

But she wasn't just running.

She was heading straight for the people who had built this prison in the first place.

She was going to confront them on their own stage.

The passage was tight, the air thick with the scent of old metal, dust, and something deeper—something damp and earthy, like the bones of Darbonne itself had been left to rot. The walls were different here, not the sleek, artificial smoothness of the containment room but rougher, more textured. Older.

Celeste moved quickly, her steps practiced, as if she had walked these hidden corridors a hundred times before. Nia followed, her breathing shallow, ears straining for the sound of pursuit. But there was nothing—no alarms, no footsteps echoing behind them, only the rhythmic churn of the ventilation system, the quiet hum of unseen machinery keeping the town's delicate ecosystem in place.

The lights overhead were small and recessed, casting a dim, reddish glow that made the narrow space feel even more claustrophobic. It reminded her of veins, of blood vessels stretching through a body, a hidden system keeping something alive. The deeper they went, the colder the air became, as if they were stepping further away from the controlled perfection above and into something raw, something buried.

"Where are we?" Nia whispered, pressing close behind Celeste.

"Below the Parish Hall," Celeste murmured, her voice barely audible over the hum of unseen circuits embedded in the walls. "These tunnels run beneath most of Darbonne. Not many people know about them anymore, not even the ones who should."

The idea sent a ripple of unease through Nia. The town was already a controlled experiment, a machine disguised as a community. And yet, even within that system, there were secrets hidden beneath the surface.

Celeste took a sharp turn, leading her through a low-ceilinged corridor lined with storage rooms. The metal doors were marked with symbols—some she recognized from old research notes, genetic markers, medical codes, while others were more cryptic, symbols carved into the metal that looked ancient, ritualistic.

Nia's stomach twisted.

This wasn't just a town built on scientific advancement. It was a place of worship.

Not for a god, but for an idea.

The pursuit of perfection, of control, of erasing the unpredictable flaws of human evolution.

Her fingers brushed one of the doors as they passed, and a memory pulsed behind her eyes.

—A room, blindingly white. Cold. A chair with straps that she had never thought to question.

"Hold still, sweetheart."

Her father's voice.

The light overhead flickered, and she had the briefest sensation of losing time.

When she opened her eyes, she was standing in the same room.

The chair was empty.

The door was locked.

And she was alone.

She inhaled sharply, pulling herself back to the present.

She couldn't fall apart now.

Celeste glanced at her but didn't stop. She led her down a final stretch of hallway, pausing at an intersection where the tunnel opened into a larger chamber, filled with rusted pipes and heavy machinery. The air here was damp, thick with condensation, the walls slick with moisture.

Celeste pulled a small, black device from her pocket and pressed it against a panel on the wall. There was a low click, and a hidden door slid open with a whisper of air.

Beyond it was a ladder, leading up.

"Where does this go?" Nia asked, swallowing back the unease rising in her throat.

"Out," Celeste said simply. "But not just anywhere."

She hesitated, locking eyes with Nia. There was something unspoken in her gaze, something deeper than just urgency.

"This takes us directly to the Parish Hall," Celeste continued. "There's a meeting happening tonight. Harris and Baines will be there. If you want answers, that's where you'll get them."

Nia exhaled slowly, bracing her hands against the cool metal rungs of the ladder.

Answers.

That was why she had come here in the first place, wasn't it?

To uncover the truth, to pull apart the carefully constructed lies that had shaped her entire existence.

Now, she had the chance to do exactly that.

She gripped the ladder, planting her foot on the first rung.

No more running.

No more waiting.

It was time to face them.

The ladder rungs were cold beneath Nia's fingers, slick with condensation, but she climbed with purpose, with certainty. The tunnel had felt like a grave, a buried vein beneath the town, but this—this was the ascent. She could hear the distant murmur of voices above, growing sharper as she neared the top, the air shifting from the stale dampness of the underground to the structured sterility of the Parish Hall.

Celeste climbed just behind her, steady but tense. "Don't hesitate when we get up there," she murmured. "You only get one moment before they try to contain it."

Nia nodded, heart pounding.

She reached the top and found a sealed hatch, a locking mechanism embedded in the ceiling. Celeste reached past her, pulling a slim keycard from her pocket and swiping it against an unseen reader. A low, mechanical hiss. The panel slid open.

Nia pushed through.

She emerged in a storage chamber—dim, clinical, lined with metal cabinets and shelves of neatly labeled files. But she didn't have time to study the details.

Beyond the door, the voices were louder now.

Harris. Baines. The town council. The people of Darbonne.

A meeting was already underway.

Nia turned to Celeste, who nodded once before slipping into the shadows, ready to handle any resistance.

This was it.

She pushed through the door and into the main hall.

The room fell silent.

Rows of townspeople sat lined in neat, orderly sections, all facing the raised platform where Harris and Baines stood, their postures rigid with control. The air was thick with expectation, with precision, as if the very fabric of this place depended on order.

And then, she saw it.

A screen.

A massive projection behind Harris, showing charts, data points, genetic lineage maps. The very foundation of Darbonne, displayed without shame, without secrecy.

Her own name was among the data.

A classification. A designation.

Not a person.

A component.

Her blood, her modifications, her engineered lineage—all public knowledge among these people.

Rage seared through her.

Harris's expression barely flickered as she stepped forward. He had expected her to stay in her cage.

"Dr. Wallace," he said smoothly, as if nothing was out of place. "I assume you've had time to reflect."

Nia let out a sharp, bitter laugh. "Oh, I've reflected." She tore her gaze away from the screen, leveling her eyes at the crowd. "How long have you all known? How long have you been part of this?"

No one answered.

Some of them looked away. Others sat still, watching, waiting.

Baines sighed, stepping forward as if addressing a difficult student. "This isn't the way, Nia."

Her nails dug into her palms.

"You took my life," she said, her voice low, steady, dangerous. "You rewrote my memories. You built this entire town on the backs of generations of people who never consented. And you expect me to just... fall in line?"

She took another step forward.

Harris exhaled slowly, not threatened. Not yet.

"You misunderstand," he said, that same measured patience. "No one has been forced into anything. Darbonne thrives because we work toward a singular goal. It has always been this way."

Nia turned to the crowd, her pulse hammering.

"You all accept this?" she demanded. "Living in a cage, having your lives, your blood, your children dictated by a council of geneticists playing god?"

A murmur rippled through the seated townspeople, shifting, uncertain.

A crack.

Nia lunged.

Not at Harris. Not at Baines.

At the console.

The heart of the system.

She grabbed the nearest piece of equipment, a heavy monitor, and ripped it from its mount. The screen shattered against the floor, sending a violent ripple through the room.

A moment of stunned silence.

Then—chaos.

An alarm screamed to life.

Baines moved first, reaching toward a panel—to override her, to contain her.

Nia was faster.

She slammed her hand against the emergency control panel, pressing every override, every emergency shutdown.

The screens flickered wildly, distorted images flashing, errors blooming across the projections.

And then—the files.

She saw them in the mess of data, hidden histories, erased records, generations of "unfit" subjects who had been removed, reprogrammed, eliminated.

And she unlocked them all.

The files spilled onto the main screen.

Names. Real names.

Not just genetic markers—people.

Townspeople gasped as faces flickered across the projection. Mothers, fathers, siblings who were supposed to have left, or died, or simply vanished.

The lie was unraveling.

The murmurs turned to shouts.

A hand closed around her wrist.

Baines.

"Enough," he growled, his voice breaking from its usual control.

She wrenched free, her breath heaving.

"You think you can control everything," she spat. "But people don't work like that. Memory doesn't work like that. You can manipulate them, you can rewrite their pasts, but sooner or later, the mind fights back."

Harris's calm had fractured. His expression was tight, no longer perfectly composed.

And then, from the crowd—

"Is this true?"

A woman stood near the back, her voice shaking. "My brother—he didn't die in an accident? You sent him away?"

The questions multiplied, spreading through the room like wildfire.

Harris opened his mouth—to soothe, to redirect. But the control was slipping.

Celeste moved beside her, ready.

Nia turned to Baines, breathing hard. "This is your utopia? A town built on lies? Built on stolen people, rewritten memories?"

Baines's jaw tightened. He looked away.

The room fractured into chaos.

Townspeople rose from their seats, confusion and anger crashing over them in waves as the truth unraveled in front of them. The screens still flickered, a broken machine trying to correct itself, but the damage had been done.

Nia could see the moment the illusion shattered.

The moment people saw the names—their family, their blood—people who had been taken, erased, rewritten.

Harris lifted a hand, trying to regain control. "Everyone, please," he said, his voice still calm, but Nia could hear it now—the strain, the urgency beneath it. "This is a disruption, nothing more. I assure you, everything you've seen tonight is being taken out of context—"

"Out of context?" a man shouted from the crowd. "My wife—you told me she was sick! That she wasn't strong enough to stay! You sent her away!"

More voices, rising, trembling, furious.

Harris lost his composure. His mask of careful patience cracked, his mouth tightening as he stepped back toward Baines, as if recalibrating, as if deciding whether to let this moment burn or force it back under control.

Baines moved quickly, his hand darting toward the console, toward whatever failsafe they had built into the system.

No.

Nia moved to stop him, but someone beat her to it.

A blur of motion—Danielle.

She appeared at Baines's side like a ghost, reaching before he could react, before Nia could even process what she was doing.

A gun.

It had been in Baines's coat. She must have known, must have been waiting for the exact moment to act.

And she didn't hesitate.

She ripped it from him, turned on Harris.

The sound of it cocking silenced the room.

Every voice, every movement, every breath stilled.

Danielle's hands trembled, but her grip was steady. Her face—God, her face. She looked like someone standing at the edge of a cliff, like she had known all along that she would end up here, that there was no turning back.

Harris straightened, his eyes darkening.

"Danielle," he said softly. "Put it down."

She didn't.

Her breath was uneven, her chest rising and falling too fast. "You knew," she whispered. "You knew what they were doing to us. You knew the people we lost weren't sick, or unfit, or weak. They were just… gone."

Harris took a step toward her. "Danielle, think—"

"I have thought!" Her voice broke, and for the first time, Nia saw the full weight of her torment. The doubt, the guilt, the years of trying to accept what could never be accepted.

Danielle had believed in Darbonne, in the vision, in the future they were supposed to be creating. But she had also loved.

She had lost people, just like the rest of them. And now, she knew why.

Tears burned in her eyes, but she didn't lower the gun.

Nia took a step toward her, slow, careful. "Danielle," she said softly. "You don't have to do this alone."

Danielle's gaze flickered to her. And there—there it was.

A moment of recognition, of understanding.

Then—

A sharp movement.

Baines.

Too fast.

Danielle turned—just a fraction too late.

A blade. Not a gun.

Nia barely processed it before Baines drove it into her side.

A sickening, wet sound—a gasp—Danielle's gasp.

The gun clattered to the floor.

Baines stepped back, his face unreadable, the knife slick with her blood.

Danielle's hands shook violently, pressed to her stomach, to the wound that was already seeping between her fingers.

Nia moved without thinking.

She caught Danielle before she could fall, lowering her carefully to the floor, her own breath coming too fast, too sharp.

"No," she whispered, her hands slick with her sister's blood. "No, no, no—"

Danielle's fingers gripped hers, her breaths shallow. Her eyes found Nia's, and there was something resigned in them.

"I had to," she whispered.

Her body shuddered, struggling, failing.

Harris exhaled softly. "A shame," he murmured.

Nia's head snapped up, rage like fire in her veins.

"You killed her," she said, her voice raw.

Harris barely spared her a glance. "She killed herself the moment she chose your side."

The words were too calm. Too final.

The room had erupted. Townspeople shouting, crying, trying to make sense of the scene in front of them. Some of them still loyal, still confused, others seeing clearly for the first time.

Danielle's breath hitched.

Her fingers dug weakly into Nia's wrist.

"I'm sorry," she whispered. "I should have..." She swallowed hard, her expression twisting.

But there was no time for regret.

Nia clutched her tighter. "Stay with me," she begged, furious at the universe, at the town, at herself. "Stay with me, damn it!"

Danielle's lips curved, but the smile was so faint, so distant.

Her next breath never came.

Nia felt it happen.

The stillness.

The moment life left her body.

The moment her pulse became nothing.

A tremor moved through Nia—a fracture so deep it couldn't be named.

Something inside her broke.

She inhaled—ragged, shaking, furious.

Her hands, covered in her sister's blood, trembled as she turned her head, locking eyes with Harris.

For the first time, he faltered—because she wasn't just angry.

She was coming for him, and she wasn't going to stop.

A crack of thunder split the air outside, as if the storm brewing over Darbonne had finally reached its peak. The power flickered again—this time, more violently. The remaining screens on the walls burst into static, then into darkness.

The town was unraveling.

Harris took a measured step back, his once-controlled mask slipping into something colder, something ruthless. Around them, townspeople moved in chaotic waves—some frozen in shock, others turning on one another, demanding answers, demanding justice.

Baines wiped his blade on his sleeve, unbothered. "This was always going to be the outcome," he said, his voice void of anything close to regret. "You just accelerated it."

Nia barely heard him.

Her body felt like it was vibrating—blood roaring in her ears, chest heaving, hands slick with Danielle's fading warmth.

Harris was still looking at her, measuring, calculating. He had underestimated her before.

He wouldn't get the chance to do it again.

Nia moved.

Her hand shot out, grabbing the fallen gun before Baines could react. She twisted, fired—

BANG.

The shot rang out, splitting through the noise, through the chaos.

Baines staggered back. His hand flew to his side, where blood bloomed beneath his coat. He let out a sharp breath, then lifted his gaze to her—unimpressed.

"Not enough," he murmured.

Harris moved.

But Nia was already turning the gun on him.

"Try it," she said, her voice flat, void of anything but certainty.

For the first time, Harris hesitated.

The crowd had shifted.

People who had once followed his every word without question were no longer looking at him for guidance. They were looking at her.

And that's when she knew.

He felt it slipping.

The control, the influence, the power he had spent years cultivating. The truth had taken root in the town's foundation, and no amount of manipulation would bury it again.

Nia took a step forward. The weight of Danielle's body, of her death, of everything, coiled inside her like a storm waiting to be unleashed.

"You built this place on lies," she said, her voice carrying across the space, reaching every ear, every shaking, breaking mind. "You convinced them that the people they lost were weak, unworthy, gone. But they weren't. You took them. You decided who deserved to exist."

Harris's jaw tightened. "You think you've won?" he asked, his voice still infuriatingly calm.

Nia felt the gun tremble in her grip. Not from fear—from rage.

"I think you're finished."

The room exploded. Not in sound. Not in movement. But in understanding.

A scream—someone lunging for Baines. Another person charging toward Harris. The once-perfect order of Darbonne fractured beyond repair, the people no longer bound by blind faith, by routine, by the illusion of safety.

And then—

The first fire ignited.

A crash—glass shattering.

The scent of smoke.

It was ending.

Darbonne was burning., and Nia was going to make sure it never rose again.

The first fire swallowed the council chamber, crawling up the walls like something alive. Smoke curled thick and acrid, choking the air, searing Nia's throat as she moved.

The town had erupted into chaos.

Townspeople surged in every direction—some running, some fighting, some simply standing frozen in the ruins of their belief.

Baines was gone. Harris too. Slipped away like rats abandoning a sinking ship.

Cowards.

Nia wanted to chase them, wanted to end this herself, but she knew—this was bigger than them now.

Darbonne was dying.

And if she didn't move, she'd die with it.

She pushed through the crowd, through the heat, the smoke, the violence, clutching the gun in one hand, the weight of Danielle's death in the other.

Then—

A familiar voice. Reed.

"Nia!"

She spun, breath catching—there.

Reed stood at the council hall's entrance, blood at his temple, a limp in his step. But he was alive.

"Come on!" he shouted.

She ran.

Out of the chamber, into the street, into the unraveling nightmare of Darbonne's final moments.

Buildings burned.

People screamed.

The town that had once been too perfect, too controlled, too unreal had finally become something human—raw, ugly, free.

And through it all, Nia felt something break loose inside her.

It wasn't victory.

It wasn't relief.

It was guilt.

She had done this.

She had set this in motion.

And now she had to live with it.

Reed pulled her forward, navigating the maze of collapsing structures and crumbling truths. "The road's blocked," he said between ragged breaths. "Only way out is the river."

The river. The same one that had always seemed too still, too controlled—just like everything else in Darbonne.

She didn't hesitate.

They ran, past houses swallowed by fire, past the faces of people she had once thought lost in their own delusions. But now—now, they were awake.

Some would escape. Some would stay.

Some would never leave.

It wasn't her job to save them. It never had been.

She had only opened their eyes.

The river came into view, wide and dark and endless. Their only chance.

Reed jumped first, splashing into the black water. He surfaced, gasping, reaching for her.

"Jump, Nia!"

She turned back one last time.

Darbonne burned behind her, flames licking the sky, the town's history turning to ash.

She should have felt free.

Instead, she felt haunted.

By the names on the screen. By the faces of the people who had disappeared before they could fight back. By Danielle's last breath in her arms.

Nia Wallace, geneticist, scientist, survivor, had thought she came here to find the truth.

But she had become a part of it.

And she would never escape that.

Not really.

With one last breath, she leapt.

The water swallowed her whole.

CHAPTER NINETEEN:

LINEAGE

Nia hit the water hard. The shock of it stole her breath, sent her spiraling down into the dark.

For a moment, she let it pull her under—let the weight of everything sink into her bones. The cold. The loss. The truth.

Then instinct kicked in.

She kicked toward the surface, lungs screaming, breaking through just as Reed reached for her, his grip solid, grounding her in the chaos.

"Got you," he said, voice hoarse.

The water was still rushing past them, cold and relentless, but Nia barely felt it anymore.

She was staring at Reed.

Reed.

Her body recognized him before her mind caught up. The slope of his jaw, the deep brown of his eyes—eyes she had seen before, somewhere far away from this nightmare.

Her breath hitched. "Reed?"

He exhaled, raking a hand through his soaked hair. "Yeah."

The word was too small for the weight behind it.

For the weight of everything she had forgotten.

Nia swayed where she sat, body still shaking from the river, the fire, the loss. But now, there was something else.

A door, opening in her mind.

A locked memory slamming into her with the force of a flood.

She knew him.

Not from Darbonne. From before.

Before all of this. Before her life became unrecognizable.

Reed Lawson. The boy she had grown up with. The one who had spent summers at her house when his father worked late shifts at the lab. The one who taught her how to ride a bike, who made fun of her for being a know-it-all but always let her win their science fair bets.

They had been inseparable.

Until they weren't.

Until he was gone.

She had thought he'd gone off to college, same as her. They had promised to stay in touch. Then—nothing.

She had searched for him once, freshman year, after their texts dried up, after calls went unanswered. But people drifted. Lives changed.

And she had let him go.

Except—he hadn't left.

Nia's stomach twisted. "What the hell are you doing here?"

Reed's jaw clenched. "I could ask you the same thing."

"No." She shook her head. "No, I came here looking for answers. Looking for my—" Her voice broke, just for a second. Danielle.

Reed's expression softened, but he didn't reach for her. "I know."

She flinched. "You know?"

A pause. A hesitation, just long enough to make her breath turn sharp.

"Reed," she said slowly, carefully, "how long have you been in Darbonne?"

He didn't look away this time.

"Long enough."

Her heart slammed against her ribs.

"No," she whispered.

Because that meant—

That meant he had been here for years.

That meant he had been here when she was searching for him.

That meant he had been here when she thought he was gone.

Nia felt something splinter inside her. "They took you."

Reed exhaled, shaking his head. "Not exactly."

She stared at him.

A familiar face in an unfamiliar place. A piece of her past buried in the wreckage of Darbonne.

"What happened to you?" she asked, her voice barely a breath.

Reed glanced at the distant glow of fire behind them. Then he looked at her. "Everything."

Reed watched her, his face unreadable, but his hands were curled into fists. Like he was waiting for her to yell, to demand answers, to break.

But she couldn't—not yet. Not while Darbonne was still burning.

The glow of the fire stretched into the sky, a beacon of destruction, of truth laid bare. But if they stayed here too long, they'd never get out.

Reed turned first, scanning the riverbank, his body tense. "We need to go."

Nia swallowed hard, forcing her mind to focus, to pull away from the past, from the questions crawling under her skin. "Which way?"

Reed exhaled, glancing toward the road—the only road out of Darbonne. It ran straight through town, through the heart of the chaos. If the council was still standing, that was where they'd be regrouping.

That was where people disappeared.

Nia knew it without him having to say a word.

"It's a trap," she murmured.

He nodded once. "The road is a dead end. It always has been."

Her pulse jumped. "What do you mean?"

Reed looked at her then—really looked at her.

"You think nobody's ever tried to leave before?"

A cold dread crawled up her spine. "They said people left all the time."

He let out a sharp breath. "They told you a lot of things."

Nia's stomach turned.

The missing people. The ones who 'couldn't stay.' The ones who 'moved on.'

But no one ever heard from them again.

She thought about Harris, about how calm he had been in that council room, even as everything fell apart. Because it didn't matter. Because there was always a failsafe.

Because the road didn't lead anywhere.

She turned away from it. From the false path. "Then how do we get out?"

Reed jerked his chin toward the tree line. "The way out is through the trees."

Nia followed his gaze, her throat tightening.

The forest surrounded Darbonne like a living wall—dense, dark, watching. It had always been there, untouched, as if the town had been built away from it on purpose.

Because it was.

She thought about all the times she had wandered to the edge of it, looking in, feeling a strange pull to go farther. And all the times someone had stopped her.

"Nobody ever goes in the woods," she murmured.

"Not unless they know how to come back out," Reed said.

She turned to him. "Do you?"

His jaw tightened. "I hope so."

It wasn't comforting, but it was better than the road.

Because this? This was the real way out.

And they had to take it before Darbonne swallowed them, too.

Nia inhaled, shoving everything down—the grief, the fear, the questions clawing at her mind.

She could deal with it later.

If there was a later.

"Let's go," she said.

Reed nodded once, and together, they ran into the trees.

The forest swallowed them whole.

Thick shadows curled between the trees, swallowing the last glow of Darbonne behind them. The air was different here—dense, electric, unnatural. And then it hit her.

The sick feeling.

It slammed into Nia like a fist to the gut. Her stomach lurched, her head went light, her vision tilted.

No.

Not again.

She had felt this before—the last time she tried to leave. The strange pressure behind her eyes, the nausea curling low in her belly, the sense that something was pulling her back. She stumbled, catching herself against a tree.

Reed was beside her in an instant. "Don't stop," he said, voice urgent. "You have to push through it."

"I—" She squeezed her eyes shut, trying to steady herself. The forest spun. "I can't—"

"You can," Reed snapped. "It's not real. It's Darbonne. It's how they keep people inside. You have to fight it."

Not real.

But it felt real.

Her skin was clammy. Her breaths came too fast, too shallow. Her legs felt like lead, but at the same time, like they weren't even hers.

Like something was leeching into her.

She forced a step forward—then another.

Her stomach twisted violently. Her vision blurred. The ground tilted—

She hit her knees.

Reed cursed, yanking her up by the arm. "Keep moving, Nia!"

She tried.

But then—

A flicker in the trees. A shadow, moving. Not Reed. Someone else.

She turned too fast, searching the dark between the trees, her pulse hammering. And for a split second, she saw them.

A figure. Still. Watching.

Someone she knew.

Her stomach dropped.

Danielle.

It was Danielle.

Standing in the trees, just ahead, staring at her with something empty in her eyes.

No.

No, she was dead.

Nia took a step forward, barely aware of herself, of Reed shouting behind her—

And Danielle moved.

She turned and walked into the shadows, deeper into the trees.

Nia lurched forward. "Wait—!"

A hand grabbed her arm, yanking her back.

"No!" Reed snarled, his grip vice-tight. "That's not her."

Nia's chest heaved. "I saw her."

"You saw what Darbonne wants you to see."

His voice was sharp, firm.

But her body still trembled, her mind still screamed—because it had been her.

Hadn't it?

She swallowed hard, fighting the sick feeling clawing through her.

Reed didn't let go of her arm, his grip grounding. "Come on. We're almost through."

Nia forced herself to nod.

She didn't look back.

She couldn't.

Instead, she pushed forward, forcing one foot in front of the other, away from the sickness, away from the illusion.

Away from Danielle.

And deeper into the dark.

Nia pushed forward, each step a battle against the weight pressing down on her. The air around her felt thick, charged, as if the very atmosphere of the forest was resisting her escape. Every muscle in her body screamed in protest, her head spinning from the lingering nausea that had wrapped itself around her like a vice. But Reed was ahead of her, moving with certainty, his grip tight on her wrist, pulling her through the darkness.

The trees stretched endlessly in every direction, their towering forms closing in, their branches twisting unnaturally, like skeletal fingers reaching for her. The further they moved, the harder it became to tell if they were making progress or simply being swallowed deeper into the labyrinth of the woods.

Then—a shift.

The air grew thinner, lighter, easier to breathe. The sickness lessened, then snapped like a thread pulled too tight.

She lurched forward as if she had been released from an invisible tether, stumbling past the final line of trees, breaking through into—

Everything.

For a moment, she could only stare.

Gone were the suffocating shadows, the eerie silence, the oppressive weight of Darbonne's fabricated world. In its place—life.

A real highway stretched out before her, slick with recent rain, its surface gleaming under the glare of streetlights. Buildings stood tall in the distance, their neon signs flickering, windows glowing with the warmth of human existence. Cars rushed past in blurred streaks of red and white, their engines roaring, horns blaring, the unmistakable hum of modern life crashing into her senses.

It was loud. It was bright. It was overwhelming.

She took a step forward, feeling the uneven ground beneath her feet shift from dirt to pavement. The sound of tires skimming across wet asphalt sent a sharp pulse through her skull. A billboard loomed in the distance, advertising fast food, something absurdly mundane, something so achingly normal that it almost sent her reeling.

This was reality.

And yet—her body didn't trust it.

Her hands clenched at her sides, her breath came too fast, her heart pounded so hard it felt like it was trying to convince her that she had made it, that she was free.

Reed stepped up beside her, his chest rising and falling just as unsteadily. His clothes were still damp from the river, his hands still streaked with remnants of the night. He looked at her, his eyes dark, unreadable.

"We did it," he said, but the words felt strange, as if he didn't fully believe them either.

Nia swallowed, her throat raw. She turned, looking over her shoulder—back toward the trees, back toward the unnatural stillness beyond the highway's edge.

She expected to see something.

A figure standing at the threshold. A glimpse of Darbonne clinging to the world just beyond reach. Some kind of proof that it had all been real.

But there was nothing. Just the thick tangle of forest, standing silent, unmoving.

And yet, she knew.

Darbonne was still there. Still hidden. Still waiting for the next unfortunate soul to stumble upon it.

She exhaled sharply, her knees suddenly weak, the weight of everything settling onto her at once. Danielle's blood was still dried on her hands. The memory of her sister's final breath was still lodged in her chest like a blade.

Reed was watching her, his expression softer now. "Come on," he said quietly. "We need to get out of here."

She nodded, forcing herself to move.

As they stepped toward the highway, she had the strangest feeling that she had crossed more than just a physical boundary.

She had escaped.

But she would never truly be free.

CHAPTER TWENTY:

Anywhere

The city lights flickered through the window, casting shifting patterns against the walls of their apartment. Nia sat on the couch, wrapped in the familiar warmth of Malcolm's arms, but her body felt distant—disconnected. She was here, in her home, in her life, but part of her was still back there.

In Darbonne.

She traced slow, absentminded circles against Malcolm's forearm, but her gaze was fixed on nothing in particular. The hum of the television filled the silence between them, the images flickering across the screen, but she wasn't really watching. Her mind had unraveled in the past week, stretching between past and present, between the world she had barely escaped and the one she had once belonged to.

Malcolm exhaled against her hair, his grip tightening around her waist, like he could anchor her back to him through sheer force of will.

"You're here," he murmured. It wasn't a question, but a plea.

Nia swallowed, guilt pressing down on her. She wanted to be present. She wanted to let him pull her fully back into this life, back into normalcy, back into the person she was before she ever set foot in Darbonne.

But that person didn't exist anymore.

"I'm here," she whispered, but even she could hear the hesitation in her voice.

Malcolm sat up slightly, shifting so he could see her face. "No, you're not." His eyes searched hers, frustration warring with concern. "You haven't been since you got back."

Nia's throat tightened. She could argue. She could force a smile, say all the right things. But they both knew the truth.

Malcolm sighed, scrubbing a hand down his face. "I keep thinking I should have come sooner," he admitted, voice thick with regret. "I should have known something was wrong. Those messages—I felt it in my bones, Nia. But I told myself I was being paranoid."

His jaw tensed, fingers pressing into his temples. "I wanted to trust you," he continued, his voice raw. "I wanted to believe that you had just found something important, that you were too deep into your research to check in. But that last post?" He let out a bitter laugh, shaking his head. "It wasn't you. I knew it wasn't you."

Nia looked away, staring at the muted television screen. She hadn't seen the latest posts—the ones Darbonne made in her name—but Malcolm had. He had spent the last week showing her everything, piecing together the gaps, laying out the careful web of deception that had kept her trapped.

It was seamless. A slow manipulation of her presence, her words, her absence.

"They covered their tracks too well," she said finally. "It wasn't just you, Mal. They fooled everyone."

"Doesn't matter." He shook his head, jaw clenching. "I should have known. I should have gone after you."

She turned to him then, resting her hand against his chest, feeling the steady beat of his heart beneath her palm. "And if you had? Then what? You think you would have just walked in and found me? That they wouldn't have pulled you under, too?"

His expression darkened, but he didn't argue.

He had no idea how deep Darbonne's grip had been.

But she did.

And now, even after escaping, she could still feel it.

The weight of the town pressing against her like a shadow in her mind, curling at the edges of her thoughts, waiting.

She wasn't trapped there anymore.

But she also wasn't free.

Malcolm exhaled, wrapping his arms around her again, pressing a kiss to her temple. "I just—I just want *you* back."

Nia closed her eyes, resting her forehead against his chest. She wanted that, too. But she didn't know if she was capable of it anymore.

The morning passed in a quiet haze.

Nia stayed wrapped in Malcolm's warmth longer than she intended, neither of them saying much. The television droned on in the background, some morning news segment about a traffic accident, a political scandal, the mundane hum of the world still turning, unaffected by the horrors she had just lived through.

It felt absurd, how normal everything was. How easy it would be to let herself sink into it, let Malcolm hold her a little longer, pretend nothing had changed.

But everything had.

She peeled herself away eventually, feeling his gaze on her as she stretched, rolling her sore shoulders. He didn't ask where she was going. He just let her go.

She spent the next hour moving through the motions of normalcy—showering, pulling on a pair of leggings and one of Malcolm's hoodies, making a cup of tea she barely drank. She stared at the phone on the kitchen counter, knowing there were messages she hadn't answered, knowing she wasn't ready to.

When the knock came, she almost didn't answer it.

Malcolm was still in the living room, giving her space, but she could feel his awareness of her, the way he watched carefully without hovering.

The knock came again.

A familiar rhythm, followed by a voice she had known for years.

"Nia, I swear to God, if you make me stand out here, I will break down this door."

A shaky breath left her lips before she even realized she'd been holding it.

She moved before she could talk herself out of it, unlatching the door and pulling it open.

Lena stood there, dressed in a casual sweater and jeans, a travel mug in one hand, her dark curls pulled back into a ponytail. The second she saw Nia, her face crumpled—the kind of relief that looked like anger, like disbelief, like something too heavy to carry alone.

And then she grabbed her.

Nia barely had a second to react before Lena's arms were around her, squeezing the breath from her lungs, grounding her in a way she hadn't expected.

"Jesus Christ," Lena murmured, her voice muffled against Nia's shoulder. "You—You just disappeared. Do you have any idea what that was like? I thought you were—" She pulled back suddenly, searching Nia's face, as if she needed to see that she was real. "I would have come the second I heard you were back, but I figured—I don't know, that you'd need time."

Nia swallowed, nodding, because she couldn't quite find the words.

Lena's eyes swept over her, taking her in—the exhaustion she still carried, the weight in her bones, the invisible thing lingering just behind her eyes.

"Okay," Lena said finally, stepping inside without asking, shutting the door behind her. "I need answers."

A small, humorless smile tugged at the corner of Nia's lips. "You and me both."

They moved to the kitchen, Lena perching herself on a stool while Nia leaned against the counter, fingers curled around her still-full mug of tea.

Lena gave her a long look before sighing, setting her travel mug down. "Alright, let's start with the obvious. What the hell happened to you?"

Nia let out a slow breath, gripping the ceramic mug a little tighter. "I went looking for my family," she said simply. "And I found them."

Lena raised an eyebrow. "That sounds like the tagline for a horror movie."

Nia let out a dry laugh, but it didn't reach her eyes. "It might as well be."

Lena didn't press. Not yet. She was patient like that—knew when to push, when to let Nia come to things on her own.

Instead, she tilted her head, studying her. "I know the basics. Malcolm's been keeping me in the loop—only what he knew, which wasn't much. You went to some town, Darbonne. And then… you vanished."

Nia exhaled slowly, rubbing at her temple. "I didn't vanish. I was trapped."

Lena's expression darkened. "Trapped how?"

"They—" Nia hesitated, searching for the words, but how did she explain it? The manipulation, the town itself, the feeling that reality had been stretched too thin? "They controlled everything. I wasn't allowed to leave. I wasn't even allowed to know I was trying to leave."

Lena frowned, but she was listening intently, taking in every word, her fingers curled around her coffee mug. "Why?"

Nia's throat felt tight.

She had been asking herself the same thing for days.

"I don't know," she admitted. "Not really. But it has something to do with me. My DNA."

Lena's brows knit together. "What do you mean?"

Nia hesitated again, looking down at the table, the knots in her stomach tightening. "There's something in my genetics. Something that made them want to keep me there. Something that made them need me there."

Lena's lips parted slightly, a sharp breath drawn in.

"They did tests," Nia continued, voice quieter now. "Experiments. I don't know how far back it goes, but they've been—watching me. For years. Maybe my whole life."

Lena's grip tightened around her mug.

She was trying to keep herself calm, to process the weight of what Nia was saying, but she couldn't hide the way her jaw clenched, the fire burning just beneath the surface.

Finally, she let out a slow, measured breath. "Nia… this sounds like something out of a goddamn nightmare."

Nia huffed a quiet laugh. "Because it was."

Lena stared at her, something shifting in her expression, something calculating. And then—

"Did they ever mention your dad?"

The question hit like a fist to the chest.

Nia blinked, caught off guard, her breath suddenly unsteady. "What?"

Lena shifted forward slightly, resting her elbows on the table. "Your dad, Nia. Think about it. If this was about genetics—about something in your blood—where does it come from? Your mom never had any answers for you, but your dad?"

She let the question hang between them.

Nia's fingers curled tighter around her mug.

She had spent years avoiding the subject.

Her father was a ghost. A name on a birth certificate, a shadow in old photographs her mother never wanted to talk about. She had told herself that was all he was.

But now?

Her stomach twisted.

Because maybe he wasn't a ghost at all.

Maybe he was just another missing piece.

Nia sat there, gripping her mug, her mind spinning in too many directions at once. The mention of her father sent something cold down her spine, something she didn't want to deal with yet.

But Lena wasn't letting her retreat.

She leaned in, fingers drumming lightly against the table, her eyes sharp with determination. "You realize what this means, right?"

Nia gave a hollow laugh, shaking her head. "Yeah. It means I'm never sleeping again."

Lena rolled her eyes but didn't back down. "No, Nia. It means you have something no one else does. Proof. You were inside something that most people wouldn't believe exists. You saw how far they were willing to go, how they covered it up, how they kept people trapped.

You can't just—" She gestured vaguely. "Go back to work like none of this happened."

Nia tensed, staring into the depths of her tea, watching the way the liquid trembled slightly in her grasp. "I barely made it out, Lena. You think I want to poke the beast?"

"I think you already did."

That made her look up.

Lena exhaled, pushing her curls back, searching for the right words. "Listen. You didn't just survive this—you escaped it. And yeah, I know you want to breathe, to feel normal again, but you and I both know you won't. Not if you pretend this didn't happen."

Nia swallowed.

Because Lena was right.

She hadn't felt normal since she got back. Every time she stepped outside, she half-expected to see Darbonne waiting for her, lingering at the edges of reality, waiting to pull her back. She felt it in the way she hesitated before opening her laptop, the way her heart jumped every time her phone rang, the way she still wasn't convinced this was over.

Lena sighed, her voice gentler now. "I'm not saying you have to go on some crusade tomorrow. But, Nia—you've spent your whole career uncovering genetic truths. And now you have one that could change everything."

Nia let out a slow, shaky breath, her fingers tapping absently against the ceramic in her hands. "I don't even know where to start."

"Then let me help you," Lena said immediately.

That caught her off guard. "What?"

"I mean it," Lena said. "I know you, Nia. If you try to do this alone, you'll lock yourself in a room, overanalyze everything, and burn yourself out before you even make a dent." She straightened, her expression serious. "But you don't have to do it alone. I've got connections. I know people who would kill to expose something like this."

Nia hesitated, rubbing her thumb against the lip of her mug. "This isn't some corporate scandal, Lena. These people are dangerous."

"Yeah, well, so are you."

That startled a small, breathless laugh from her.

Lena grinned, but the fire in her eyes remained. "I'm serious. You've got something here, Nia. And you don't have to go back there to destroy them—you just have to shine a big enough spotlight that they can't hide anymore."

Nia inhaled deeply, letting the words settle, trying to ignore the instinctual fear clawing at the back of her mind.

She thought of Darbonne. The town that wasn't real, but had somehow existed in the shadows. The experiments. The people who had disappeared.

The ones who never got out.

The ones who never would.

Lena was right—she couldn't just walk away.

The weight of it settled in her chest, but beneath the fear, beneath the exhaustion, something else stirred. Something like purpose.

Anywhere But Here

She set her mug down, meeting Lena's gaze. "Okay," she said, her voice steadying. "Let's do it."

Lena grinned, raising her coffee mug like a toast. "That's my girl."

The conversation with Lena left Nia feeling something she hadn't felt in days—momentum.

It wasn't enough to erase the exhaustion in her bones or the grief pressing against her ribs, but it was something.

By the time Lena left, they had sketched out the beginnings of a plan. Nothing concrete, nothing reckless. Just the first steps—pulling records, finding patterns, leveraging Lena's contacts in investigative journalism to see how deep this rabbit hole really went.

Lena hugged her at the door, her grip tight. "We're gonna tear them apart," she murmured before stepping back with a smirk. "And you're gonna make history."

Nia only managed a small, tired smile in return. She wasn't thinking about history. She was thinking about Darbonne. About everyone still trapped there.

Malcolm had been quiet during the conversation, letting Lena push when he knew Nia needed pushing, but after Lena left, he finally spoke.

"You're sure about this?" he asked from the kitchen, watching as she stared at her phone, debating whether she had the energy to go down this path again.

Nia glanced up. "Would you believe me if I said no?"

Malcolm sighed, walking over, resting his hands on her shoulders. "You don't have to be sure. You just have to be ready."

She nodded, leaning into his touch for a second. "I think I am."

She wasn't. Not really. But she had run out of options.

As Malcolm pulled away, heading toward the fridge, her phone vibrated on the counter.

A text from an unknown number made Nia's stomach drop. She stared at the screen, pulse thudding in her ears. The message was short and simple. But it sent a shiver down her spine.

UNKNOWN: *You think it's over. It's not.*

Nia's hands clenched around the phone, her breath catching in her throat.

Another vibration.

UNKNOWN: *Darbonne lives.*

A cold sweat prickled along her spine.

She looked up at Malcolm, but he hadn't noticed her reaction yet, hadn't seen the way her fingers had gone white around her phone.

Her heart pounded as she stared at the words on the screen. It wasn't possible. She had burned it down. She had exposed them. She had escaped.

But maybe… that was the mistake. Maybe Darbonne was never about the place. Maybe it was about the people.

A third message appeared.

UNKNOWN: *New leadership. New plans. And you're still part of them.*

Nia's breath came sharp and shallow, the room around her tilting slightly. A pit opened in her stomach, swallowing any shred of victory she had clung to. She thought she had won.

She thought she had destroyed them. But Darbonne was still out there, and they were waiting for her.

The city pulsed around her, neon signs flickering against the wet pavement, car horns blaring in the distance. She had left the apartment. Left Malcolm's warm, worried gaze. Left the weight of Lena's certainty pressing against her ribs.

She needed air.

She needed to be alone.

The phone in her pocket burned against her thigh, those three messages looping in her head like a song stuck on repeat.

Darbonne lives.

New leadership. New plans. And you're still part of them.

She walked faster.

The streets of the city—her city—should have felt like a barrier between her and everything she had left behind. But they didn't. Because suddenly, she wasn't sure she had left at all.

Her fingers clenched inside her pockets, nails biting into her palms. She counted every step, grounding herself in the rhythm of her boots against concrete.

The air smelled like rain. Real rain. Not like the damp, curated scent of Darbonne's controlled ecosystem.

"This is real," she whispered it under her breath, like a mantra, like an anchor.

A streetlamp flickered overhead.

Nia stopped walking.

There was something off about the sidewalk in front of her. Something subtle. A barely perceptible shift in the way the concrete met the curb, in the way the traffic lights swayed even though there was no wind.

The air felt denser.

She turned slowly, scanning the street. People passed her in a blur—normal people, bundled in coats, staring at their phones, hailing cabs. But something was wrong.

Her stomach turned as she caught sight of a man across the street. He was standing completely still. Not checking his phone. Not adjusting his bag. Just watching.

She took a step back, and then—he smiled.

It wasn't a normal smile. It was knowing.

Like he was waiting for her to figure it out.

A chill ran through her spine, and suddenly she was moving again, walking fast, turning down a side street, her breath coming sharp and uneven.

She pulled out her phone, her fingers shaking as she dialed Malcolm's number.

A ringing tone.

Then—static.

Her pulse thundered. She yanked the phone away from her ear, staring at the screen. The call had connected, but all she could hear was white noise.

She swallowed hard, turning a corner, moving faster. The city was closing in now, the skyscrapers towering higher, the streets stretching longer than they should.

No.

No, no, no.

She reached another intersection, her heart hammering as she looked up at the street sign.

Main Street.

She blinked—turning to ice.

Because she had just been on Main Street.

She hadn't turned that far.

Her breath came too fast, too sharp, her fingers tightening around her phone. She turned in a slow circle, scanning the buildings, the passing cars, the people— then she saw her.

A woman standing at the next intersection. Facing away from her. Hair the same length. The same build. A deep, sinking feeling slid into her gut before her mind could catch up.

The woman turned slightly, head tilting as if she sensed Nia watching.

The woman had her face.

It was her.

Standing across the street. Staring back at her.

Nia staggered backward, hands shaking.

The world tilted.

A car horn blared past her, tires screeching against wet pavement. She turned, breath coming ragged, searching for something, anything to ground her.

She needed Malcolm. She needed Lena. She needed proof that this was real.

That *she* was real.

She reached into her pocket, feeling for her keys, something solid, something hers. But instead—

Her fingers grazed something smooth and small.

She pulled out a keycard.

It was impossible. She had left it behind. It should have burned with everything else.

Her fingers shook violently as she turned it over. A name was printed on the front.

Her name.

Dr. Nia Wallace.

But below it—

Her title had changed.

Director.

The wind howled through the streets. The city around her blurred, lights twisting into something unnatural, something too clean, too perfect, too designed. Nia's breath stilled.

No.

No.

She hadn't escaped.

Anywhere But Here

She had just moved up.

The world around her shifted—just slightly. Just enough. And then, in the reflection of a shop window, she saw the man from before.

Still smiling.

Still waiting.

Nia squeezed her eyes shut, the keycard burning in her palm. When she opened them again—the city was gone.

About Myunique

Myunique C. Green is a versatile and celebrated author whose work spans across genres, including mystery, thriller, young adult fiction, dystopian science fiction, and personal memoir. She began her literary journey with the independently published *Bloodlines: Everything That Glitter* in 2012, which climbed to the Top 10 on Amazon Kindle's Bestseller list. Since then, she has continued to captivate readers with her unique voice and compelling storytelling.

Her titles, such as *713*, a chart-topping mystery short story, and *Grand Rising*, a dystopian epic, showcase her ability to explore complex themes and engage audiences with fresh perspectives. Myunique's deeply personal memoir, *To Mend a Broken Heart*, stands out as a powerful testament to resilience and healing, inspiring readers with her honesty and courage.

When she's not writing, Myunique is a dedicated teacher, student, and parent, continually pushing boundaries and inspiring others to find strength in their own stories. Through her work, she strives to connect with readers, leaving a lasting impression of hope, resilience, and the power of storytelling.

Stay Connected

Hey there, amazing reader!

I hope you enjoyed diving into my world of stories as much as I loved creating them! Your thoughts and feedback mean everything to me, and I'd love to hear what you think. Whether it's a review, a favorite quote, or just a quick "OMG, I need more!" I'm all ears!

Your Reviews Matter! If you loved what you just read (or even if you have thoughts on how it made you feel), leaving a review helps more readers discover my books. Plus, it totally makes my day!

Let's stay connected! Follow me, tag me, and send me a message. I love chatting with fellow book lovers!

Blog: MyuniqueGreen.com
Instagram: @_cmajor_
Snapchat: Cece_major

Can't wait to hear from you! Until next time, keep turning those pages!

Made in United States
North Haven, CT
25 May 2025